NOT FOREVER DEAD

With best wishes,

Jules Langton

JULES LANGTON

EARLY REVIEWS

Oh my goodness! I can't begin to tell you how much I enjoyed this! I had high expectations, after I'd enjoyed the first one so much, but it has exceeded those expectations! ... Thank you for letting me read and review this - I'm already looking forward to renewing my acquaintance with Ellie, in the future!

I definitely loved it as much if not more than Dream Die Repeat. It was certainly a page turner and I could not put it down until the last page.

I really felt I was in the book with Ellie and her friends, the descriptive writing of all the places visited was so vivid and makes you want to follow in their footsteps on my next holiday.

The story follows effortlessly from the first book and surprised me with some of the plot twists, which means, you have to finish the book.

I like the way it is written, it really keeps you engrossed and the writing style is very recognisable as Jules Langton following on from Dream Die Repeat.

Cannot wait for the next book.

The follow up to DREAM, DIE, REPEAT, the second in the trilogy, was well anticipated and lived up to expectations. It was exciting and fast paced.

A spellbinding read with a frizzle of excitement.

This book is the second in the series and is just as amazing as the first, if not better. The descriptive writing allows you to immerse yourself fully in the book. It's almost as if you are with Ellie on her journey.

Uprooting her life seems to be normal for Ellie these days since finding out she is a witch. There is such a twist which answers so many questions but in turn raises more questions. I can't wait to read the next book.

It's a simultaneous ease in of characters as well as multi-level/dimensional stories within a story that had me needing to keep turning the pages to ease my curiosity. I felt the characters were well thought out and each had their own appeal/intrigue and were woven well into the storyline. The main character, Ellie, had a lovely depth and emotion which made you invested from the start in wanting to know what happens and hoping for a "happy ending" outcome.

I really enjoyed the modern/old world weaving and felt it was creatively done without losing the story or leaving you confused. What I also liked was just when you thought you had the plot sorted, you find you don't, and another surprise and intriguing turn pops up.

It had the same page turning vibe as the first book with very different paths you're taken down, which is a credit to the author in being able to avoid repeating "similarities" from the first story, but building on that with a clever combination of calming your curiosity, bringing some context to things and still leaving the pages ahead for you to follow with new intrigue and need to knows! Really enjoyed both books and looking forward to seeing the last chapter with book 3!

Published by Goldcrest Books International Ltd
www.goldcrestbooks.com
publish@goldcrestbooks.com

ISBN: 978-1-913719-85-2

In memory of three wise souls:

My hero, my late father Joe. A child refugee who travelled the world during his childhood, his own journey is a story in itself. The star in the sky that shines the brightest.

My late in-laws, Janis and Ken, they believed in soul mates meeting throughout eternity, I'm sure you will meet each other again.

"I cannot express it: but surely you and everybody have a notion that there is, or should be, an existence of yours beyond you."

Emily Brontë

PROLOGUE

The tastefully decorated room – green and white palm wallpaper and several carefully placed, flourishing potted plants – gave a deliciously chic indoor-garden vibe. The floor-to-ceiling bi-fold doors opened smoothly for me, and I stepped out onto the spacious balcony, where a lounger with vibrantly coloured cushions matched the chairs set around a small table. The view beyond the immaculately kept grounds was stunning. Another gorgeous spa retreat.

It should make me happy, it always used to, and the fact that it didn't now makes me sound like an ungrateful bitch. This place certainly didn't disappoint in wall-to-wall comfort, nothing was too much trouble, and by now I was an expert, having spent so much time in similarly unique places dotted around the country, no rhyme or reason as to the location, but I always picked carefully, with privacy in mind; I preferred off-the-beaten-track places with tight security. Since fleeing from Yorkshire, so much of my life had been spent looking over my shoulder. I wasn't imprisoned, but I might as well have been. I was like a bird in a gilded cage. At each new location, it was only when I was safely through security that I relaxed a little, some peace of mind until the anxiety set in again, and I knew I was ready for the next move. I never stayed anywhere for more than a couple of weeks.

Obviously, I used my magic where I could, changing my appearance on a whim, but my tattoo and heart-shaped mole were a spell too far, problematic as they could identify me, easy to spot. I'd booked in incognito to a plastic surgeon, to be fair she didn't ask too many questions – did she get it? I had a couple of painful and expensive sessions, which resulted in the successful removal of both my tattoo and the distinctive heart-shaped mole on my breast. There was nothing out of the ordinary in a lone female checking in for a spa stay, a sanctuary away from everyday life. The staff were used to women booking in, whatever the reason – a relationship breakdown, time out of the rat race, or maybe just a while away from family dynamics. I kept my head down, didn't ever ask any of the other guests why they were there, and they didn't ask me. I avoided conversation as much as I could, I'm not sure what reaction I'd have received if I'd said I was on the run, fearing for my life because I was being hunted as a witch. Maybe I wasn't the only one?

One of the things I particularly liked about my current accommodation was that it seemed to be run like a convent. As I was shown around, I noticed no unnecessary conversation and signs everywhere respectfully requesting silence. A mobile ringing loudly earned its owner a frown from the young woman who was giving me the conducted tour. I liked that. I'd enjoy the tranquillity and certainly didn't want to make new friends. The selling points of the places I picked were rest and recuperation, making them perfect havens for me to hide in plain sight. I'd also discovered the benefits of yoga and meditation, both of which were helping me in my recovery from the trauma I'd experienced.

I still had nagging fears and doubts each time I moved on. Where best to go, who to turn to, was there anyone I could trust? Important questions I asked myself each time I settled into yet another luxury room, not a home, just another temporary stay until such time as I felt safe enough to stay somewhere for longer. Having fled from the danger that was Seb and the shadowy witch hunters, I had no idea who were the good guys and who were the bad. Thinking of Seb, my soulmate, filled me with horror – were we destined to meet through time, again and again. How many lives had we shared, and did they all have the same grim conclusion? Would my life end the same dreadful way for all eternity?

I desperately missed my beautiful home. I could weep just thinking of Lavender Cottage, my perfect retreat; it had broken my heart to leave. I'd spent blood, sweat, and tears on making it my forever home, a place in which to grow comfortably older, not to mention the connection with both Hettie and Anna, previous residents themselves. I pictured myself, serene and grey-haired, like Agnes,

Hettie's mother, an old woman completely at peace with the land, foraging, making my own bread and spending the evenings in a rickety old rocking chair next to a roaring fire. I added a hairy wart to my chin for full effect and set a broomstick in the corner of the cosy room. Then reality kicked back in and the faint smile on my face faded. I was no longer living at my cottage. I had no contact with Seb; my former life had been left behind, the dream turned into a nightmare, my lover into my enemy, my perfect man into a wolf in sheep's clothing.

Wearing dark sunglasses and a peaked cap, whatever the weather, I realised that in aiming for incognito, I might achieve the opposite, looking like a celebrity trying to stay under the paparazzi's radar. But possibly that was as good a disguise as any. I was petrified that Seb was on the hunt for me and the thought of looking into those cold wolf eyes again made me shudder. I was thankful for my magic which meant for each move I made, I was able to change my look using a few simple transformation spells. Despite that, I never felt secure, avoided people as much as possible, and made a point of never conversing with the staff wherever I was staying. There were times when I yearned for an invisibility spell but feared that it was way beyond my current capabilities, let alone the logistical problems that would arise. For now, I'd have to be satisfied with changing my look at the drop of a hat and praying Seb wouldn't be able to sniff me out.

There was no fault to be found with my new accommodation, yet I woke up the following morning feeling particularly melancholy. After a shower, which did nothing to make me feel any better, I spread out the newspapers I had delivered daily and looked through them as they lay on the bed. It was important to ensure I kept track of what was going on and followed stories online. To my horror, history was repeating itself; women were being persecuted and prosecuted as witches, neighbour turning on neighbour, suspicion rife. The media had whipped up a storm and weren't going to let it abate. They were having a field day, and it was providing a thrilling agenda, raising arguments both for and against the draconian new laws which were dragging so many, both men and women, before judge and jury. Even more concerning were the increased reports of drownings and other unexplained deaths – mainly women – noted as accidents or suicide clusters, although I knew they were connected to the Purge and the fanatical hatred of the people behind it. I gathered up the papers and closed my iPad, I didn't want to see any more, it wouldn't do any good.

My floor-to-ceiling window showed a spectacular day, but despite the sun, a black cloud was hovering over my head. Glitz, glamour, and luxury were hollow without anyone to share them with. I thought back to my spa stays with the girls, I missed them so much. More painfully, I'd also left behind my newly discovered birth mother, Anna. We'd had so little time to get to know each other, and where was my half-sister, Lottie? I even missed my parents, and that was saying something, but contacting any of them would bring danger to their door.

I knew it wasn't the best or most sensible time to check out the minibar while I was feeling like this, but I needed to blunt the fear and loneliness. A few sips of bubbly usually helped a bit, and the small bottle was only one glass – it was a classy place so only the best champagne. Sitting on the bed with its luxurious high-thread-count Egyptian cotton duvet, I kicked back and, having drained the first, I opened a second bottle – it'd be rude not to – and tried to focus on my breathing as I'd been taught in the oh-so-many meditation classes I'd been attending. I couldn't even be bothered to explore my latest stop. I knew what I'd find, and I'd given my usual reason when I checked in. I was here for work, and the "do not disturb sign" was often going to be on my door. Housekeeping would have to work around that.

There were only so many books I could read, music I could listen to, and Netflix series I could watch, not to mention that a body can only take so many pampering treatments. Things I used to love to do no longer pleased me. Not only was moving from place to place completely unsettling but creating a different look for myself and making actual physical changes meant I didn't really know who I was any more. I had nothing to look forward to in the future, didn't even know whether I had a future, I suppose it depended on how long I could keep running. Sipping the champagne, my mind was free to roam – there must be a way of getting out of this situation, a spell that would help. I deliberately hadn't thought too much about the old Book of Knowledge Hettie had directed me to at Lavender Cottage. It was currently concealed in my suitcase, and deep in its spine, I'd hidden the delicate necklace. Wearing it might have brought some comfort, but it wouldn't be wise to be seen wearing anything remotely mystical. Even keeping the book was a risk, it had slipped to the back of my mind, I'd have to do something about it. A safety deposit box, somewhere ultra-secure would be sensible. Even though I'd zipped it into the lining now my clothes were in the wardrobe, it felt more exposed. I'd decided that safely storing the book away would be my next move, no time to waste. I rang down to reception to ask if they could send up some strong packaging and tape to get the ball rolling. It had to be kept secure and stay unseen, it was way too precious to fall into the wrong hands.

I was wary about lifting it out of the case, but I wanted one last look. Placing it on the bed, it fell open to the middle pages, all still heavily dust-coated, it had never felt right to try and clean it, the dust carried its own history. Almost without thinking, I studied the symbols and words before me. I'd grown used to using the book for an assortment of spells, including my forest faeries effort, but it must be said that much of the book's content hadn't been that useful for a twenty-first-century urban witch. No end of an asset if you were looking to spoil crops, curdle milk, or banish a mean spirit, but not hugely relevant today. As for the love potions, well, I'd tried one of those and that hadn't gone too well either. Now, I frowned at the page before me, leaning over the book to look more closely. How odd. Since it had come into my possession, I'd always been able to easily – perhaps too easily – interpret the spells from the book. From the beginning, it had felt familiar, every word, each symbol. But not only could I not recall this particular page, but I could make no sense of the symbols and script, although it was no more faded than any of the other pages. How ridiculous, it may as well have been written in another language. I focused intently, and as I did the vibe in the room shifted. I sensed someone behind me, and my blood turned cold.

Had the cat-and-mouse game ended? Had they hunted me down? I didn't dare turn around. Those few seconds felt like long minutes; frozen like a rabbit in the headlights, I was motionless apart from an almost imperceptible internal shivering. Had they been waiting for me in this room since I checked in? Had I been watched while they bided their time? I turned slowly to face my fate but could see no one. There was nobody there. I grabbed one of my trainers from the floor, not much in the way of a weapon but the only thing to hand, and began to move cautiously around the room. I looked behind the curtains, in the wardrobe, and snapped on the light in the bathroom. There was no one, nothing out of place. The door to my room was still locked, and I had already closed the bi-fold doors, I double-checked, they were still closed. But I knew I wasn't mad. Scared stiff, but not mad.

Every one of my senses was alert as I listened and looked; there was no mistaking the shift in the air, in the energy; someone or something was here. My witch's heightened sense of smell picked up a distinctive aroma, an earthly, outdoor, lavender smell, and a distinct whiff of poor feminine hygiene. It was a smell I knew, but so out of context in this hotel room, I searched my memory, and as I did, the shock ran through me from head to toe. It was Hettie, she was here, with me in the room; how was that possible? Then, so light I nearly missed it altogether, there was a touch on my neck, as soft as a breeze.

"Hettie?" I whispered, "I know it's you, but I can't see you." Initially, there was no response at all; I didn't move, hardly breathed, and waited. Then, so quietly that I wasn't sure whether it was wishful thinking, my own ears generating what they thought they should, I heard a soft, repetitive sound, slowly growing and gaining in volume from a low buzz to a clearer whispering. It increased, filling the room, surrounding me as I understood what I was hearing. An incantation, ancient magical words carrying the weight of the years and the rhythm of the women who'd recited them. These were, I knew beyond a shadow of a doubt, from the page I'd been unable to read. She was repeating them over and over, implanting the spell again and again in my mind until it was as much a part of me as it was of her. However she'd reached me, whatever unseeable form she'd taken, it didn't matter. She was here to help, transferring the age-old words from her mind to mine.

I closed my eyes, the better to focus and understand the power of what she was giving me. I instinctively knew she had never used this herself. Why? Surely the strength of the spell meant the ending of her story could have been so different. The magnitude of the knowledge she was imparting felt like it could be a game-changer in the war against the witch hunters. I had so many questions, and even though I knew it would probably be futile, I spoke the most important aloud anyway.

"Hettie, why didn't you use this to protect yourself?" I

expected no reply and didn't receive one, just the repetition of the incantation almost like a recording playing over and over, stimulating faint echoes in my mind, even as my head was spinning. This was the spell, the power of which could save me from the inevitable – a get-out clause, the answer to my prayers. For whatever reason, Hettie's fate had been sealed; I was determined mine wouldn't be. I fully understood the risks, but I had no choice, I had to move quickly before it was too late.

Feeling lightheaded and weak, I took a deep breath, hands shaking, heart pounding. But now I knew there was a glimmer of hope, a path out of my predicament – that is if it worked. But I had to dismiss doubt, and just as importantly knew I had to eat and drink before I fainted, my stomach was rumbling as I brought my focus back into the room. I grabbed and ate some snacks from the minibar, then downed the second bottle of champagne for Dutch courage. A little tipsy by now, I felt my mind calming as I sat back once again on the luxurious, plumped-up pillows. I knew time was short, and I had to make a life-changing decision, possibly the most important I'd ever make, but there was no doubt I felt more alive and with a sense of urgency that had been missing for so long. I'd been trapped, but perhaps now I had the key to my freedom, to resuming a normal life.

I knew the dire risks carried by the spell. Hettie would have done too, maybe she'd considered it just too dangerous, and if she'd had a change of heart at the last moment, it would have come too late to save her. She had my trust, though. She'd led me safely to Lavender

Cottage, to the Book of Knowledge. I was confident she would never deliberately cause me harm or show me anything that was beyond my capabilities to control. With that in mind, I knew my first task was to hide the book. If I survived, I could retrieve it and use it for good, change the war against witches. But I was getting ahead of myself, first and foremost I had to use it to see what happened – and I was petrified. I understood that to initiate the spell I had to have total faith, and trust that the power released would be enough to save me.

I knew exactly where I needed to be, to do what had to be done. It had to be the Thames, and I knew the perfect, secluded spot. The more I understood, the more I realised that it wouldn't be a pleasant procedure, in fact it was incredibly treacherous, I was going to have to technically drown myself, there was no alternative. I just needed the courage to put it into practice, and I now knew Hettie was there with me, that really helped. Softly, I went over the incantation and didn't hesitate over a single word – it was firmly in place now.

The following day I checked out, hoping it was going to be my last luxury hotel stay for a good while – you can sometimes have too much of a good thing. As I drove towards London and my fate, I was comforted by the fact the Book of Knowledge would be safe, first stop was to place it in a secure safety deposit box. My aim was to change history and change the way my past lives had always ended, but I had no idea of what the implications might be for my future.

Of one thing I was certain: I simply wasn't prepared to

play the victim any more and the knowledge I'd acquired could protect me for my lifetime and beyond. I only hoped Hettie could take some comfort in the fact that she'd saved me, and maybe our future lives, even if she couldn't save herself. I couldn't be harmed by anyone, no one would be able to take my life, in any way, as long as this spell worked. Shaking away any doubts, feeling relieved that the book was now safe and sound, I reached the designated well-concealed spot. Away from prying eyes I stripped off, my cold flesh instantly goose-pimpling, but I knew I had to be naked. Slowly and clearly, I recited the words that had to be spoken, and slipped into the water.

CHAPTER 1

Spiralling out of control, freefalling into the abyss, around and around, on a non-stop roundabout, I couldn't get off. A nightmare? Real life? I really didn't know for sure, but it didn't seem like my familiar dream world. I couldn't process any information and the brain fog felt impenetrable. Or maybe it wasn't just a dream, perhaps the world and I had simply gone totally crazy.

There was one lucid thought, but I didn't want to acknowledge that: was I dead? Was this really what was on the other side, a continuous maelstrom? Was this heaven or hell? Into my bruised mind flashed visions of coffins and funeral cars – my funeral? I hoped I'd had a good send-off. I couldn't quite fathom it out, but there was no doubt that something had gone drastically pear-shaped. I only wished I knew what. Trying to grasp a thread of memory seemed impossible.

I waited in limbo, real or metaphorical. There seemed

little else to do, and after a while – minutes or hours, I had no idea – there was a glimmer of light through the fog in my head. Snippets of thought, clearer than before, came, but went too swiftly. It felt as though I was waking from a deeply drugged sleep. What was wrong with me? Either this was an exceptionally long and lucid dream, or I was dead and in heaven, hell, or purgatory. Then the faintest hint of memory, enough to tell me I'd gambled on something, taken a huge risk. I instinctively felt something traumatic had happened to my body. Did this mean the gamble had paid off or confirm it hadn't?

After a while, I felt I could open my eyes and I was glad I did. The scenery around me was heavenly. I was sitting in the type of small rowing boat common on the narrower parts of the Thames. And I was sure it was the Thames, although instead of the murky grey water, it now flowed with rainbow colours. I wasn't rowing, the boat seemed to be steering itself, moving steadily on the water. Well, I thought, perhaps I'd hit the nail on the head – I was dead. Whatever trauma I'd been through, it would seem I hadn't survived. But it wasn't an unpleasant feeling, to be honest. I felt calmer than I had for a long time, I'd embrace the afterlife and go with the flow.

What the hell was I wearing though? A vintage, calf-length floaty dress, jewel-encrusted pumps, and a large, floppy straw hat were on the seat next to me. It was an outfit perfect for a society country wedding, so pretty and so not me. Having said that, with the sun beating down, I was cool and comfortable, and I felt free, although I had no idea where that thought came from. I put the hat on, shame I didn't have some shades to go with it, that would be perfect. Then I spotted a glasses case in the exact spot where the hat had been and inside, a pair of oversized sunglasses. I'm sure they weren't there before, was my magic still working? Another thought crept in, was magic what this was all about? Be careful what you wish for. Although this was blissful. Shaded comfortably from the sun, I realised what was missing – sound. Silence surrounded me, you could hear a pin drop, not even a solitary bird singing, or a plane overhead, not a soul to be seen or heard. It was a dreamy scene, peaceful, and I yawned. I knew I was on the Thames, that bit was familiar, but gone were the drab London colours, the buildings grimed by the years, and the sludgy shade of the river. The sun brought out the rainbow colours of the water so vividly that I was glad I had the shades.

Then the smell hit me – in a good way, I should add. The scent of a delicious, enticing sweet shop, the doubly delightful combination of candyfloss and doughnuts. My stomach rumbled; I had no idea when I'd last eaten nor where I'd smelt that delicious aroma before. I'd been resting my arm on the side of the boat, fingers idly dangling in the water which felt like warm jelly. I licked my thumb with cautious curiosity, the taste was exquisite; I could have happily stayed there indefinitely, just drifting and licking sweet nectar from my fingers.

But then the water started flowing more swiftly and the scenery flashed by faster. The boat seemed to have a mind of its own and was following the current, and I could now faintly hear the sounds of the river flowing.

When the boat slowed and drifted to the shore, I gasped. My surroundings were breathtaking. If this was heaven, I never wanted to go anywhere else, it was the perfect place to spend eternity. There were flowers of every colour, like psychedelic lollipops from Charlie and the Chocolate Factory, it wouldn't have surprised me one little bit if a group of Oompa-Loompas had emerged, singing, from behind trees that appeared to be made of spun sugar, their delicate leaves tinkling in a soft breeze. Perhaps I could simply sit here all day and partake of the delicacies around me. But an odd note struck me, if this was heaven, surely I couldn't be the only one here? Maybe I wasn't dead then, but why was it so silent, and what was with the lollipop surroundings? In the background, a song I hadn't heard since childhood gradually grew louder both in my mind and in my ears, "Lucy in the Sky With Diamonds" by the Beatles, one of my parents' favourites, and here I was amidst a magical world – maybe this was just another dream? I smiled serenely at this dream-like scene, I wanted to climb out of the boat and explore, but try as I might to steer the boat to the shore, it seemed to have a mind of its own, and I was jolted forward. We were again midstream, and I had to accept this was a journey that wasn't going to stop.

Faster and faster, now sailing at speed, the boat was violently rocking from side to side, and I had to cling on for dear life, although briefly, I reflected, if I was already dead, that was possibly irrelevant. Gone in an instant were the vibrant rainbow colours. Everything was stripped back to stark grey and white, the air was heavily charged, and lightning streaked the sky, followed almost instantly by a huge crash of thunder reverberating through me. The wind was viciously whipping trees and flowers to the ground, and the smell of sulphur made me gag. The elements had turned malevolent and, lashed by wind and rain, the boat lurched ever more violently until I inevitably lost my grip on the wet, slippery wood of its side and was hurled into the water. I knew instantly that I stood little chance against the churning current but I had to try and swim against it because what lay ahead was far worse than I could imagine. I was aware of being pulled down and down into the blackness of the murky water, and the weeds from the riverbed reached up to greet me, winding round and binding my legs.

It was hopeless; struggle as I might, there seemed to be no way to fight my way back to the surface, and my strength was running out. I held on to what would probably be my last breath until I could hold on no longer, and then I gave in to the inevitable.

CHAPTER 2

And I found I was able to breathe. I took great big gulps of air and exhaled. With relief, I realised the water wasn't flooding my lungs. I just had to hope against hope that when I was eventually found and dredged up from the Thames, the paramedics would find my pulse, however weak it might be.

It was all coming back to me now, brain cogs grinding gradually back into gear. The cold water must have shocked everything back into action, although I was still unable to move my body. The spell hidden in the book, which Hettie helped me understand and implement, was the answer to my prayers, even if it had called for me to drown myself first – pretty drastic, I know. But it hadn't detailed how long I'd be in this state of seemingly suspended animation. My biggest fear was being found and pronounced dead. Neither was I sure if what was happening right now was what was supposed to happen.

What I did know instinctively was that if I'd used the spell correctly, it promised absolute protection for the rest of my mortal life. I'd be safe from harm, and death from drowning, or indeed any other murderous intent, was now no longer inevitable for me; my destiny would have been changed. The spell didn't promise immortality, I could still die a natural death. But hopefully I'd broken the cycle. I knew the witch hunters wouldn't have disappeared, but I'd be steps ahead of them, my power would have increased, and maybe I'd even be able to help others.

All I could do right now was concentrate on the immediate, although the downside was that while I still couldn't move, my other senses were working, and the putrid stink of centuries of discarded waste was doing me no good. I felt my body was in some form of hibernation; things were changing and having cast my lot at the same time as the spell, I had no choice but to see how it played out. I'd chosen the Thames because I thought there was a good chance of being found. I didn't want to end up as just another "jumper", a suicide statistic, too often seen as an inconvenience to commuters trying to get to work across the city. It was a fact that there'd been a shocking increase in deaths by drowning, but jumping in front of trains had become increasingly popular, and women caught up in "accidental" house fires, that sort of thing, along with other gruesome unexplained deaths. Death by train, I couldn't think of anything worse. Suspicions were that they were being furtively pushed onto the tracks, not just in London but across the entire rail network; what a macabre way to go. Theories put forward suggested that loneliness and perhaps lack of family support were to blame, even shame at having been outed as a witch was put forward as a reason, which was bizarre. But I knew the truth, that the newly introduced draconian laws and the Purge had encouraged the vigilantes. They were running amok, yet there was frighteningly little being accurately reported. Just like in Hettie's time, a blind eye was turned, and they were getting away with murder. Seb insinuated himself into my mind, I remembered him saying Revenge is a dish best served cold. If I could have nodded agreement now, I would have done. And Seb would be first on my list! Revenge would be my mission, on behalf of myself and all the other witches and the completely innocent women who were being caught up in what was happening. Consumed with rage, resentment, and love – love? Revenge against Seb – who was I kidding, my head or my heart? I felt my thoughts slowly drifting away before everything went black.

I came back to earth with a bump, woken up from a deep slumber, not sure how long I was out for. I wriggled fingers and toes, but still nothing. I felt I was floating, moving upwards to look down on a hive of activity below. An out-of-body experience? Was that a good sign or a bad one? I was looking at what seemed to be a film set for a horror movie, or maybe a murder mystery, and suddenly I knew exactly where I was. I was behind the Prospect of Whitby, the Thames-side pub and not far from where I'd entered the water and set the spell in motion. My location of choice, it was here that I'd had my leaving party, which seemed so long ago, a different life. Maybe I should have just stayed where I was? There was a large white tent on the bank and lots of people. I floated through them like a ghost. Then the reality hit me: this was not a movie set. I hadn't been prepared for what I was seeing.

Four naked women were laid out in a row on a blue tarpaulin, all dead. Their bruised, battered, and injured bodies, bloated from time in the water, made them unrecognisable, apart from one. The body at the end of the row was mine. The small scar on my breast left by the removal of my heart-shaped mole was unmistakable against the blue-white of my cold flesh. Our bodies were assorted shapes and sizes but shared with the other women were purple bruising and blue lips, we looked like discarded shop mannequins, no longer fit for purpose, no longer even remotely lifelike.

I was in deep trouble. I looked as dead as the others, just another corpse. A group of uniformed police didn't seem overly concerned with what they were seeing, there was no horror on their faces, it was just another day at the office. The overwhelming relief I should have felt at being found had deflated like a pricked balloon. I still had confidence that I was not as dead as the others, but how could or would anyone else know that? I'd completed the first part of the spell, but what a sorry state I was in.

I needed to attract attention, so I did what anyone would in the circumstances, I screamed as loud and as hard as I could, again and again. But to no avail, nobody batted an eyelid. How could I make anyone realise that I wasn't dead, was hanging on by a thread, and needed urgent medical attention?

One of the men – no uniform, so I assumed CID – was obviously senior. The others moved swiftly out of his way as he looked briefly at the bodies before turning away and taking out his phone.

"Another four, can you send someone down?" He paused, then answered irritably, "Course I'm sure they're bloody dead, wouldn't be calling you otherwise. Yeah, same as usual, but we can't move 'em till we've got confirmation and certificates. Thanks." He moved away from the bodies, and I screamed again, "Not dead, not dead, please, please help me!"

The senior officer left swiftly with a couple of uniforms accompanying him, and scene-of-crime specialists head to toe in white protection garb moved in, exchanging banter with the couple of policemen remaining. Everyone was acting as if this was all routine, an everyday occurrence, it was bizarre. With only two left, I screamed again and thought I saw a slight flicker of a reaction on the face of the younger of the two men, a tall, dark-haired, good-looking guy, young enough to be just out of training school. He glanced up momentarily, looking puzzled, then resumed his conversation. The other policeman was older, certainly, a lot bulkier and looked as though he'd been around the block more than a few times and seen all there was to see. I zoned in on what he was saying.

"They've had to open a temporary morgue, did you hear? To cope with what's coming in. I know they're trying to keep it under the radar and out of the press. But surely" – he jerked his head towards the bodies – "they can't all be witches? Doesn't make any sense."

The older man's shrug indicated he wasn't that bothered either way, and he swung round to face the senior officer who'd returned, caught the end of their conversation and was frowning.

"That's enough. You need to be policing, not gossiping like a couple of old women. Roads blocked off, but the press always finds a way in, so keep an eye out." He turned to go, stopped by the young officer.

"Sir, what d'you reckon it's all about then?"

"Official line's the current economic climate. There's always been jumpers, nothing new there."

"But—"

"No buts," he paused at the tent entrance, "just get on with the job, keep your mouth shut, and make sure the doc gets them signed off as soon as possible, otherwise we'll have the next lot on top of us before we know it."

This was incredible, I couldn't believe what I was hearing; something had to be done to expose this travesty, this mass dehumanisation. Surely the great British public wasn't going to buy into this deception.

The younger officer waited until he was sure his superior wouldn't make an unscheduled reappearance, then said something in a low voice to the other man. I could only just hear him but moving in closer, I brushed past his hair, and again he gave a baffled glance behind him. Had he felt my touch?

"One of these bodies could be my mother or my sister," he muttered.

The older man moved away but turned back, "Matt, listen, just keep your opinions to yourself, will you? I don't want any more stick. Keep your head down, just follow orders, or you'll end up with more trouble than you can handle."

It was clear from the look on Matt's face he remained unconvinced. Had he felt my touch? Maybe he was the answer to my prayers, my saviour. I just needed to get his attention. I wondered if he'd accompany me and the other bodies to the morgue. I already knew he was perceptive; I'd taken rather a shine to him, it's amazing what you observe about someone when they're unaware you're there – apart from which, he seemed to be the only one who cared one iota for the women lying at his feet.

They were interrupted by a short, stout man bustling into the tent as he pushed glasses up onto a shiny bald head. Sweating profusely, he already had his medical bag open and briefly acknowledged the two policemen before donning gloves and mask and crouching over the women, I could smell his foul body odour. His checking of the bodies was so quick and cursory, and so obviously box-ticking, that it chilled me to the core. As he reached my body, I waited for him to sound the alarm, "Wait, this one has a pulse, get an ambulance." But his examination was as brief as it had been with the others, and all he said was "ID?"

"Nope, nothing." It was the older officer who answered, Matt had turned away.

What the fuck, I wanted to kick and scream and smash him in the face, this gross little putrid-smelling man currently bent over my body, "We're not all fucking dead!" But there was no way of reaching him.

He was already brushing the knees of his trousers where they'd got muddy, discarding his mask and gloves into a plastic bag. He was irritated. "Dental records then, that's always a bloody nuisance." He nodded briefly on his way out adding, "Vans are here," as I tried to take in what had happened. Oh, dear God, what would happen to me now? Buried alive or cremated? I suppose I should have had faith in Hettie and the spell, but this was such uncharted territory. My feeling of sheer helplessness was appalling.

As I floated out of the tent, I saw the vans had pulled up outside.

I made one last desperate bid, "Matt, I'm alive, I'm alive. Don't let them take me." For a moment, his face went blank as he focused on what I was saying, then he shrugged, and my last chance faded as the black body bag was zipped up over my deathly white face. They lifted me onto a stretcher and slid me smoothly into the back of the van.

CHAPTER 3

Well, I wasn't going to let my body go off without me, so I followed it into the van. And even in those awful moments, a small part of me wanted to laugh at the sheer absurdity of what was happening. We swept at speed through the bustling streets of London and finally pulled up to a large, prefabricated building which was the temporary morgue set up to meet demand.

If I'd been attached to my stomach at that point, I knew it would have been knotted, as it was, I felt a wave of fear wash over me. What was going to happen to me now? I had no choice but to keep the faith and try desperately not to even think of the word autopsy. Surely, they must detect signs of life before that – I mean, there must be procedures and careful double-checks?

My body was taken out of the van, and I was swiftly wheeled inside the building. I was overwhelmed with the metallic smell of blood, human waste, and a mix of strong disinfectants. Weird, I had no idea whether in reality, I was able to smell in my current state, or whether it was just some sensory memory – whatever, I knew it was making me feel worse and worse. And I'd watched enough TV dramas to know what came next – indeed, I could see equipment on portable trolleys set next to stainless-steel tables all gleaming coldly in the harsh artificial lighting.

Everything was spotless, even if the place had been put together in a rush, it certainly looked fit for purpose. The other women's bodies were being brought in, and two assistants were already draping them with starched white sheets up to the chin. With relief, I noticed that Matt, my friendly policeman, had also turned up, although I could see he wanted to be here about as much as I did. I don't know why I was pinning all my hopes on him, hoping he'd hear me before it was too late, but I did know he sensed something, and I knew he had a kind heart. Bizarre as it may sound, I know I felt a connection even in my sorry state. What could I do to get his attention? I felt this was fate's sick joke. Yes, I'd been saved from drowning, but look what was happening instead. Things were extremely grim.

I studied Matt as he stood huddled in the corner, quietly speaking to the morgue attendant, or diener as they were called, the word meaning "corpse servant" – how gruesome. They were discussing everyday stuff, football and the like, as the last woman was brought in to join us. Four bodies in a row, our modesty preserved by white sheets.

"This the last one then?" the attendant said. "Been a busy night again on the river."

Matt nodded, "It's relentless, isn't it, but I don't think the divers are going down again today. And I got the short straw coming here."

The attendant grinned at him. "You get used to it eventually." I thought how ridiculous it was that Matt had come to guard us; what did they think we were planning – we could hardly jump off the table and run away. Although perhaps, in my case, that wasn't so far out, at least I hoped it wasn't. I willed my useless body to do just that, but nothing, no movement whatsoever.

As I'd heard his colleagues address him, Stuart looked to be in his thirties, although it wasn't easy to tell as he was getting fully gowned up in white scrubs, pulling on latex gloves. The banter continued, I suppose you had to keep cheerful surrounded by so much that wasn't. I'd heard it said that more care and attention was given to a body than a living patient in a hospital bed, with so many rules, regulations, and procedures to be followed. It seemed ironic that more time might be spent on the dead than on the living.

I'd zoned out for a moment or two when I heard Stuart say, "They all have to have an autopsy, an official practice now, dotting the i's and crossing the t's." He glanced at the clock, "Boss's late, usually here by now." Matt nodded absently, he wasn't paying attention.

Stuart continued. "We used to have an hour and a half per person, been cut down to an hour now, and that includes sorting notes and pictures and writing it up, and," he added, warming to his theme, "all before six in the evening, thank you very much. Boss's rules, work-life balance and all that won't work any later, however busy we are."

"Will you have time for all of them today?"

Stuart laughed, "Probably, slick as a whistle he is when he gets going. One in one out. We'll get this lot sorted." Unseen, I quailed, and Matt looked around; maybe he'd caught my grief. How could I watch as my once beautiful, alluring body was cut up in front of me?

I was certain Matt was aware of my presence, so I shouted out again, and YES, there it was again, that look on his face, he'd heard something. But he couldn't register where it was coming from. He must be what they call a sensitive, but unless he boosted his skills a little more, he was going to carry on being bewildered, and that was no help to me at all. To be honest, I was pinning all my hopes on this wet-behind-the-ears, handsome guy. I loved the way he brushed his hair away from his eyes, I knew he was a kind person too, I'd already seen the evidence. All I had to do was use all my energy to make him at least hear me, even if he couldn't see me.

As Stuart busied himself, making sure everything was in place for the pathologist, Matt commented, "Can't wait to get out of here, wash my clothes, the smell always lingers, takes ages to get rid of it."

"You get used to it. I don't smell it any more but my girlfriend makes me get straight in the shower when I get in, says I smell of death. We get through gallons of disinfectant, but it only masks it, doesn't get rid. You'd be surprised how quickly decomposition sets in, it's that you can smell."

Gross, I felt like retching and I could see from his face that I was only echoing Matt's disgust. I think he was relieved when this cheerful conversation was interrupted by the entrance of the pathologist. Fully masked and gowned, he was a man obviously stressed, anxious to get on with things but at the same time well aware of his own importance.

He mumbled impatiently, "Right, four today, is it?" as he swiftly made his way over to Stuart, his assistant for the day.

"Sorry, sir?"

He said it more sharply this time, "I understand you have four women for me?"

"Yes, four, sir."

"We'll start with this one." He indicated the body on the right. Stuart removed the starched sheet from the corpse furthest away from me and was now taking shots from different angles. I felt sick, not shots I'd want in my album! Gone was the light banter from before, this was serious business. I could only thank God I was to the far left, I wouldn't be dealt with next, which gave me a little more time.

The pathologist nodded to one of the assistants. "Music please, The Planets, op. 32, Mars the Bringer of War." Music? He'd be cutting us up to music. Great! I'd been force-fed classical music at boarding school, so I was familiar with Holst, it set the seal on the whole macabre scene, and the room suddenly sprang into action as the dramatic music boomed from the sound system.

I was startled by a high-pitched whining competing

with Holst and saw Stuart had handed the pathologist a medical saw which he was using to open the skull of the first woman. I couldn't watch. I had to swiftly leave the building, sickened to the core. Did I have to accept the inevitable? My once sassy persona, Ellie, the real me, would be just another number in the pitiful death toll. From my viewpoint outside, I could see London life was going on as normal, traffic-jammed, people striding, everyone with places to be, oblivious of what was happening in the building behind me.

I pulled myself together and went back in. It was not in my nature to give up, and maybe all was not lost? Once more, I was pleading with Matt, "Double-check the last body on the left. I'm begging, please." I thought he'd heard and seen me for a moment, but hope died as he scratched his head; he still didn't get it. Below me, the dreadful procedure on the first body was nearly completed. Another sorry death dated and documented. Stuart placed the skull carefully back in place, replaced the scalp flap then moved to sew up the Y-shaped opening from sternum to pelvis. He worked with speed and precision, and while he was attending to the first body, the pathologist had already moved on to the second.

It seemed no time at all until work on the third woman commenced. Fuck, I was next! After finishing with her, he discarded his latex gloves and mask, wiped his hands carefully with an antiseptic wipe, and left the room. He didn't say a thing to Stuart. Presumably even pathologists needed to answer the call of nature now and then. I looked at the clock; the hours had ticked by since he started his work.

A thought suddenly occurred, maybe this was all part of the spell, or was that just wishful thinking? With my life hanging by a thread, was it possible that I had to be even closer to death? Could it be that drowning wasn't enough? Nothing to do now until the pathologist came back. One by one, the women who'd been worked on were placed on stretchers to be returned to their refrigeration drawers, awaiting identification and the undertaker.

Then it was my turn; I couldn't look away. Surely there could be no going back from here – where would I be? Would I be forever a ghost-like creature, neither in heaven nor hell, but condemned for eternity to hover between, purgatory maybe? I hadn't been bad, but neither had I been an angel, if these things counted. The music track changed. Beethoven's Fifth was to be the soundtrack to my final few moments. Stuart handed over the small saw. I didn't have a religious bone in my body, but from somewhere a prayer came to mind. It seemed appropriate at a time like this, maybe I'd get brownie points for wherever I was going. I watched in horror as the pathologist bent over me, the saw whined, and I stared death in the face.

CHAPTER 4

Then a miracle, some sort of divine intervention, my prayers answered, or was this just the next part of the complex, ancient spell? At the very moment the music reached its crescendo, and the pathologist lowered the whining saw to my skull, my comatose body suddenly sat bolt upright on the mortuary table, and my eyes opened, staring glassy and unseeing.

Water started seeping out of my mouth, a slow trickle at first, then gushing out of every orifice of my body, hitting the floor with such force that it splashed before flowing everywhere. Hallelujah, I was alive! To say I was freaked out was an understatement, even though I'd been hoping and praying for something like this. The shock nearly killed the pathologist, the saw clattered noisily as it dropped from his hands, and he leapt back from the table as if electrocuted, yelling, "Jesus, she's still alive," then promptly collapsed, crashing to the floor. Stuart thankfully didn't lose consciousness, but he started to shake uncontrollably, muttering to himself, "Best turn off the music so we can concentrate."

As swiftly as I'd bolted up, I slumped down again, my body hitting the table hard, eyes shut, limbs all over the place, the white sheet crumpled down around me, and no evidence of further movement. But I'd been seen, at least they knew I was alive!

Matt was already on his radio. "PC 3401. Ambulance to the morgue right away. Yes, it's an emergency – one of the women from this morning, she's alive!" Stuart with a shocked expression said, "What the fuck happened there? I've never seen anything like it, she only bloody well sat up, didn't she?" Matt nodded in agreement not quite believing his own eyes, he then pointed down at the Pathologist crumpled on the floor. "...and what about your boss?" Stuart bent downwards and belatedly checked for a pulse.

"Is he OK?" asked Matt. "An ambulance is on its way they can check him over too."

Stuart nodded, "Just fainted, can't blame him." They both turned to look at me apprehensively, although I knew I looked anything but alive and healthy. Stuart took charge, pulling up a chair for the pathologist, who was coming to, as one of the other assistants rushed over with a glass of water. I could see the pathologist's hand shaking badly as he took it. The realisation he'd been about to saw into my head while I was still alive had obviously shocked him to the core.

I checked my body for any more encouraging signs.

Weirdly my lips were in a gruesome trout pout, and from the corner of my mouth, water was continuing to flow.

"Sir?" Stuart turned to his boss.

The older man shook his head quizzically, "No. Never come across this before, not without pressure being applied to the lungs." He stood, moved forward reluctantly, and turned my head to one side, "Don't want her drowning again."

Stuart lowered his voice, "Sir, you know all this talk about witches, you don't think …?"

"Oh, don't be so ridiculous," the pathologist had regained some of his colour but was still trembling. "I can't believe the doctor on the scene missed this; someone's going to be in deep trouble, have to hope it's not us." Then they all nearly jumped out of their skins – if it hadn't all been so dreadful, it would be comical – as I started hiccupping, regular and loud, my body jerking with each aggressive spasm. Well at least it would reassure them I wasn't dead yet and should certainly minimise my chances of being dissected alive.

CHAPTER 5

One year and ten months later
I knew how long I'd been here, there was a clock on the wall with the date tormenting me day in and day out as time passed, seconds, minutes, hours, days, weeks, and months – tick by tick. Trapped in my useless body in a hospital bed. Yes, I was still in a coma, alive but in purgatory, much of the time I felt it would have been easier to die.

My only reprieve was my out-of-body experiences. Unfortunately, as time went on and my physical body became progressively weaker, so did my ability to travel; no longer able to leave the room, I was a prisoner. I was in big trouble. I knew I must be heading towards the end, maybe I'd just gently and peacefully fade away to nothing. Perhaps for the best, I'd been in this state far too long now. It wasn't a regular coma, I was stuck in the spell, but there was no way the specialists would know what to do, I was a medical conundrum. They were dealing with magic, or witchcraft (although I know that has a bad name), which had gone badly wrong.

I'd been taken from the morgue to the Coma Specialist Centre in London, flashing blue lights whizzing me across the city. It seemed this was the only place for me, but I knew, from seeing my body on the bed, it would be fruitless. In normal circumstances I was probably in the best place; what they didn't know about brain injury or disease wasn't worth knowing, their success rate was high, their dedication second to none, although I'm pretty certain they'd never worked with a failed witch before, who was literally spellbound.

The specialists were amazed I'd survived being immersed in the water for so long. The water still in my lungs had taken me to the point of death, and in the ambulance I'd gone into cardiac arrest. They'd managed to bring me back, but the trauma was such that they couldn't be certain there was no brain damage. I was wired up to any number of monitors and understood from what I overheard that because of the swift reaction of the ambulance team, my heart had sustained little damage, but I was deeply unconscious and, of course, they couldn't have known I could still see everything, as "ghost" Ellie. I was so thankful I still had a window on the world, even though it was only in this room. I'd given up on trying to get them to see or hear out-of-body me, and, as time passed, I could feel myself fading in and out like an old movie.

By now, to say I was a coma expert was an under-statement. I knew everything there was to know, having learnt from the best – the specialists who visited my room regularly. When I was first admitted, they'd been fairly positive I could recover quickly, but as time passed, I'd hear how puzzled they were; I simply wasn't responding as I should. I was battered and bruised from the continual moving and prodding. They wouldn't leave me alone. "Something's not right. She really should have come round by now. Her body has recovered from all the initial injuries; there's something else going on." They'd shake their heads. There were four main stages of a coma, and I seemed to have stopped at stage one. Unresponsive was how they termed it. Stage two was early responses, stage three agitated and confused, and stage four was higher-level responses and on the road to recovery.

You might wonder why I didn't use my magic and try another spell to escape this predicament. It wasn't that easy; my magic didn't work in my comatose state, I was trapped in limbo, and I couldn't attempt even the simplest things. So frustrating.

Since this was a teaching hospital, I'd heard it all from the specialists and their students congregated around my bed – nothing like rubbing salt into the wound. They shared experiences of those who had recovered from comas. Some former patients spoke of being able to hear everything, others of strange mental experiences – vivid dreams or hallucinations. Others were unaware they were in a coma, they thought what was going on in their head was real life, and couldn't believe when they woke up in a hospital bed just how much time they'd lost. The experts endlessly went through long lists of symptoms and complications in front of me, not sensitive that I may be able to hear every word they spoke. The tragedy was that when a tear slipped from the eye of the unconscious Ellie, it was dismissed as an autonomic reaction, no indication of anything else.

For some reason, I felt positive today, but that only lasted until the consultant neurologist, Mr Kapashi, came into the room, a sombre look on his face. He was my favourite, the most positive and upbeat of them all, so his long face spoke volumes. He had named me Jane, as they didn't know my identity – after all, I had been brought out of the river totally naked. But it still felt strange; Jane didn't suit me at all. But after all this time, I felt a connection with Mr Kapashi, who always took the time to speak to me as if I was a person and not just a body on a bed.

Perched on the edge of my bed, surrounded by his entourage, he was serious, and I had a feeling of foreboding. I sometimes felt like a piece of meat as I was regularly turned to stop the bedsores. Some nurses were kind, chatting as if we were having a two-way conversation. Others just bustled around, ignoring the fact that lying there was a real person with emotional needs. Mr Kapashi always took time to speak to me. But not today. Something was very wrong.

Mr Kapashi had a beautiful voice, a soothing nature, and a fabulous bedside manner. He even sent me to sleep sometimes with his musical voice, like a trickling stream. He was patient with his students, always taking the time to explain. Some of the students I recognised, others had moved on, but you know you're getting older when the trainee doctors look like they should still be at school. They treated Mr Kapashi as a superior being, hanging on his every word. I think nearly all of them, guys and girls, were a little in love with him. I was a bit too, he was an attractive man with a ready smile. Today that was noticeably absent, and I knew it was bad news. I spent a lot of time reading body language these days.

"Patient progress has been minimal," he said. "Now would be a good time to pray for a miracle. We will, however, continue with the routine response tests." A student raised a hand with a question, but he shook his head. "The tears were simply an autonomic response." While he was speaking, he was holding my hand, stroking it gently. I couldn't feel a thing, but I heard the regret in his tone, "Time is running out." I wondered what it would feel like to be dead. Would it be a big nothing, or was there life afterwards? Would it be different for a witch? Would I be visiting my past and future lives? The way it was looking, I'd find out soon enough.

CHAPTER 6

As I said, few of the staff took the time to speak to me, even though it was a known fact that coma patients could often hear what was going on. I understood why they'd spend more time with their other patients, the recovering; it was bound to be more satisfying when someone could communicate. So they often whizzed in and out, made sure I was comfortable and stable and were gone before I knew it.

Occasionally a kind soul would switch on the TV, which at least drowned out the ticking clock for a while. They'd tune it into a news or current affairs programme as they plumped up pillows and smoothed the covers over me, not realising how much I appreciated their kindness. I dipped in and out of listening to these programmes, trying for a while to concentrate on what was going on in the world outside. I was desperate for this to end, whether in recovery or death.

Unsurprisingly, the world had moved on while I'd been here, and now witch stories were yesterday's news; I just knew it had been brushed under the carpet. A problem they were solving under the radar. The undercurrent of news was more worrying, the suicide contagion that seemed to have taken hold around the country. Women everywhere were being washed up on riverbanks, as I had been, or other gruesome "suicides" were reported. It seemed no one was asking the question, why? Why women, and very few men? I tried not to worry, relieved when they turned the news to something more mundane. After all, what could I do?

By this time, I was ready to give in, but I didn't seem to have the option. Even my dreams had stopped. No more dreams of drowning and no sign of Hettie and past lives. I was a nonentity, a body the staff tended to, day in, day out. I deeply regretted using the spell; I shouldn't have dabbled with magic in the first place. It had certainly ended in tears for me. With deep regret, I know my mother was right, I'd had a gilded life and I'd thrown it all away on a whim. What I'd give to just live a normal, boring life. But then, just as my spirits had sunk about as low as they could, something started happening – or was I just imagining it? I sensed a presence in the room. There was no one to be seen, but at odd times a feeling of peace would creep over me, as if someone was there, someone looking out for me. Maybe it was simply a side effect of the coma, but I felt oddly comforted. And then, one day I felt a touch on my cheek. I almost missed it, a light feathery touch on my out-of-body self just for a second or two. Was that possible? Was it the ghost of a long-dead patient roaming the wards, or was it something or someone else?

I'd recently caught snatches of conversation; although I didn't know for sure, I was certain something was going on. I needed to stay alert to hear what was being discussed. First in the room was Mr Singh, my second-favourite consultant; he had a good bedside manner, although I still preferred Mr Kapashi. Seating himself on the side of the bed, he said, "Jane, if you can hear me, you might feel a little disturbed with what we are discussing today, how the new regulations affect you as a patient. Protocols have changed radically. If there is no improvement after two years, all care and medical assistance will be withdrawn." That was that then, if nothing happened within the next couple of months, I was a goner. Hearing him clearly, but being unable to respond, was unbearable.

While waiting for his team to arrive, Mr Singh tested my reflexes, seeking resistance in my hands and reaction in my elbows. Then he gently pulled the blankets back to tap my knees and run an instrument under each of my feet, but still nothing. He replaced the blankets and then shone a light into my eyes, disappointment on his face as my pupils remained fixed and dilated with no reaction at all. I shared his frustration, after all, I'd had this routinely repeated countless times through the years.

Time to concentrate, as the rest of the team and students surrounded my bed. I'd seen them all before, even knew most of their names. Mr Singh updated them on my current condition, my prognosis, and the new regulations on care for coma patients. It was confirmed that I only had two months left to make a miraculous recovery. One of the student doctors stated the obvious, "If we stop all treatment, will Jane die?"

Mr Singh nodded. "I'm afraid so." Not sure I wanted to hear much more, Mr Singh was merely confirming what I already knew. I zoned out, their words blending into one – blah blah blah. Then, as if by magic, a new cleaner arrived. There was something about her, but I couldn't put my finger on it. How funny she chose this moment to make her way into the room, totally bad timing. The team seemed oblivious, like she wasn't there, invisible. She carried on with her job, keeping my environment clean and tidy. The cleaner also seemed unaware, or so I thought, to what was happening around her.

I'd had plenty of time to study people, it was the only hobby I had. On the surface, the cleaner was fairly nondescript, the type of person who could easily pass unnoticed as she silently carried out her work, weaving in and out of the medical team. She wore oversized glasses, far too big for her mousy face. I had a sudden strange thought; she looked like Rose West, the infamous serial killer. I remember watching a documentary about the Wests, and the incredible thing was how Rose got away with murder simply by looking so ordinary. No one noticed or remembered her.

I re-focused on Mr Singh as he continued to talk. "In two months, we will have to start end-of-life care, turn off life support and withdraw feeding tubes."

One of the students asked, "Are there no other tests that can be run?"

"I'm afraid not. There's nothing left to do apart from making her as comfortable as we can."

Well, I recognised a death sentence when I heard it. What struck me as odd was that while this sensitive subject was covered, the cleaner made no attempt to leave the room, continuing to clean around them, although nobody paid her any attention. It was as if they couldn't see her. Her cleaning was certainly meticulous, an improvement on my usual cleaner, Steve, who managed to knock over more items than he cleaned. Who was she? Finishing off in the bathroom, she put all her cleaning equipment back into her trolley and left as quietly as she'd arrived, not a second glance. She seemed oblivious of what had been going on around her. What was strange was that about fifteen minutes afterwards, Steve turned up. I wanted to tell him not to bother, it had all been done – and a lot more efficiently – but of course, he couldn't hear me. Maybe their shifts had clashed – it happens.

CHAPTER 7

Mr Singh and his team left the room, and Steve did a quick dust around, not that it needed it. I could see he looked puzzled, something didn't look right, the room was too tidy, not to mention clean and sparkly – not his usual style. "Must be going mad," I heard him mutter. "I've already done this one, but I don't remember coming in here." Shrugging, as he realised there was little left for him to do, he left with a smile at the prospect of getting home earlier than normal.

Almost as soon as he'd gone, the new cleaner came back into the room. Had she forgotten something? As she shut the door behind her, she turned and locked it, checking the door handle to make sure it was secure. What the hell was she up to? That's when she looked straight up at me – yes, the "me" floating outside my body! And did I feel the air shift around me? Was there someone else there as well as the rather odd cleaner and me?

Then she spoke, quietly but urgently, "Ellie, we've got very little time, you need to listen carefully.' For a moment, I didn't register that she was talking to me, I think I'd rather lost the art of conversation, but she called me Ellie. How could she know who I was when no one else did?

I yelled with excitement, "You can see me, wow, wow, wow, I can't believe it. How do you know my name? How did you find me?" I reached for her hand, but mine just went through hers.

She was impatient, no longer the meek little mouse who busied herself around the room. "My name's Carol, and that's all you need to know. I'm here to help. I've got your back, but you're in grave danger. You attempted the spell without really understanding it, stupid."

"You're a witch?"

She put a finger to her lips. "Shush, no time for explanations. Just believe in the magic like you always have, Ellie, that's all you need to do."

"I don't understand."

"You don't need to," she said briskly. "Now, no questions, just listen." To say I was confused would be an understatement. I'd been in that room for so long now it was hard to take in what was happening.

"Look, you're shocked and confused, and I haven't got long, but I know exactly who you are and how you got here." Her whole attitude and persona had changed, her voice authoritative as her slightly hunched form straightened before my eyes, revealing the powerful witch now in front of me.

"Oh my God," I said, "you're the first person to see me, in all this time, the only one, but you heard the consultant – I don't know what can be done."

"Well, I do, but there's no time to waste. Stay alert, I'll be back as soon as I can."

Maybe it was a defence mechanism, but the Ellie of old with her kick-ass attitude came back.

"Err, help me how? I'm a lost cause!" – I paused – "I'm not sure you understand the gravity of the situation." I was starting to feel spooked. If I didn't know who she was, or how she'd found me, how did I know whether she was here to help or harm? Had I been tracked down to ensure I was bumped off for good and all?

"Ditch the attitude," she said sharply. "You'll just have to trust me. You don't have a lot of options, do you?"

"So you're going to perform a miracle? Because that's what I need right now."

"Careful. You don't want to offend me, because I can walk out of here, not come back and leave you to cope on your own."

I thought it best to backtrack. "OK, I'm sorry, I'm scared and can't see how you can make things right."

"I have the benefit of experience, I've used this spell and, I might add, more successfully than you. I know where you went wrong, and I can put it right." Then, in response to my sceptical silence, "What, d'you think you're the only one, Ellie? The chosen one?"

I was about to let loose a little more sarcasm, but she didn't give me time. "There's no such thing as a miracle, but if you stop looking down your conceited little nose, you might see I'm your fairy godmother." She laughed.

"But you heard," I said, "they're going to pull the plug. I'm going to die in a few weeks."

"Not if I can help it," she said firmly.

I decided she was right, and I did need to shut up. I didn't know who or what she was, but I couldn't look a gift horse in the mouth. I did know Carol probably wasn't her real name, and she was certainly not your average cleaner, but I had to face it. Currently, she was the only game in town, although what she said next knocked me sideways.

"Before I go, I need to clarify something. Your plight is just the tip of the iceberg, and I hope you'll see fit to contribute to our charity. I know you're not short of a penny or two." She continued, "The money will cover travel and safe houses for vulnerable women. Nothing comes for free, you know, and helping correct the spell is dangerous. Financial reparation is only fair. You may have missed what's happening to witches; I'm risking a lot." She was interrupted by someone trying the door handle of my room. She swiftly crossed the floor and unlocked it. Reverting to her cleaner persona, she apologised to the nurse and was once again the quiet little mouse.

When she left, Carol didn't close the door behind her, and I caught a glimpse of her in the corridor, talking to a woman in black. They were in deep discussion for a few moments, and then they both seemed to disappear, although that may have just been a product of my muddled mind. I'd have to ask Carol about the mysterious woman next time she chose to drop in.

My mind was whirling. I felt remorse that I'd been

so rude, but she had caught me off-guard, and I was understandably a little twitchy, what with the death sentence and all, plus the ransom money. Could I trust her with my bank details and password? Still, I should have been more receptive, especially as she was the only one who'd been able to see and acknowledge me. Despite myself, a tiny flame of hope had been lit, although I couldn't believe she knew the same spell I'd found in the hidden book at Lavender Cottage. On the other hand, if she disappeared, so did my last chance of regaining my life. I was between a rock and a hard place.

CHAPTER 8

One month later
I was devasted. She wasn't coming back. She'd abandoned me. But had I expected anything else? Maybe I'd imagined the whole thing? Could Carol the magical cleaner simply have been a side effect of the coma, a wishful figment of my imagination? I prayed that wasn't the case. I wanted to be saved, not left to die.

Steve, the burly cleaner, was in my room again, as usual; he knew nothing of my dilemma. He'd become increasingly annoying as he bumped into everything, and he was singing, "I'm H.A.P.P.Y., I'm H.A.P.P.Y." What an insensitive prick, his singing was worse than his whistling. I shouted, "Shut the fuck up because I'm not feeling frigging H.A.P.P.Y.," but of course he couldn't hear me. I felt he could be the last straw, I'd had to put up with him for nearly two years now, and patience wasn't a virtue of mine.

Just as I'd given up all hope, Carol reappeared, as unremarkably as she'd left, a nondescript woman who blended in so easily she was almost invisible. She entered the room cautiously.

"It's OK," I said, "they've finished with today's rounds." I didn't want to reveal my delight at seeing her.

"Good," she said. "I've had a nightmare few weeks, another emergency."

"What, worse than mine?" I suppose she knew I wasn't going anywhere!

She sighed. "Things are escalating. Honestly, I'm all over the place. So many needing help." I wondered who'd made her the witch saviour, she didn't look the part. What was so special about her? She seated herself on my bed, automatically straightening the sheet, which amused me, she'd obviously been playing the cleaning part a bit too long.

She opened an envelope she was holding. "Right, let's get this show on the road!"

"OK," I said cautiously.

"Please read the terms and conditions." It was a professional terms of service contract, and the amount stated as a fee was fifty thousand pounds, which was extortionate. But what choice did I have? I was on a sinking ship, tethered by a swiftly fraying rope.

"Look," she said, "I'm happy to help, but each case is charged according to means. It's not all for me, you know, I pass it along to those who most need it, although I more than cover my expenses." She smiled as she moved towards the door. "I'll leave that with you, though as you're not really in a position to sign, verbal confirmation will be splendid." Wow, super-efficient, cold, and calculating, an attitude that didn't seem to fit her appearance.

"If I agree to these terms and conditions, are you one hundred per cent confident this will work, and I will be released from the spell-induced coma?"

She nodded briefly, and I noticed a trace of relief on her face. Maybe she thought I'd baulk at the price. "That goes without saying. I'll be back as soon as I can."

"Wait," I said. "Not that I don't trust you, Carol, but could you just do a little magic?"

She looked insulted. "Really?"

"Really," I said and watched as she cast a few simple spells, changing the room's colour from clinical white to bright sunflower yellow. She did a quick transformation spell on herself – suddenly in front of me was a glamorous rock chick clad in leather jacket and trousers, Carol, the dowdy cleaner, had disappeared. As she impatiently changed everything back to normal, I said, "There's something else, I've felt a presence in here, as if someone else is in the room. Can you feel it? I saw you talking to a woman in black, last time you were here." Carol gave me a look, but chose not to answer, instead wheeling her trolley ahead of her out of the room. I honestly didn't know when or if she'd return.

Three days later
I'd been counting seconds, minutes, and hours, so I knew just how long it was before Carol came back. This time

it looked as though she meant business. She was dragging one of the huge laundry trolleys the porters used. It was certainly big enough to hold me. As usual, she locked the door behind her and barely acknowledged me. There was a sense of urgency about her as if something significant was about to happen.

She swiftly removed a load of sheets from the trolley. I was relieved to see it was clean laundry. Not leaving anything to chance, she'd done a quick spell, and there was now a brick wall making up the side of my room where the door had once been.

"I can see where you went wrong," she said matter-of-factly, and gave a rare smile. "You were so nearly there."

I had to ask,

"Are you sure you know how to resolve it?"

"How rude to even question my integrity, I can still walk away if you continue to insult me."

I apologised. "I am so sorry, I'm just so anxious, I hope you understand."

She didn't reply, and I gasped as she took action, swiftly but carefully detaching the drips that were keeping me alive, and the wires that recorded my condition. I heard the ancient words she was chanting and realised it was simply a minor error I'd made, a couple of words transposed which had cost me nearly two years of my life – not to mention fifty grand.

Things were now happening at speed. I could feel the out-of-body me being sucked back into my physical body, and I instantly lost vision. After almost two years of seeing myself lying prone on the hospital bed, I suddenly couldn't see anything. Then I felt tingling start in my fingers and toes, gradually travelling through the rest of my body like a massive surge of electricity. My eyes shot open – and I could see again.

The coming round was weird, nothing like waking up from a deep sleep. It felt as if I was thawing from a big freeze. I raised my head, not expecting much, but it felt normal, not as if I'd spent years immobile on a bed. The spell had worked, well at least this part of it, anyway. I tried out my voice, it was a little hoarse, "Thank you, Carol." I sat up on the bed, swung my legs around and tentatively put my feet on the ground. Then, after a moment's hesitation, I stood up. I felt slightly off-balance but nothing more than that. With apprehension I raised my eyes to my reflection in the mirror, and was shocked, I actually looked better, younger, as if the enforced rest had done me some good. I knew I'd been looked after amazingly well, my body regularly massaged with rich body lotion, my food intake just right, with all the correct nutrients pumped into my body daily, but I'd never been able to appreciate any improvement. I'd been merely an extension of the technology that was keeping me alive, tightly tucked into the bedding that was regularly changed, and it had been hard to see my full body.

Carol, digging deep into the laundry basket, brought out clothing for me. OK, not my usual thing but it would have to do, we didn't have much time. The underwear was like something I'd have worn at boarding school, not my usual sexy silk undies, but this wasn't a time to be choosy. Carol had known my size, maybe it was expecting a bit much for her to get my style too. I mentally resolved to buy myself a whole new wardrobe. Meanwhile, I found I was moving with total ease, with no stiffness anywhere.

"You shouldn't have any side effects," she said. "You're physically back to normal, you just have to be able to get your head around what's happened." I laughed, it sounded a little manic I will admit.

"Shush Ellie, they'll hear you!" She wasn't seeing the funny side at all. "We have to move, we can talk later, now pull yourself together."

"Sorry, I'm just deliriously happy." It was true, my emotions were in tatters, and tears of joy ran down my face. Taking a last, quick glimpse in the mirror, I could see that even with eyes red from crying and my hair all over the place, there was no doubt that I looked good. I was ready to face the world again.

"Quickly," she said, helping me onto the bed so I could climb into the laundry trolley. I followed instruction, having to almost double up, knees to chin, and she piled sheets back on top of me.

I couldn't see a damn thing, but I heard her chant another simple spell to reopen the doorway. Once outside the room, she resealed it, buying us some time and aiding our getaway. Urgently on the move now, her slight body pushed the trolley along the corridors with surprising strength. I knew she thought of me as a loose cannon, and she'd put a silencing spell on me to make sure I couldn't make a noise and attract unwelcome attention.

The laundry was on site, and she had parked her van near its entrance. I heard a vehicle's doors being opened and creaking as I was wheeled up a ramp. Once inside the van, she removed the sheets and helped me out of the basket.

"Make yourself as comfortable as you can. I'll drop the trolley at the laundry, back in a moment."

As she closed and locked the doors, I moved to the back and, feeling around, found an old duvet, it smelt mouldy but would have to do. The van itself smelt pretty foul; goodness knows what she kept in there. I started to shiver from nerves or cold and was grateful to wrap myself up; at least I was warmer, even if I had to hold my nose.

Carol returned, slipped into the driver's seat, and turned the key, but nothing happened. I heard her swear, she tried again and, thank God, this time it started. I thought wryly that perhaps she could treat herself to a new van once the money had been transferred. The van crunched into gear and lurched forward, and then we were on the open road. I kept my fingers crossed that we wouldn't get stopped by the police. She may have been able to do magic, but she wasn't a great driver – too fast and erratic. If we were stopped and they found me in the back, it would look suspiciously like a kidnap.

I was being swung from side to side, we must have been travelling on exceptionally winding roads. I normally avoided these like the plague, they made me feel sick at the best of times and not being able to see now made the journey a real roller coaster of a ride. Several times I thought I was going to throw up, the smell and motion were really getting to me. Mercifully I managed to hold on, I didn't want to lie in my own vomit. Just when I'd reached the point of thinking the horrible journey was never going to end, the van came to an abrupt halt and, to my relief, Carol unlocked and opened the door. With an overwhelming sense of relief, I knew now everything would be all right.

CHAPTER 9

Feeling dizzy after the tension of the escape and the journey, it took a few moments for me to force my cramped limbs to move. Discarding the warm but pongy duvet, I crawled towards the open doors. Freedom! The mouldy smell seemed to have become a part of me, and I was grateful to get out into the fresh air. I quickly drank the bottle of water Carol passed me and accepted the tissues she handed me to wipe my face. I felt very shaky as reality hit home. Carol had removed the voice-silencing spell. "I feel strange," I said when she asked me if I was OK. "That smell in the back of the van was gross. What do you keep in there?"

"Sorry, all sorts of things, but we had to avoid anyone seeing you." She didn't elaborate further, and I looked around as I started to feel a little better. It was dusk, and we were somewhere in the countryside. I asked where we were, but she either didn't hear me or chose to ignore the question. Switching on a large torch, she locked the van and set off down a tree-lined lane. I wasn't going to get any more information right now, so I followed quietly behind her. It was pretty spooky moving down the lane. There seemed to be no one else around.

After a while, by which time my shoes were totally mud-clogged, I saw a tiny Victorian cottage set a little way back from the lane. It looked almost derelict, certainly in need of some TLC, and more than just a lick of paint. It was certainly secluded and, with no sign of nosy neighbours, she could live her witchy life here quite peacefully. We entered the tiny front garden through a rickety wooden gate, which could have done with some lubricant. As I followed her inside, I could see it was a two-up two-down sort of place. The door opened into a tiny living room, and the stairs were straight ahead.

"I'll show you up to your room," she said, and I followed her up the stairs to what must be her spare room. There was a pile of ironing on the bed which she shoved straight onto the floor. "You can use this room, and the bathroom's just there to freshen up. I'll put the kettle on. Tea or coffee?"

"Coffee would be lovely, thank you." I almost licked my lips at the thought of the simple pleasure I'd not enjoyed for so long. I hoped it wouldn't be a disappointment, I was quite the coffee connoisseur but I suspected it was more likely to be a budget instant blend.

She left me alone, and I scanned the twee, old-fashioned room with its shabby carpet, decor, and battered pine furniture. A single, wrought-iron bed, a bit like the one left at Lavender Cottage, dominated the space. It had a rose-patterned duvet. The only other furniture was a tiny single wardrobe and a bedside table on the threadbare pink carpet. As I moved, I saw my reflection in a long mirror on the wall – I was wrinkling my nose because, unfortunately, the room smelt like the van.

I hurriedly nipped to the sparse bathroom – thankfully, it was clean. The same carpet ran through into this room. Who the heck has carpet in their bathroom these days? Hardly hygienic.

A quick freshen up later, I made my way down the steep stairs. Delicious cooking smells were wafting up and making my mouth water and my stomach rumble. I hadn't realised how much I wanted food. Carol was bustling about in the tiny galley kitchen, but I saw she'd placed a steaming cup of coffee for me on the small coffee table in the cramped lounge. It was a bookish room with different-sized volumes occupying every square inch of space.

Carol called out, "Coffee on the table and mind the cats, they're around here somewhere, and they rule the roost. Supper ready in a minute."

I hoped she'd hurry up, I was ravenous. I took a few welcome sips of the coffee. Heaven! OK, it was budget, but that didn't matter, it was nectar as far as I was concerned.

A welcoming fire had been lit, warming up the room nicely. Evidently, she lived here alone as I couldn't see any sign of anyone else. Out of the corner of my eye, I noticed movement and smiled to myself as I saw the cat was black – naturally! It was sitting near the fire, eyeing me up, staring at me with its knowing eyes. From the cat hair all over the sofa, it was clear that this was kitty's bed. The cushions, once velvet, were now worn and stained – urgh! This lady needed a home makeover, but maybe she liked it like this. Each to their own, I suppose.

The cat stalked over to me and jumped on the sofa as if it owned the place – well, it probably thought it did. It gave me a disgusted look as if I was intruding on its territory. I outstared it and it jumped down and stared unnervingly for a moment before heading upstairs, obviously thoroughly offended. Although the sofa had seen better days, it was super-comfy and I just sank into it. It was much warmer in this room than upstairs, and I felt myself nodding off. But before I did, Carol came in with a full English, maybe a bit late in the day for breakfast, but it had been a choice that was quick and easy for her to cook, and it smelt divine. There wasn't a dining table, so she put the plate full of food down on the coffee table. She then brought cutlery and a plate piled high with doorstep chunks of bread richly buttered. I had seen Nigella on TV recently double buttering toast – she would have been proud, it looked delicious!

Carol smiled, for the first time a warm smile. Maybe now she was at home, she could be herself, whoever that really was.

"I hope you are not vegetarian or vegan Ellie, I haven't really got much in other than what you have in front of you. As you can see, I'm a little remote here, there's not a village shop for miles, and I don't really do online shopping."

I smiled back. "I am not fussy, and certainly not vegetarian or vegan, plus I'm absolutely famished for some real food, not the drip that's been keeping me alive for forever."

"Well then, eat up while it's still hot."

I didn't waste any more time and tucked in.

The texture felt strange at first, chewing and digesting, but like riding a bike it all soon came back to me. The modest meal in front of me might well have been served in a top restaurant, crispy bacon and the bright yellow egg yolk brought back memories of my student days. We girls had often come home in the early hours, and then it'd be a hair of the dog to help the hangover, then over to the student canteen for a full English – true heaven. We'd even tried black pudding until we found out what it was made from.

Since uni, I'd become far more health-conscious and very rarely fell off the sensible food wagon, but I decided today was an exception, a celebration, and, I reasoned, I did need to plump up a bit.

As I finished the last morsel on my plate, a satisfied burp popped out. I was mortified.

"How rude, sorry about that."

Carol laughed. "Belch away, you've had a traumatic time, it needs to come out. I'm glad you enjoyed it." However embarrassing, my burp seemed to break the ice, and I realised she did have a sense of humour, she was still laughing to herself when I took my plate into the kitchen and started to wash up. She followed and stopped me resting her arm on mine, an intense look on her face. She looked into my eyes as if she could see right into my soul.

"No, you don't need to do that. Get yourself to bed, you must be shattered after all you've been through, you need a good night's natural sleep."

"Are you sure? I don't mind helping. I'm not tired, and it's early." I glanced at the clock on the mantelpiece.

"I don't want to hear another word," she said. "We have a lot to run through in the morning. You'll be leaving here in the afternoon ready for your new life." I must have looked puzzled. "Well, you didn't think you were staying here forever, did you?"

"No, obviously not, it's just I still feel a little disorientated."

She patted my arm again. "You'll sleep like a log and feel far more like your old self in the morning." I nodded. She seemed insistent, and I didn't want to appear rude.

As I headed for the stairs, I paused and turned, "Carol, just a quick question, how did you find me?"

She shot me a warning look. "I think I told you before, I can't say, but you should know there are people out there who have your back. There are still good guys around."

"But how on earth will I know who they are?"

She shook her head impatiently. "It'll soon become clear enough." She moved forward and gave me a gentle push in the direction of the stairs. "Go on, you need your rest, but if you're not ready to sleep, there's a selection of books in your bedside cabinet, and you have a good reading light by your bed." As I suddenly yawned, she laughed. "I don't place bets but if I did, I'd put money on you being asleep before your head hits the pillow."

Despite myself, I laughed too. I could see I wasn't going to get any answers tonight, so I said, "Goodnight – and thank you," and made my way upstairs.

CHAPTER 10

The following morning, I woke from a blissful dream with a smile on my face. Carol was right, I did feel refreshed; I'd had an amazing night's sleep. This time the dreams were happy ones, not my pre-coma haunting, drowning nightmares. I clearly remembered it featured Alice, Sarah, and Lizzie, my besties. We were back in Whitby for Goth Weekend, for Alice's hen party, we were having a lot of fun, laughing and joking, dressed in our Victorian finest. My smile faded, it was just a dream, not real life. Sadness washed over me, I had no idea when it would be safe to see them again, and what on earth did they think had happened to me? Did they think I was dead?

I decided against using the shower. It looked archaic, and the old enamel bath not much better, stained and chipped. I shuddered and settled for a strip wash using the toiletries Carol had left out, along with a rough, faded towel and flannel. Both felt like sandpaper, definitely not the standard I'd become used to in the many spa retreats I'd frequented since I fled Yorkshire.

I'd arrived at Carol's place with virtually nothing, just the clothes I stood up in, and they smelt a bit rank now, so I was reliant on what she'd left out for me, clothing-wise, to freshen up. The underwear was hardly what you'd call sexy, Bridget Jones-style oversized pants and a basic bra, like one of those trainer bras your mother gave you as a teenager. But they did fit, as did the sweater and leggings – not my usual attire though. She'd even got my foot size correct for the trainers. As I made my way downstairs, I could hear activity in the kitchen, the crashing of pots and pans. She wasn't what you'd call a delicate lady, even though she was so small and skinny. As I looked around the lounge, it seemed even shabbier in the light, dust particles shining as the sunshine came through the window.

Carol emerged from the kitchen. "Morning Ellie, how're you feeling?"

"Not too bad. I had a wonderful sleep, just as you said!"

"You're virtually recovered from your ordeal, and you'll feel stronger every day."

I smiled. "It's starting to seem like a lifetime away."

"Look," she indicated a small case on the floor by the sofa, "I've put together some basics you'll need until you get settled." She looked stern. "You now have the protection of the spell. It will last your lifetime and is extremely powerful. Use that power wisely to help others."

I nodded, it had crossed my mind that maybe I was subsidising all the other unfortunate women who needed her help but didn't have the funds. But I wasn't moaning, it was money well spent. But was I really protected? I didn't want to try it out again, once in a lifetime was more than enough. I turned my attention back to what she was saying, she must have read my mind. "A word of warning, you are not immortal." Then, totally changing the subject, back to her brisk, organised self, "I've booked you into a hotel near Hampstead. It was heavily booked around there, so there wasn't a lot of choice of rooms, but I think it's a good place to start."

I was a little confused. Back to London? Hampstead?

She continued, "I'd recommend you look at either buying or renting in that area, but recharge your batteries first, give yourself some breathing space before making any big decisions."

"Why Hampstead? I don't know that part of London very well."

She shrugged. "Just an area that seems safer than others at the moment. It makes sense to blend in with a crowd and become anonymous, hiding in plain sight. Although I don't doubt the witch hunters will be sniffing around there before too long."

I opened my mouth to ask for more information, but she only said, "Once you get back into the big bad world you'll understand more. You need to find out for yourself, keep your ears to the ground."

I realised just how cocooned I'd been in the hospital; I had a lot to catch up with.

She bustled back into the kitchen and brought out a bowl full of what looked like grey sludge, which I identified as porridge, reminiscent of boarding school offerings where you had to finish what you were given. I'd have to find a way of eating it and keeping it down. I didn't think she had anything else in the house, but thankfully, she also suggested some toast and marmalade. After I'd washed it all down with coffee, I had to admit I felt a lot more on top of things.

Carol seemed quite comfortable with silence, but when I'd finished, she said, "The advice I give all my clients is to be ultra-careful. You won't believe what's been happening while you've been in a coma, but you'll cope, I can tell you come from good magical stock. Now, I've given you the number of a couple of contacts who can help get you up to speed if you need help."

I was about to ask who they were, but she'd already headed back into the kitchen and, over her shoulder said, "Another coffee, before I drop you at the station?" I declined, my heart pounding a little, and it wasn't just the caffeine – I was going today then. "I've bought you a ticket to St Pancras and your hotel's booked for two weeks, which will give you time to find something more permanent. I'll be billing you for the expenses." I nodded, why would I have expected otherwise? "I can't emphasise how important it is to be careful with your magic. You won't know who to trust and," she smiled wryly, "maybe stick with safer spells from now on. They can't kill you now, but they could make your life very difficult."

She turned and started fumbling around in her oversized

handbag. Tissues, a blackened banana and a packet of cough sweets were amongst the things that went flying before she said, "Ah, here it is. A mobile phone for you. I've put a couple of contacts in there, they may be useful to you one day. Don't use any previous numbers you may remember; it wouldn't be safe."

"Is one of these numbers yours?" I asked.

She shook her head. "I said earlier, we won't meet again after today and that reminds me, please can you transfer the funds as soon as you get to a bank."

I hesitated because I wasn't sure how she'd take this. "Yes, I'll head to the bank once I get to Hampstead. I might have some explaining to do as I haven't used the account in nearly two years. I'll tell them I've been working away and had an overseas account."

She tutted. "It's a good job I trust you, Ellie. Here, this will tide you over." She handed me a bundle of notes. I counted £200 and reflected that wouldn't have lasted me five minutes in my old life.

"Thank you." I was genuinely grateful. "I'll add it to your fee." I was still curious about the contacts she'd given me. "I'd like to know something about these numbers," I held up the phone.

"Sorry, can't give you any more right now, but you'll find out when or if you need them. Only you will know when the time is right, if ever. You're very capable, even though you failed dismally at the spell, but that one was always pretty tricky." She paused as if wondering how much more she should tell me. "You do know our movement has gathered momentum. You'd be most surprised at who is supporting us, openly or undercover." She left that hanging in the air.

She had a great deal of practical information to offload before we parted.

"For now, Ellie, all you need do is concentrate on your future and think of the phone I've given you as backup only."

I sighed. "I'm feeling a little overwhelmed at the thought of going back out there."

She ignored my concern, intent on practicalities. "You have your hotel booking to start you off and then I'll leave it to you to look for somewhere long term. I realise you might not think much of the hotel, but I'm afraid there was no other choice, and there's little more I can do to help."

"Presumably if there are any problems with the transfer, I can call you?"

"No. I've told you, you won't see or hear from me, nor will you contact me. As long as you use the correct account, I can't see what could possibly go wrong."

Changing the subject, making it clear the previous topic was closed, she said, "Can you do a transformation spell, change how you look?"

"I think so," I was hesitant. "It's such a long time since I've done any magic, I'm probably a bit rusty."

"Nonsense, it's like riding a bike, it'll come back to you. Now, I suggest you keep your own name for your documents and such, but you must make sure you change your appearance. Try it now, show me." I was a bit slow off the mark, and she snapped, "Now, no time to waste. Look," she grabbed a magazine and stabbed a sharp fingernail at a group of women in a Boden advert. "Try the yummy mummy look." I still hesitated. "This isn't a game, you know," she snapped, so I took a deep breath and went for it. She nodded approval, and I was ridiculously pleased by that.

I'd never been under the illusion that Carol would be a friend, but I had thought she could be an ally – provided the financial settlement went through. What I hadn't anticipated was the way she was wasting no time in throwing me out. Maybe I was just too much of a risk, and she was certainly efficient with her arrangements. She'd even already booked a taxi to the station so I wouldn't miss the train that would take me to my new life.

CHAPTER 11

Carol hadn't been wrong about the hotel she'd booked. I wasn't thrilled at all. Advertised as being in Hampstead, in reality it was just outside in a much less salubrious area. It was both noisy and smelly, being right on the main road and surrounded by several takeaways; the mixed aromas made my stomach heave. As soon as I'd arrived, I tried ringing around other local hotels for an alternative, but everything seemed to be booked several weeks in advance. The area was popular with tourists and a good base for sightseeing in the city, and Hampstead was a lovely, leafy enclave.

The hotel would have to do for the time being, although not up to my usual standards, and I knew it would have gained an immediate thumbs down from the girls. Sitting on the bed – the only option other than a rickety chair that looked as if it might collapse if I even thought of sitting on it – I flipped grimly through the greasy and stained guest information book. The hotel had a three-star rating, although I'd have downgraded it to two. I noted that despite stating it had a pool, it was a pool with no water as it was closed for maintenance. The gym offered only a battered treadmill and exercise bike, both of which had seen better days, but as I needed to get some strength back in my arms and legs, I'd have to use what was available. There was also a cheap, not-so-cheerful restaurant smelling strongly of yesterday's chip oil. I certainly couldn't see myself enjoying a meal at one of the battered tables.

I put the ancient kettle on and found the best cup and saucer on the tray, the one with the least stains and chips, yes, it was that bad, but I was so parched that I was prepared to settle for the cheap instant coffee and tiny capsule of milk. I'd get something better from the local shops and pick up my own mug too. I could, of course, use a little magic to spruce things up but realised it would only raise suspicions if the cleaners walked in to a full-on style transformation. Once I got my energy back, I'd look for an apartment to rent. All I wanted right now was to catch up with my sleep; at least the bed was comfy, but I wouldn't stay for a moment longer than I had to. I revelled in the thought of going into a luxury rental apartment before long.

Over the next few days, I didn't give much thought to the two contacts, whose numbers Carol had put in the ancient, brick-like mobile. I'd left the phone in the zip-up compartment in the small suitcase and hoped it wouldn't be necessary to use it. Even though she hadn't given me the choice I knew it would be better to cut all ties with Carol, especially as she'd told me that due to her use of transformation spells, I'd never recognise her even if I did bump into her again. I was thinking hard about getting back into the midst of a witchy life, not sure what the score was in Hampstead. I wondered if Carol had picked the area specifically because it was a safe haven and relatively witch-free. For now, at least, I decided I wasn't taking any chances in my new life, I wanted a clean slate and from now on felt happier as a sole traveller. I was an independent, badass woman who planned to find her way in the new world order, not look backwards.

I felt a frisson of excitement as I thought of what might lie ahead. Maybe I didn't want to go back to a safe, mundane life? After all, even after the bank transfer, I had loads of money, plus the properties in Yorkshire.

Maybe my vocation was living life in the danger zone, helping witches less powerful than me, especially as I now had the protection of the spell. Thankfully my mind, body, and soul were now connected, there was just the odd pocket of brain fog remaining, and I was sure that would clear soon as I felt an improvement every day. Almost back to normal, whatever normal would be in these uncertain times. I knew that having been safely cocooned in the hospital for so long, I'd become institutionalised – I'd need to take baby steps to acclimatise.

I wasn't bothered about going out that much, at least not until I had somewhere to stay permanently, but I had become obsessed with the news, downloading all the apps and binge-watching Sky. I was on alert for any mention of magic. To be honest, it was a bit of a let-down, most of the news was of everyday dramas and scandals, nothing out of the ordinary. Was the witch issue being swept under the carpet? Was there a news embargo? Were they playing down the havoc spreading across Great Britain and beyond? Why, if it was getting much worse, was so little being reported?

There was a full-size mirror in my room, and I liked what I saw – even though the yummy mummy look was not my usual style, I wore it well. No one would recognise me as Ellie, not even my mother, or in my case, both my mothers. I inspected my face, ticking off the things that needed doing. My eyebrows were quite bushy, my hair had grown unruly, and I desperately needed a pedi and manicure. My hospital care had included a beautician and hairdresser, but the results were rudimentary, and my spells could only do so much. I had benefited through catching up on my sleep, the comfy bed providing nights of blissful, dreamless slumber, just what I needed. I had to get my energy back. Mercifully, my nightmares were receding, and my past life experiences hadn't been repeated either. I was sure I would never see Hettie again. She had warned me: her job was done.

Carol's help had been invaluable, and I'd always be grateful to her, despite the cost, but I had to accept that my life would be different from now on. In the back of my mind, I knew I had more power, I was protected, and no one could do me any harm. It was a comforting thought. I had successfully come out the other end, not forever dead. Or had I? A flicker of doubt crept in; I didn't want to go through the drowning experience again to test it out, but on the other hand, could I one hundred per cent trust Carol that I was fully protected? Niggling in my mind was the remark she had made that they could make life hard for me. What could they do, I wondered? I decided I'd put it to the back of my mind, I couldn't live my life looking over my shoulder. From now on, it had to be all about the present. I needed to focus on such trivial things such as hair and beauty treatments. Spending time being pampered would do me good and, first things first, I needed to start looking for somewhere to live.

I spotted a chic hair and beauty salon on one of my exploratory trips and decided to drop in later to arrange a mammoth appointment, and then I could start feeling like the old Ellie again. I smiled as I realised there had been several incarnations: the professional, city advertising executive, all power suits, and Louboutin's with their distinctive red-soles, then there was the Yorkshire Ellie rocking the country-casual, home counties look, before going over to the dark side with the goth look. The latter was the look I'd liked best but recalling Carol's advice, I knew it was important to blend in rather than stand out. I'd already spent time outside local coffee shops in the nicer part of Hampstead, shades on, book in hand, surreptitiously people-watching, picking up on what I needed to do to fit in. Looking around, there were headbands, big floaty blouses with oversize bows, short miniskirts, tights, and cute pixie boots. Hair wasn't being worn particularly long but was cut in choppy layers – a Meg Ryan look from back in the day. I was ready for a mega shopping spree.

With beauty treatments booked, a clear idea of what I would be looking for clothes-wise and several local letting agents on speed dial, I now just needed to get my finances in order. My first appointment was at the bank. The funds for Carol still had to be dealt with; I certainly didn't want to let her down, she knew where to find me, and I wouldn't like to have a taste of her magic if she was angry.

I still had the apartments I'd purchased in Whitby, which were being managed by the agency I'd appointed. I assumed they were paying bills and banking rental income for me and, hopefully, the funds would have accumulated and been paid into my account. It would be interesting to see what the value of the properties were now, maybe it was time to sell the apartments and my beloved Lavender Cottage.

I felt a knot in my stomach as I walked into the bank. I was concerned they'd quiz me about the lack of everyday spending on the account, but I had a backup story ready – I'd been living abroad using funds in my foreign account. My old bank card had expired and apparently a security flag had been put on the account. I had an appointment with the bank manager to sort it out. As I only had a temporary address at the hotel, I'd have to explain that I was only in a hotel until I could find permanent accommodation. I hoped that would be OK. As if by magic, Carol had already sorted out a passport and driving licence with my new image so I could use them for identity verification. Thankfully, the manager was happy to remove the security flag and order a new bank card, asking only that I pick it up from the bank and let them know my permanent address as soon as I had one. As I left the imposing building, I felt lightheaded with relief – I was one step closer to a normal life again.

CHAPTER 12

Five weeks later

Awesome – I had picked up my keys to the most incredibly perfect penthouse apartment in the heart of Hampstead, boasting its own roof terrace and underground parking. I'd been thrilled and relieved to find this gem and to be taking another big step on the road to normality and full recovery. I felt I could finally put down some roots and was determined not to let negative thoughts creep in again.

My apartment was in an old Georgian mansion, once the residence of a wealthy London family but since converted into individual apartments. It had recently undergone a total refurbishment and was technically a new build but with the original, listed Georgian facade remaining. Internally it was twenty-first century with lots of exposed brick and added metal beams to give it an industrial look. They had built upwards above the original roofline and deep underground to create underground parking, a gym, spa, and pool. This was pretty common in this area, and indeed in parts of London where there were private homes with mega-wealthy owners – we are talking billionaires now. I'd had a call from an excited agent who told me the penthouse had originally been let but the tenants had backed out at the last moment, hence it was back on the market. I didn't hesitate, I knew something like this didn't come around too often. As well as a roof garden, there were also stunning communal gardens to which residents had the key. It was meticulously maintained with lush greenery, benches, and ornate tables and chairs dotted on the pristine lawns. A great place to sit and get lost in a novel; I had a few to catch up on, too, I'd been buying books while holed up in the hotel with nothing else to do. My current book obsession was with the Brontës, the fact that they'd originally had to publish as men seemed incredible, but maybe not when I thought of what was happening to women in this day and age. My challenge was to read every single one of their novels. They reminded me of Yorkshire. Wuthering Heights was based around the West Yorkshire moors, but the description was similar to my beloved North Yorkshire. On my first visit to the penthouse, I'd wandered around the grounds while the agent took a phone call, noticing a couple of mature, well-heeled ladies sitting at one of the tables, dressed to the nines, giggling as they clinked their glasses together. Gin for elevenses – my sort of place.

The agent had explained that the inside of each apartment had interior design to die for, top-end premium appliances and cutting-edge technology. Blah blah blah, the list went on. I was a visual person and could tell from the first look that this was the place for me. I smiled while the agent made lights flash on and off, blinds go up and down, and music fade in and out. He made it clear that each tenant had to have a certain amount in the bank or have a professional occupation. The unsaid implication was to keep the riff-raff out. There was to be no subletting and there were rules and regulations covering noise levels, antisocial behaviour and the like, but all of that was fine for Ellie the recluse.

The roof garden was one of the best features of the penthouse, with spectacular views. I felt I could live here like the queen of the castle, observing all those around me going about their day. It didn't have quite the river views of the Thames like my previous apartment, but it was huge and secluded with all the mature greenery, and furnished with egg chairs, a large table and chairs, and squashy leather sofas on the patio area, with an electric awning for excessively hot or rainy days. I noticed a gas barbeque, a pizza oven, and even a hot tub in the corner, brilliant for entertaining. I could have fun throwing parties if only I had any friends, I thought sadly. A pang of loneliness enveloped me. I just needed to meet a few locals to enjoy it more fully, and I would be well away. Start afresh. I could do it – after all, I'd done it before, hadn't I?

I was relieved to leave the budget hotel. My stay lasted longer than I ever intended. I'd also got a good deal on the apartment because the agent was relieved to have it taken on at such short notice. The helpful concierge had taken my suitcases to the apartment, and I'd picked up some supplies from the deli: freshly baked croissants, artisan butter, French raspberry jam, with the seeds in of course, coffee beans for the machine, organic milk, and the daily papers from the newsagent. I just needed to get the coffee machine working.

There was a laundry service on site, which pleased me. I felt all my clothes smelt of the greasy food smell that had permeated the whole of the hotel at any time of the day or night. Getting everything laundered and ironed on site was the icing on the cake! There was also a twice-weekly cleaning service, so I wouldn't need to lift a finger on housework either. The apartment was fully equipped with anything I might need, from fluffy towels to hi-spec TVs and speakers. It wasn't as cosy as Lavender Cottage, but I appreciated its spaciousness, and it was in a perfect location.

With the help of my magic, the beautician, and the hairdresser, I now looked like a new and improved Boden-clad yummy mummy, just without the babies. With my new, preppy look, I felt I'd fit in well with the women around here, but even though everyone seemed friendly, it was a bit random to stop passers-by and introduce myself. How do you start making friends again when everyone seems to be in their own clique?

I liked the London vibe, it felt good to be back, and I'd come full circle. I might decide to go back into the world of work again, or maybe I'd find a way of investing my money so I didn't need to work at all. I had mixed feelings about getting back into the rat race. I bought a dark grey, convertible Mini with a black roof. It was the smallest car I'd ever owned. Perfect for nipping around the city, as parking spaces were at a premium, and it was just right for the small underground space I'd managed to bag with the apartment.

London was becoming much more continental; the outdoor cafe culture was popular come rain or shine. A spot of rain, and staff quickly came out to put up the awnings. I'm sure they'd be constantly doing this job with the good old British weather. I'd found Friday's were as good a day as any to get out there and people watch. I also found getting back into a routine was good for me, and I'd found my favourite haunt to people watch, Otters of Hampstead, an artisan deli and coffee shop on the High Street, the place was buzzing. A beaming waiter came over to take my order, not one of the regulars. I couldn't quite place his accent, French perhaps. I smiled back at him and ordered a skinny latte, extra hot, and a glass of sparkling mineral water. He nodded and went back into the cafe. Conversations from surrounding tables mingled and wafted over. Behind me were three guys. "You've gotta leave it," said one, intriguingly. To the side of my table was a group of women of mature age, discussing music festivals their teenagers wanted to go to. At another table, someone wound up a story with,

"... but they only had one key to open the bloody door." There was laughter, the clink of glasses and the scrape of cutlery providing an almost musical background. Life was happening around me, while I kept myself to myself, on the periphery of society.

Sipping my coffee, I observed the flower shop on the opposite side of the road. It was gorgeous, with exquisite bouquets and freshly watered house plants of all sizes. I liked to guess who the customers who went in and out all day were buying for. The suave guy with sunglasses and a sharp suit, buying a white bouquet for his illicit lover? The middle-aged woman buying bright blooms, maybe cheering up a sick friend or relative? The pretty young lady with a satisfied look on her face carrying a box full of succulents bang on trend for her new pad? My personal favourites were lilies, which I bought weekly, loving their heady scent, although I remember my mother banning them from the house – she said they reminded her of funeral parlours.

The florist came out to rearrange, restock, and water the flowers and plants and, recognising me, smiled and waved. She was incredibly knowledgeable. When I'd bought some succulents recently for my new terrace and confessed that I was certain death to plants, she'd laughed and told me they were really hard to kill and neglect was good for them.

All in all, summer in Hampstead was delightful, but I knew I needed to interact with others, not just the cafe waiting staff, beauticians, and boutique owners. I was surrounded by normality, everyone getting on with their day, yummy mummies chatting animatedly with little cuties in designer pushchairs, whistling delivery drivers, and ear-podded joggers and cyclists whizzing by on fitness crusades. Then there were the suited and booted men and women, coffee and sandwiches in hand for a working lunch. Everyone seemed happy. There was no suggestion that anyone lived in fear or even had a clue about the witches and their plight.

The stories about the Purge and witch-hunting had become old news – after all, the first inkling of a story had started in Whitby over two years ago. No news story, however horrific, kept the news headlines for that long. What was more worrying in the news was the increase in drownings and other suspicious deaths, mainly of women. It was being explained officially as suicide contagion, and allegedly women everywhere were getting on the bandwagon. But I knew better. The official witch trials were still going full steam ahead, but it seemed, from what I read, that they had the witch problem under control and that the new laws were enthusiastically being used to make sure offenders were given the full force of the law for their wrongdoings. But the truth was, as I've said before there was more going on under the radar, there was a full- scale murder of witches, the vigilantes were running amok, and a blind eye was being turned.

I felt in some way that I ought to use my power to help, but it didn't look like anyone around here would be sympathetic to the cause, or even let it concern their pretty little heads, and I certainly didn't want to bring attention to myself. I wasn't even sure that anyone in Hampstead needed my help, it seemed unscathed. They appeared to live a trouble-free, charmed life, all about meeting up with friends for lunch, and having fun, from what I could make out from the buzz of the place. Maybe ignorance was bliss.

I bought the local papers as well as the nationals,

scouring the news gave me something to do at the local cafes, a good way of people-watching. I hadn't yet come across anything untoward, or the least bit weird around here, but on the other hand, this pastime meant I was getting to know the waiters and waitresses pretty well; we were all on first-name terms. Scanning the local papers, the worst I could pick up on in the area was the banning of electric scooters in pedestrian areas and a tougher attitude to chewing gum on the pavement – trivial issues. Although, from what I could see, everyone was pretty well behaved around here, and the place looked clean and tidy. I hadn't seen any visible issues with antisocial behaviour or vandalism. The occasional extra lively and boozy work party was all. Maybe the council in this upmarket area were on it as soon as they saw a problem.

Taking all of this into consideration, it seemed on the surface an excellent place to settle. But first I needed to pull myself together, concentrate on making friends and see what the locals were really like, not just from afar. I needed to meet people before I decided if it was the right place to put some roots down. I'd bide my time about buying a home again, as I'd need to sell Lavender Cottage to be able to afford anything around here. Plus, I still didn't feel one hundred per cent certain that anywhere was a particularly safe haven. I knew things could turn bad at any time, and then I'd have to be gone before you could say abracadabra. And who knows what misadventures I'd get myself into in the meantime, I thought wryly.

There was no doubt I was missing my support group and I spent a lot of time wondering how Alice, Lizzie, and Sarah were faring. I hoped they were OK. I promised myself that one day I'd be in touch again with my old friends but in the meantime, I wouldn't risk putting them in danger, however much I yearned to see them. In the happy chatter of the deli, I understood the busiest of places could also be the loneliest. I had to get out there more and make an effort, groups of congenial people weren't going to come looking for me. Surely there were a few others in the same boat as me?

CHAPTER 13

I'd started the ball rolling, the first baby steps of socialisation. I wasn't going on a date or anything exciting, but I'd been researching Hampstead and its Victorian influence, which was why a poster advertising a ghost tour around Hampstead Cemetery caught my eye and made up my mind.

I'd always been interested in the Victorian attitude to death, so different to how we handle it nowadays. This alternative way of looking at things was epitomised in the death portraits – photos of the dead celebrating their lives. These sepia photos of people with dark clothing and frozen expressions fascinated me – macabre, I know. When I was clearing out Lavender Cottage, I'd found several of them, and Pannett Park Museum in Whitby had been delighted when I donated them. They were so important, often the only photograph of a loved one the family would ever have. For this reason, they went to town with the tribute to the dearly departed, often festooning them with flowers, even decorating closed eyelids with fake eyes. It was seeing a couple of those that had particularly freaked me out, once seen, some images can never be unseen. Another particularly uncomfortable memory was of a picture of twin babies, one alive and the other flower-entwined, and dead.

Before I had time to think, I dialled the number on the poster.

"Hackett's Funeral Directors, how can I help?" a woman said.

"I'm so sorry, I think I must have the wrong number – it was on a poster for—"

"The ghost tour," she interrupted. "No, you're in luck, right number and John has a space left for tonight – cancellation, someone died."

"Oh." I was disconcerted, but she was brisk, and I found myself giving my details and card number and promising to be there on time.

If I had more time to think, I might have backed out; a funeral director tour guide was a bit creepy. Also, on second thoughts, was it wise to be out after dark in the city on my own? Hampstead Heath did have quite a dubious night-time reputation. On the other hand, while I hadn't spent all my life in graveyards or ghost hunting, this did bring back fond memories of the one the girls and I had done in Whitby with Will – although admittedly, that had been more fun than frights.

This one promised to be a more sophisticated affair. I'd passed Hampstead Cemetery several times, admiring its

Gothic Victorian splendour. Hampstead had always been an affluent area, therefore most of the residents buried here were either wealthy or famous; maybe that was why there were no pauper's graves. Impressive as it was, it was full to the brim with no spare space for anyone wanting to get in at a later date. They had to go to the new and far less grand cemetery a short distance away. The poster stated that our guide John Hackett, who did these tours in his spare time, was raising funds for the much-needed cemetery restoration; after all, it had been going since 1876.

John was the third generation of Hacketts in the funeral business and seemed to have his quota of online ghoulish followers. Those who'd previously taken the tour had only good things to say about him: "There is nothing John Hackett doesn't know about the history of the cemetery or its inhabitants.", "John, what a legend, such a spooky tour.", "... loved his morbid sense of humour." It seemed I was in for a spine-tingling evening and history lesson combined. I spent the rest of the morning researching online. I suppose my interest sprang from my own experiences, and my research brought back some gruesome flashbacks to my out-of-body experience, looking down at myself on the mortuary table, and the crescendo of music as the technician raised the drill above my head.

As I got ready, finding some warm clothing as it was starting to get nippy at night, I put on an eerie track on Spotify to get myself in the mood. The soulful piano piece Gnossienne No. 1 came up, and I started to feel I was bringing back a little edginess to my life. A frizzle of excitement ran through me, and I knocked back a shot of whisky – Dutch courage – at the last moment. Making my way down to the taxi, I had a moment of doubt but ignored it.

People were already gathering at the cemetery gates where we were to meet up. A couple of young guys, eighteen or nineteen, looked pretty grungy. It was evident from their body language that despite their larking about they were scared shitless, and I'm ashamed to say I was tempted to creep up behind them and go "boo" but I restrained myself. An older man and woman, wearing sensible matching outfits, looked relaxed in each other's company; they'd done this before. Two pretty blondes around my age were keen to show they were a couple with a public show of affection. It looked like I was the only sad loner. There was a feeling of nervous energy, everyone on tenterhooks. They wanted to be scared but at the same time were not sure, maybe having second thoughts. Smiling to myself I thought, what would they do if they did see a ghost?

"Welcome to Hampstead Cemetery, our very own garden of the dead." John Hackett looked precisely as you'd expect, in working attire, black velvet top hat, red velvet waistcoat, and long black overcoat with velvet collar. He was in his sixties, and beneath the gloomy look, there were clues to his real persona – tattoos on his wrist, another partially concealed by his shirt collar and on the fingers of each hand, letters spelling "dead end". Surprisingly, the addition of metal and leather bracelets and a long grey goatee beard tied with silver beads made him more approachable and less scary, more human. Outside work, I imagined him headbanging at a Rammstein concert and riding a Harley-Davidson, wearing a battered Hells Angel's leather jacket.

He smiled as I approached, a clipboard in his hand, "You must be Ellie. Excellent, now we're all here."

"Sorry," I said, "hope I'm not late." I'd deliberately cut it fine because I hadn't fancied the idea of hanging around the graveyard on my own.

He smiled, displaying a gap between his front teeth, which lent his speech a slight whistle. "Not at all, I think everyone else was just a little early. Thank you for joining us." Was he being sarcastic? I couldn't tell. He gave me an odd look, almost as though he knew who I was. I'm sure I hadn't imagined it, but I was certain I'd never seen him before. It made me feel decidedly unsettled. Gathering the group together, he introduced himself formally, "John Hackett, director of Hampstead Cemetery Trust, and a living, breathing funeral director; most people are dying to meet me!" Nervous laughter from the group. "Now, shall we begin? It's a perfect night for it."

As I looked around, I could see what he meant, the mist over the gravestones certainly added to the spooky atmosphere, and I shivered.

"Ah," he said, looking over at me with a theatrical wink, "I think someone just walked over Ellie's grave," cue more nervous laughter as he continued, "I must warn you all, ghosts and apparitions have been sighted on these tours; please don't be disappointed if nothing happens tonight, but don't be alarmed if something does. Sometimes it's a sighting, sometimes just feeling a presence. The spirits have treated us well in the past" – he paused for effect – "I would suggest you leave now if you feel this might be too much for you." He laughed, "No hard feelings." And probably no refund, I thought to myself. "But whatever we see or don't see, because obviously, I can't just summon them up, you'll be hearing some fascinating history." He looked around, "All staying? Good, and please feel free to ask any questions you want, I won't bite." He paused for a beat, then added with a ghoulish laugh, "At least not very hard." I wondered how many times he'd run through this same script.

There was a feeling of considerable serenity about the place in the misty darkness as we followed John's lead, weaving between tombstones, memorials, statues, and Celtic crosses. He knew his stuff, I had to give it to him, as he regaled us with murders, sudden deaths, suicides, or just people reaching a ripe old age. As the cemetery was located in one of the most prosperous areas of London, especially in Victorian times, he told us about the morbid rise in grave robbings by opportunists hoping to find valuables buried with the dead.

"And here," announced John, "lies poor old Albert, Bertie to his friends. After his wife Elizabeth passed away, unable to bear his grief any more, he took his own life, and passed away right here on her grave … The poison of choice was potassium cyanide. Buried together now for eternity." He lifted his hat in respect as if to an old friend.

Moving on, he next stopped before the graves of

Charles, his wife Violet, and son Henry. "Another tragic story I'm afraid. Charles regularly visited the grave of his young son Henry, he'd died of a childhood illness some years before. Violet thought he had left for work, but later received a telegram from Charles saying he was going to visit 'our Henry'. Sadly, poor Charles was found stone-cold lying next to Henry's grave." He paused. "This time prussic acid was the poison of choice." We walked a little way, and then he waved his arm again. "Not all deaths were macabre. Here lies Cyril, he was on duty as a policeman. There had been a spate of thefts and vandalism. He simply keeled over from a fatal heart attack."

By this stage, we'd been walking for around an hour and a half, my feet were aching, and I was grateful when we paused again in an area John told us was in the middle of the cemetery. So far, we hadn't seen anything remotely ghost-like, not even a chilly presence. If anything, I found it genuinely peaceful after the hustle and bustle of life amongst the living. Some bright spark started taking photos, and John was happy to pose, looking solemn. We all saw the funny side and quickly snapped him as he posed for his audience.

"Now, this is an interesting one, 'moaning Maud', they call her, on account of sighting of her spirit – she has been seen wandering around the cemetery softly moaning. During her life she was a music hall star, her funeral brought this part of London to a standstill. She was adored by the public, but her private life was rather colourful. She died in her early fifties and it was rumoured that a rather energetic session with her husband, a jockey –

twenty years her junior – and a judiciously applied riding crop, hastened her premature death." A riding crop – I didn't know whether to laugh or cry. Poor Maud.

Towards the end of the tour, I noticed that John changed the tone of his voice; he became gentler as he brought us to a standstill in front of an art deco statue of an angel, her wings spread wide, with the most delicate stone face. Although made of stone, the figure looked exquisite, with a hint of 1930s sophistication. We all gasped in admiration.

"As you see, I have left the best to last; this is the pièce de résistance, the most beautiful statue in the cemetery and the saddest story." Was there a tear in his eye? "You are looking at the memorial for Madeline, known as Maddie to her friends and family. She died in childbirth, giving birth to her second child. Her husband commissioned this most magnificent statue in her memory." He gave a proud smile. "We have recently used funds from the ghost tours to renovate Maddie's statue; it had seen better days and was partially covered in ivy. We are gradually working our way around the site. I think you will agree she has now been restored to her true beauty." The way he spoke, you would think he was in love with the statue, and maybe the woman buried underneath?

He composed himself and said, "OK, that's all, folks, we will make our way back to the front gates, please follow me," and I saw him blow a surreptitious kiss to the statue before moving swiftly away from it. "Thank you for being respectful visitors to this site. Sorry I couldn't conjure up a ghost or two for you!" We all laughed dutifully. "Joking apart, your support is much appreciated; if you want to support the cemetery further, there is a donation site via the website."

Suddenly there was a commotion on the edge of the group. Someone screamed, and then there was a bump. What a surprise, it was the spotty youths; I knew they'd cause trouble, they couldn't hack a ghost tour. John rushed over to see what was going on to hushed silence.

"Are you ok, lads?"

One of the young guys had fainted but was slowly coming to; he looked bewildered and was trembling as he pointed, "A ghost, a woman, over there!" He picked himself off the ground, and he and the other lad scrambled as fast as they could out of the graveyard before John could say another word.

"Oh dear, Maddie, what have you done? You've scared two of our friends." He smiled, and we followed his gaze, staring in wonder at the most exquisite, ethereal, ghostly white creature floating amongst us and then through us, although I couldn't feel a thing.

"Don't worry," he reassured us, "Mournful Maddie won't do you any harm; she's eternally searching for her lost child." I was mesmerised, as was the rest of the group; you could have heard a pin drop. Maddie was dressed in a long sheath dress, her hair in Marcel waves, like something you'd see a debutante wearing at a ball in the 1930s. She had a dreadful look of sorrow. The middle-aged couple had their phones at the ready, trying to get a snap. John smiled, "Sorry guys, you won't get a picture; she's very camera shy," and then he laughed out loud at their expressions when their phones showed no pictures.

We had certainly had our money's worth on this tour; what a turn-up for the books, although I felt sad seeing the mournful beauty eternally searching. As Maddie disappeared into the distance, I wondered if she stayed in the graveyard or wandered further afield. As we strolled back to the gates, John said, "We were so fortunate to see Maddie tonight, she hasn't been seen for a while now." He added, "I rather hoped she had finally found her child and could now rest in peace."

"Where else has Maddie been sighted?" I asked.

"Only in the graveyard," he responded. "Nowhere else as far as I know. I had wondered whether we might spot Esmerelda, a Victorian ghost, jilted at the altar, couldn't bear the shame, and took her own life. She wanders here a lot, but Maddie is a scarce sight indeed. You have been honoured tonight."

When the taxi dropped me home, it was very late, and I was shattered and felt I deserved a stiff drink. I was still emotional; even my magical and past life experiences hadn't prepared me for my first ghost, and how beautiful was Maddie. I sat on the bed and yawned, the drink doing the trick and knocking me out, and my head had hardly touched the pillow when ...

I was back in the cemetery. This time, it was daylight and looked very different, more like the pristine country garden of a stately home than a graveyard. Neatly manicured lawns around the tombstones and an abundance of bright flowers all in glorious bloom – so different from the mist and darkness of my last visit. It was a green and pleasant place. The sun was shining brightly and the sky was azure blue. It felt so real, but I knew I was dreaming.

First to show her face was Mournful Maddie, no longer ghostly but appearing as a living, breathing woman. She was wearing the same dress, but this time I could see it was vivid green shot silk. With a beaming smile, she was twirling around as if dancing to a tune only she could hear. She called to a boy of about four or five, his head bobbing up from behind one of the tombstones. His hair needed a good brush, and his face was stained red from the strawberries he was stuffing into his mouth.

"Henry, there you are. I've been searching everywhere, and look at you," she said. "Come to Auntie Maddie, darling. I'll look after you. Your hair needs brushing, and your face could do with a good wipe." He jumped up into her arms. "I'll take care of you until your Mama arrives," she murmured as she held him close.

Other people had started to arrive, dressed in their Sunday best, but they were not of this era. Initially, there were just a few surrounding Maddie and Henry, until others joined them. When the crowd parted, I knew it was for the star turn. Maud Avery, queen of the music hall, resplendent in a dress with a tight bodice and wearing an oversized hat on dark, ringleted hair.

The crowd seemed to gather around a recently dug, still open grave with a closed casket, but the scene had changed when I looked up from the freshly turned earth. Gone were the vibrant flowers and manicured lawns, the tombstones and statues were covered in weeds and ivy; the cemetery looked utterly neglected, the sky black, and the mist from the other night was swirling back in. I saw with horror that the people surrounding me were no longer alive; their elegant clothing had been shed, and now they were just misty figures, their ghoulish features ferocious. Then, from the ground, came a deep wailing, and a loud scratching, as if someone or something was trying to get out of the closed casket. The crowd began to sway and moan, they were chanting, "Traitor, traitor, traitor," over and over again. The scene was sinister, the crowd increasingly menacing, I turned to run, but my feet were rooted to the spot. The crowd turned to face me ...

CHAPTER 14

I woke up with my heart beating and my head banging. It took me a few moments to realise that this was just another lucid nightmare, such a strange and spooky dream. Maybe a warning I should stop trying to scare myself, I hadn't had such a bad nightmare for so long. The dead had all been saying the exact words over and over, but for the life of me, I couldn't remember what they were. I told myself I probably had to have a rethink and start getting to know some real-life people instead of messing around with the dead. In the meantime, my priority was painkillers, and I was right out of those.

The local chemist was delightfully traditional, with bottles of different sizes filled with different coloured liquid on the shelves and antique scales in the window. It was called Hackett's Pharmacy and I thought it likely there was some family connection rather than just coincidence.

There were no other customers in the shop today,

which was unusual. The pharmacist, a lady around my age, was always friendly and helpful. I could see she was preoccupied with prescriptions in the back, in her own little world, so I selected what I needed, together with a bottle of water. I needed those pills sooner rather than later.

"D'you mind if I take a couple now?" I said as the pharmacist rang up my purchases.

"Heavy night?" she said with a smile.

"You could say that. I was on a ghost walk last night. The local funeral director runs it." She gave me a puzzled look. "I noticed the sign above your door; it was John Hackett who took us round last night – any relation?"

The colour drained from her face, and she took a step back. "John Hackett was my father, but you must have made a mistake."

"Sixties, goatee beard, tattoos on his hand?" I smiled. "He looked more like a biker than a funeral director."

"My father died just over ten years ago, the tours stopped then, and we sold his business. Look, I don't know—"

I interrupted – if this was a joke, it wasn't very funny. "Well, he was alive and kicking last night, and he deserves his good reviews. We even saw Mournful Maddie ..."

She'd retreated further behind the counter and turned paler still. If this was a prank she was pulling, she was throwing herself into it.

"I don't know who you are or why you're doing this, but I'd like you to leave."

I stared at her, completely confused. WTF! I put a £10

note on the counter, more than enough for my purchases and, as she started to cry, I left.

I went straight over the road to the cafe where I'd seen the ad. It wasn't in the window but of course that didn't mean anything. The tour had been and gone. I moved away slowly – was she crazy, or was I? Hurrying back to the apartment, I didn't even bother to take my coat off but had the laptop open to the reviews. It was a huge relief to find they were still there, at least I hadn't imagined them, but what I hadn't checked were the dates – the last review was just over ten years old.

But I'd paid by card over the phone, which would be on my bank account. I signed in, but the transaction wasn't there, not even hanging around in pending. There was no sign of any payment to Hacketts Funeral Directors; neither was the Uber payment for my taxi last night there. OK, my phone wouldn't lie; I had taken a few pictures of John Hackett, along with the other ghost hunters. But, as I scrolled through my phone, there were no pictures. My mouth was dreadfully dry, and the headache hadn't receded. I took a deep breath, divested myself of my coat, grabbed a black coffee and googled. Then wished I hadn't.

John Hackett had run up gambling debts he couldn't handle and had borrowed from people he couldn't handle either. They had him over a barrel, and his facilities to "dispose" of people was exactly what they needed. It soon became known that anyone who crossed the gang ended up in the crematorium. Maybe he'd outlived his usefulness, or perhaps he turned uncooperative? Called out one evening to a fictitious death, he was ambushed, bundled into the back of a van, and ended up back at his premises. He was unceremoniously dumped into one of his coffins, brought to the local cemetery and buried; unfortunately, he wasn't yet dead. Whether that was deliberate was a moot point, but by the time the police located him, even hardened officers were shaken by such a terrible end.

I slammed shut the laptop, although that didn't eradicate the pictures in my mind, nor the indisputable fact that I seemed to have slipped back in time without even knowing. It was so subtle this time, as I had only travelled back ten years. Was I meant to learn something from John Hackett? Or maybe Mournful Maddie, the beautiful ghostly creature, had been trying to tell me something? I was starting to freak myself out. At least when it had happened before, I'd known. I'd been unaware this time, and on top of it all, I'd now have to find another chemist to go to. That poor woman, I felt awful. Then I thought of the dream, the ghosts wailing, the banging from the open grave, John Hackett desperate to avoid his dreadful death. Dabbling in the ghost world was not good, I needed to stop it. The John Hackett I'd seen last night was even more terrifying; he knew me, recognised me – now that wasn't good.

CHAPTER 15

Trying to distract myself, I decided to start running again, get into some sort of routine. I didn't want to join a gym, especially as I had Hampstead Heath on my doorstep. The heath had a dubious reputation come nightfall, but during the day it was a unique green space full of people enjoying fresh air and exercise.

I settled into a routine of running in the morning, whatever the weather, then picking up the papers and having a leisurely coffee either at one of the local coffee shops or on my own rooftop garden.

The endorphins were gradually having an effect, and on this particular morning the weather was balmy, the bright sunshine was not too hot and perfect for a run. I ran up to the Hill Garden with its Georgian arbour, terrace, and Italian columned pergola. At the women's pool, there was lots of splashing and frivolity going on; I wondered if it would be a good way of meeting new people. I used to swim with the girls at uni but loved the idea of using a natural, unchlorinated pool. On Parliament Hill Fields, people were already eating and drinking, the perfect place for a picnic. Children were shrieking with enjoyment at the model boating lake, and it seemed the world and his dog were out and about, enjoying the sunshine.

Later, sipping my coffee on my terrace, I remembered Carol mentioning a great local Pilates class. Suiting action to thought, I looked up the number and called, only to be told there were no spaces in the class. I was disappointed. "My friend Carol recommended you, but is there anywhere else around here?"

There was a brief pause before the woman, who'd introduced herself as Kat, said, "Oh, I hadn't realised you knew Carol; let me see if I can squeeze you in." There was a rustle of paper. "How about my last class at 7.30 pm on a Monday? Starting next week."

"Perfect." I wasn't going to look a gift horse in the mouth even if the way she'd changed her tune seemed odd. "See you then."

I have to confess, I wasn't expecting much as I made my way to my first class, but she'd only taken payment for the first lesson, so if I didn't like it, I could look elsewhere.

The studio was above one of the high street shops; it was typical of a workout studio with its mirrored wall, which I wasn't particularly thrilled about. I felt a little self-conscious for the first time, still not used to who I saw in the mirror. As I was here a little early, I snuck in, picked up a mat, block and blanket and laid them right on the back row, choosing, for a change, not to be a show-off at the front.

I shouldn't be condescending, there seemed to be a good mixture of people in this group, and on first impression, they didn't seem unfriendly, apart from the two beauty queens at the front of the class. Oh my God, did they fancy themselves – a bit like the old Ellie, maybe? I bet this is how I had come across to others, I was nicknamed "Beautiful Ellie" after all. I nearly burst out laughing but had to check myself and pretend to cough, I didn't think they'd appreciate the joke. I noticed they came in last, but their place was bang in the middle of the front row where a double space had been left. Obviously, they took this space every week and didn't have to worry their pretty heads about where to put their mats. In the group's pecking order, they were the queen bees. I'd best steer away from them then, I thought ruefully.

There was a smattering of guys dotted around the room; they didn't seem to be a particular type. Just there for no-nonsense exercise, by the looks of it. Friendly to the others around them, but not in any particular clique. Maybe they had partners at home and didn't want the women in the room to get any ideas. I didn't pay too much attention; I wasn't looking to get romantically involved. No more complications were needed at this point. One of the guys on the next row looked familiar. No, surely not, it couldn't be? John Hackett, the funeral director, was dead, wasn't he? No, surely I hadn't dropped back in time again? As he turned around, I knew I was mistaken, he was a dead ringer, though it gave me a start. He gave me a welcoming grin – no gap in his front teeth – before turning back to the front. He had taken his place with the earth-mother types and didn't look out of place with his goatee beard and faded t-shirt.

Looking around the room, everyone else looked harmless enough. I certainly didn't get a witchy vibe from any of them, although I could see why Carol had recommended this particular class in this area. It seemed a perfect hiding place for anyone who didn't want to attract notice. At the front of the room, Kat was ready to start and, in response to her "All set?" received enthusiastic nods. She followed the warm-up with some pretty intense stuff, and I felt the burn. It was tough, using muscles I'd not exercised for some time. I was also well aware I was Billy no mates at the moment, without my usual support network, and did need to get back out there and make some friends. I couldn't say anyone in this group was immediately appealing, but immediately after that thought, I gave myself a bit of a talking to; I shouldn't make snap judgements. And then something extremely odd happened. Kat abruptly stopped instructing. I glanced at the clock, it was exactly 8.15, still fifteen minutes of class to go, but she headed for the door and locked it. Now that was strange, and so was the atmosphere in the room, which had changed completely.

Back at the front of the now still and silent class, Kat said, "I'd like to introduce a new member, Ellie; please make her welcome." A sea of faces turned towards me as they acknowledged I was one of them. There was the unmistakable crackle of magic in the air, and I suddenly saw through the normality to what lay beneath. So good had they been at blending in, I'd never have suspected a thing; they were experts at hiding in plain sight. Carol had known exactly what she was doing when she recommended Hampstead, and she'd known I'd find out soon enough. Meanwhile, Kat used a transformation spell to completely change the studio to an over-the-top party room. I thought briefly about how dangerous this might be, but I knew I'd come home to a witch community. Was this what I wanted, though? Hell yes, my new life was verging on the boring side.

As much for my benefit as for everyone else's, Kat set about bringing us up to date on what was happening that was relevant. Not everyone in the room was a practising witch, but those who weren't were staunch supporters. The single aim of this group was to derail witch hunters however and whenever possible, the movement Carol had mentioned. Everyone knew the risks they were taking but, behind closed doors, felt free to enjoy their magic. I was once more amongst my own and determined to see if I could help the cause.

CHAPTER 16

Life in Hampstead with newfound friends was good. I finally felt happy and settled and couldn't think of anywhere I'd rather be. The Hampstead witches had nailed it; they were always vigilant, brilliant at being ordinary – even I'd been fooled, and I was an insider. So far, our community within a community hadn't been affected by the Purge, and there was the comforting thought that should someone dangerous like Seb venture to this neck of the woods, they wouldn't suspect a thing; all they would see around them was bland and vanilla. The Stepford Wives came to mind.

From what I'd seen so far, this group was not as experienced as the Mystical Ladies in Whitby; I thought of them as apprentices, although I couldn't be certain whether or not they were unleashing their true power or holding back. I certainly thought I could be helpful to them, but I'd discounted using the protection spell for the time being, I didn't trust it – had Carol really known the spell or just got me out of a sticky situation? It wasn't right to put anyone else through what I'd experienced. But that didn't mean there couldn't be a way to use it in the future to protect our heritage. Currently, all seemed to be well in our area, but I had a feeling in my bones – that sixth sense again – that things might change, and when they did, maybe it was worth the risk to try the spell out again. If it worked, I really could use my knowledge for good. For now, though, I'd park the idea and concentrate on developing friendships with my new magical friends.

In the main, my Pilates mates were a great bunch of people, and my social life was now buzzing. It was a tight-knit group, and to be included meant they trusted you one hundred per cent. I don't know how Kat did it, but she ensured that there was no way anyone could infiltrate the group, and we were all grateful for the security. Even so, I missed the magical times I'd had with my friend-turned-half-sister Lottie and my birth mother Anna; I knew our relationships would have gone from strength to strength had they been given a chance. I wondered if Lottie had ever returned home but realised I might never know, although I made up my mind that I could look for them one day when the time was right. For now, I had to put all thoughts of the past to the back of my mind, at least until the next time I started to worry about them all over again!

While we all had a chance to showcase our skills at the end of the Pilates classes, outside meetings had to be kept discreet. Although I hadn't yet attached myself to any particular group, some of us frequently got together privately to have some fun experimenting with our magic. To a chosen few, I had also shared a whitewashed version about my time in Yorkshire and the reasons for so abruptly disappearing, although I was careful not to go as far as talking about the protection spell, or Seb, for that matter. Some things were better left safely in the past.

Secrecy was now more important than ever. Nick, one of the Pilates guys, was a solicitor; he told us it was illegal to try witches in any way other than via the law of the land. Unfortunately, people didn't always stick to the law and in many rural areas, they were allegedly taking matters into their own hands with kangaroo courts and the like. They didn't need to tell me, I'd seen the rise of the "accidental" deaths, the protagonists were getting more inventive – you can add cliff falls to the wide range of apparent suicides, it was gruesome. It couldn't be proved, but we were fairly certain there were a number of people out there prepared to make and take their own decisions and actions on the witch problem. It was a terrifying thought.

Our solicitor friend said if we needed him, he'd keep the costs down, and at the first hint of any trouble, we shouldn't hesitate to get in touch. I looked around the room while he was speaking; everyone looked stunned, trying to grasp the reality of the situation. It looked as if things could go from bad to worse. I still had faith in my own magic and crossed fingers I was protected against the murderous intent of the witch hunters, but was all too well aware that others might not be so fortunate or as skilled at their craft as I was.

On a lighter note, I now knew the queen bees in the

class were Laura and Tess, who had perfected the yummy mummy look and stood out from the start. Watching them became my new obsession. They had perfectly toned limbs and figures to die for, boasted natural tans and perfect hair which stayed in place even after forty-five minutes of exercise. They never seemed to sweat or look the least bit dishevelled. How did they do it – maybe magic? One evening after class, Laura strolled over and asked in her cut-glass accent whether I'd like to join them for a glass of wine at Olivia's, one of the coolest places in town. I nearly declined; I didn't feel these two were my type at all. Then I thought, why not? I wouldn't do it again if they bored the hell out of me with their beige lives, and on this occasion, I could always fake a headache, and that would be that.

Surprisingly, I was completely wrong, and it turned into a truly magical evening. We finished at Olivia's and continued to Laura's apartment, not that far from my own, and that first outing turned out to be just the first of many girls' nights out. It soon became apparent their perfect look was a clever front, deliberately conforming to a stereotype, and it was brilliant. I'd certainly been taken in, hadn't I?

They were great fun to be around, and our evenings reminded me of my times with Alice, Sarah, and Lizzie, which made me nostalgic but grateful at the same time to have found new friends. We spent time together regularly after Pilates as well as on other evenings. They wanted me to teach them some new spells, and I could also pick up a few from them.

All this was, of course, discreetly behind closed doors.

Far from being beige, these ladies rocked, and we let our hair down, the three of us having fun with some of my favourite outfit change enchantments. Funny, I really thought they knew these spells, their outfits were perfect. When I first demonstrated what I could do, the girls squealed with excitement. They were quick learners, and I enjoyed coaching them, and they, in turn, showed off some of their own signature spells, so our sessions turned into magical workshops. I saw them in a completely different light, the real women behind the mannequin-like facades. One thing that wasn't in any doubt, they were both capable witches.

Tess, Laura, and I made a good team. They, too, were young, free, and single, with no children. With this in common and our magic, we all just jelled. Unlike some of the women I met who had to juggle so many different things daily – partners, children, nannies, and the rest – these two had only themselves to think about. This made it much easier for us all to meet up, often at a moment's notice. We were comfortable in each other's company, there was no rivalry between us, and they were happy to see me separately or together. Their aim in life was to have a blast while they could. In the back of their minds, they knew, as did I, that this happy-go-lucky lifestyle might not last forever.

We'd even spoken about going away together, just the three of us, for an early autumn break, a girls' road trip, or as Laura said, "Witches on tour!" Tess had added, "I need to get out of this godforsaken place, let my hair down!" We all laughed, and I had dreamy visions of somewhere hot and exotic, the Maldives or Mauritius, I'd heard Goa was idyllic. It was a place I'd always wanted to visit but had never got around to. But then I realised that while I might be able to afford that sort of exotic trip, the other two probably couldn't; they'd both at different times mentioned that their salaries never went far enough. It was a bit of a reality check for me, and I made sure I bit my tongue before I said something insensitive.

I always found conversations about money a little awkward. I'd never had a problem funding whatever I wanted but came to understand that Tess and Laura, despite their cultured and well-groomed appearance, didn't have spare cash to flash; London life came at a cost. By the time they'd paid their extortionate Hampstead rents for their tiny apartments and enjoyed a busy social life while keeping up their immaculate image, there wasn't much left for holidays. They'd even talked about pooling their funds by house-sharing to cut costs, maybe renting a two- or three-bedroomed apartment. They had asked if I wanted to come in with them but, call me selfish, however much I liked them, I loved living on my own and didn't want to share. I made the excuse that I was tied into a long lease.

The girls knew I was in a better financial position, but both had pride and wouldn't dream of letting me treat them or not paying their way when we went out. I had to admire the way they stretched their cash so well, even jokingly asking them if they had magical money trees growing in pots somewhere. As the three of us became closer, they let me into some of their secrets: both of them used upmarket charity shops and dress agencies, and that, plus a little bit of magic, allowed them to endlessly adapt their wardrobes. I was impressed by how brilliantly they made it work.

In my family, there had always been a bit of a taboo about wearing second-hand clothes, even if you knew where they came from. I went to boarding school, so most of the parents, apart from those of the kids who had won scholarships, were on the same socio-economic scale, and clothes were all too often throwaway items or were handed over to someone else when the original owner grew bored. I'd do the same to them. Then, once I got to uni, we swapped clothes all the time, but I'd had to keep it a secret from Sandy, my mother. She'd asked me once about a new pair of trousers, and I'd had to make up a story as to where they came from. It felt as if she was testing me.

I was careful because of one particular heated argument as a teenager. She had insisted I give back the most beautiful silk skirt to a friend. She was mortified. "My daughter does not wear hand-me-downs," she said, "hand it back to your friend immediately." The whole fuss seemed ridiculous to me, my friend had put on a bit of weight, and I was super-skinny – too skinny at the time – and the exquisite skirt, in the tiniest of sizes, fitted me perfectly. It hadn't even been worn, it still had its shop label. I made a dreadful fuss at the time, but to no avail, Sandy was adamant and eventually I did what she asked. But how could I explain to my friend when I didn't understand my mother's reasons myself? I decided it would just be too awkward and embarrassing. So I kept the skirt hidden in my wardrobe. I could never wear the skirt because of a combination of guilt and reluctance to face my mother's anger. The whole episode left a bad taste and a lasting memory.

I'd always put Sandy's view down to her upbringing, living in dire poverty with her alcoholic mother. The difference between my childhood and hers had been drummed into me from an early age. I don't want to sound ungrateful, but it was rather like a broken record – rubbed in my face, again and again. It was her opinion that I'd been born with a silver spoon in my mouth and maybe she was right, I was certainly a long way from standing in her worn-out shoes. I'd wanted for nothing – apart from love.

My mother, as a child, had had to rely on the kindness of others when it came to what she wore, and beggars can't be choosers – until she had honed her skills on the sewing machine, she had to fit into whatever was given to her. She told me her own mother didn't give a toss about anything other than where the next bottle of vodka was coming from or the next hit for which she had to beg, borrow or steal money. Although Sandy did her best to keep herself clean and tidy, she struggled with a lack of toiletries, not to mention hot water. That was just one example of her mother's total neglect. The cruel schoolgirl label of "fleabag" had haunted her ever since, and she never let me forget it. It was always new designer threads for me, the height of fashion. But perhaps I should accept that times were changing, and there was no denying that recycling was a more eco-friendly, socially responsible option than adding to landfills with endless new purchases. Even the stars were recycling and hiring dresses for red-carpet events. Gone were the days when they worried about the paparazzi photographing them in an outfit they had worn to a different event. Now it seemed that the more recognisable the dress, the more kudos earned.

Tess and Laura both had an excellent eye for what would work and what wouldn't, which was why they always looked on trend and immaculate. In fact, as with my first impression, there may even have been a hint of envy on realising that sometimes they looked better than I did, so you can imagine it was a revelation to be let into their fashion secrets. I didn't mind admitting I could learn a thing or two from them. They tried to persuade me to go with them on some of their designer bargain hunts, but even knowing preloved was prevalent, it wasn't for me. I'd stick to the divine boutiques in the high street for the time being, my comfort zone.

Our talk of holidays made me restless and got me thinking. Having been literally grounded over the past couple of years with all that business of the coma, it seemed so long since I had been on a proper, relaxing break. When I thought back, the last time I had been away had been Alice's hen party, then the short trip to Edinburgh for the wedding, but neither had been relaxing and, lovely as they were, neither could be called far-flung. Since I'd recovered from the coma, I'd not considered travelling, but now I was gagging to get away. OK, maybe Europe then, rather than further afield, would be in budget? One of our group had recently returned from Turkey, she'd described the area she stayed in as a lush Turkish version of the Cotswolds, or we could look at the Amalfi Coast, you couldn't beat Italy, could you? I'd leave it up to them and just go with the flow, anywhere would be a break, wouldn't it?

CHAPTER 17

Late September

We really were going on a witch hunt! We'd arrived in New England in the fall! There couldn't be a better time to visit, and we happily blended in with the other leaf-peepers. We'd flown into Logan Airport from Heathrow, picking up the SUV we'd hired for the duration. I'd insisted on paying. I wanted to travel in comfort and safety.

I was surprised to find myself so excited when heading towards our first stop, Salem. Straight into the eye of the storm, not my idea! It was great to be there though; better still, Tess had been true to her word and organised everything, she had volunteered and for once in my life I had taken a back seat. I hadn't had to lift a finger other than doing my own packing. It felt liberating being outside of the UK for the first time in what seemed like an age, for me anyway. Life had stood still on the travel front for much too long. I was buzzing.

I'd admitted to the girls that I was more than a little nervous about driving. I'd rarely driven abroad. As a young adult when I was with my parents Sandy and Geoff, Geoff always took over the driving and Sandy the navigating. I'd never really taken any notice of directions, and later, travelling with friends, especially Alice, Lizzie, and Sarah, we tended to stay put at a location, only moving off the sunbeds for drinks and food before going out to party at night. I was delighted to hear that both Laura and Tess had driven extensively in the past in Europe, so they were completely confident about driving on the wrong side of the road. I did say that if they were really tired and had had enough, I'd give it a go, but they gave me a look indicating they didn't fancy that one bit and politely declined my offer. That left me free to sit back, relax and take in scenery ablaze with autumn colours as we headed to Salem.

Laura was driving with Tess providing directions, but she wasn't going to let that stop her from handing out a history lesson along the way. I confess I tuned in and out as she droned on, she was making me sleepy.

"So," said Tess, and I was amused to hear she'd adopted the slight sing-song rhythm of a professional tour guide, I wondered if she realised. "At the time of the Salem witch trials, there was Salem Village and Salem Town, but some sixty years later in the early eighteenth century, Salem Village was changed to Danvers, but Salem Town is still called Salem to this day."

Laura said, "I bet they wanted to disassociate themselves from their gruesome past."

Tess continued, satisfied that she had the right answer, "Wrong! It was more to do with religious and economic reasons. Salem Village was a small farming community, they followed a Puritan doctrine, and were against economic prosperity and the 'new worldly' ways, whereas Salem Town was a larger, more prosperous, town, it had grown rich from a thriving merchant trade. Salem village didn't want to share taxes with Salem Town, simple as!"

We still didn't have an explanation for the name change. I supposed it would only be polite to show my interest with a question. "But why Danvers, sounds a bit random."

Tess turned and gave me an appreciative look – there's nothing like a responsive audience. She smiled. "That is a simple explanation too, it was named after one of the settlers, Danvers Osborn, in 1752."

She had certainly done her homework. "Then," she added, "Europeans continued to settle here – look out for the English-sounding place names we pass."

Laura, who was now trying to concentrate on her driving, interrupted, "OK, Tess, enough with the history lesson. Which way up ahead?"

The clement early autumn temperature was divine, the trees against the backdrop of a cloudless sky were perfect and, once we got out of the city, the white clapboard homes with their wrap-around porches completed the picture. I had already checked the weather app, and it looked like this weather would follow us. Visitors from around the world came to see and admire the fiery reds, vibrant oranges, and mellow yellows of the fall but to have great weather too was the icing on the cake. Tess and Laura were the perfect tour guide and driver, and we stopped several times when we spotted a stunning picture opportunity, with the bonus that we could breathe deeply and take in the salty sea air.

The scenery was magnificent, but I can't say the same about our first stop. It was gross! I should have taken more of an interest in the accommodation choices. To put it bluntly, it was basic, more of a motel than a hotel. I'd never have chosen something like this. My first thought was to call the nearest Hilton and pay for us all to abscond, but would that be totally insensitive? After all, Tess and Laura had a budget, and I'd appear stuck up and ungrateful. That was the old Ellie resurfacing, wasn't it? I decided to suck it up and hope things improved as we travelled. If they didn't, I might have to say something, unable to help myself. Although our rooms appeared clean, there were no luxuries, and the towels had seen better days, they were rough and threadbare, and the bedlinen scratchy – no Egyptian cotton here – and the trickle of water that came out of the shower was hardly worth bothering with. There was even a Bates Motel-style shower curtain, no expense spared. I sheepishly peeped in. Phew, no knife-wielding maniac!

As we met outside, ready to head for a late dinner, Tess must have seen my look. "Guys, this place looked so much better in the pictures. I'm sorry, it's a bit grim, isn't it?" We both grimaced as she continued, "We only have three nights here, and then we are heading to Cape Cod. Can you bear it, or do you want to go somewhere else?"

Seeing her sad face, I knew it was down to me, and I was getting better at holding my tongue.

"Don't worry, Tess, I stayed in far worse when I first came to Hampstead. I just hope the next place is better!" I thought back to the grimy hotel in Hampstead that was on a par with this, although this one was marginally cleaner.

Laura agreed. "Sweetie, I think we can bear it for three nights. After all, we'll only be sleeping there. I know you have so much planned for us." We had seen Tess's notes. She had us going from one place to another over the next two weeks. So much for that relaxing break!

Returning to the room after a delicious meal and a couple of glasses of wine at the restaurant, and viewing the room through rosier-coloured lenses, it didn't seem quite as bad. Each room had a connecting door, and Tess was next to me, so if I got a little worried about the Bates Motel comparison, I could knock on her door and bunk up in her room. On the other side were unknown neighbours. There were all sorts of bumps and noises from that room, an energetic night of sex or something more sinister. I wasn't prepared to speculate. So, tired after an early start, a seven-and-a-half-hour flight, a drive, and nicely relaxed from the alcohol, I put my earpods in my ears, put a sleep story on, and settled back on the pillow.

After a good, dreamless sleep, I felt surprisingly fresh in the morning, ready to seize the day. The only thing going for this room was that the bed was comfortable, and that always scored brownie points with me. A good night's sleep for me was so important. I had the briefest of showers – it really was just a trickle – not bothering to wash my hair, just a few sprays of dry shampoo and a quick spell, and I was styled! I hoped the next place was a little more luxurious, but another night or two wouldn't kill me. I wasn't that spoilt.

Today was all about the history of the Salem witches. We had our very own historian in Tess, who was in her element, keeping the history alive and interesting. It was a subject close to our hearts. Could we find a commonality between the plight of these poor souls and our own situation with the Purge at home? We were doing the tours to find out more. Little did they know that three badass witches were amongst them, finding out about the hysteria and trials of 1692. Tess knew her stuff and had done her research so well I could forgive her for the budget room. She told us that in the seventeenth century, many British settlers came to this area after they were persecuted for their religious beliefs. Salem Village was a rural area at the time, while nearby Salem Town was much more industrial, with trading ships arriving and departing. I hoped Salem wouldn't disappoint, as had happened when my parents took me to Niagara Falls. The Canadian side was commercialised, full of casinos and souvenir shops, and although the falls themselves were stunning, we didn't stay too long. Now I am sounding like a spoilt brat, I was lucky to have these experiences, I know.

On our schedule was a two-hour guided walking tour called History & Hauntings of Salem, run by a local historian; it would be dark by the time we joined, and we would be led by lantern light making everything spookier. The reviews, Tess said, were awesome, and we planned an early supper. Most of the restaurants cashed in on the witches, it was so strange for us, having come from England where nobody wanted the word witch to pass their lips. We could embrace our heritage around here in a safe environment. Tess read the tour literature to us, we'd be visiting sites including the Burying Point Cemetery and Witch House and pass through the historic McIntire District and the Ropes Mansion gardens, all of which had a reputation for paranormal experiences and, of course, you remember what happened the last time I went round a cemetery. Would I see ghosts again? I hoped so!

Tess had researched restaurants, and the one she'd chosen for breakfast didn't disappoint. We needed to fuel up because we had a morning tour as well. American breakfasts were to die for, and on the basis I'd need my strength, I couldn't and didn't resist stacked pancakes with maple syrup, peanut butter, bananas, and blueberries. This calorie-laden tasty treat would negate any fitness benefits, but at least I wouldn't be tackling things on an empty stomach. The morning outing was with the Bewitched Historical Tour, gathering outside the store of the same name downtown. It was jam-packed with witchy souvenirs for the discerning collector – not our thing, seeing as we were the real deal.

It was, though, an opportunity for Tess to take a break from history lectures, although, bless her, she couldn't resist a summary. Laura and I grinned at each other.

"The Salem witch trial started in 1692, and by 1693, more than two hundred people, mainly women but some men, had been accused of practising witchcraft."

Tess pointedly ignored our smiles. "The hysteria started in Salem Village, but, as often happens, suspicion soon spread outwards, and twenty people out of the two hundred accused were executed." That wiped the smile off our faces. I was curious now, "What was the catalyst for the hysteria?"

"Most of the early settlers came from England." Tess said slowly. "They'd already fled religious persecution back in the old country. Once again, they believed that their way of life was under attack, this time by the devil himself. Those stirring up the unrest made it clear that if this continued, they would lose control of their puritan way of life."

"You explain things so well, Tess," Laura said. I wondered whether this was a path Tess might want to follow once back home, but that thought led me back to Yorkshire, my history degree, and Seb.

"You OK, Ellie?" I must have lost colour because both girls were watching me. "You looked as if you'd just seen a ghost," Tess said.

"No, I'm OK. All this is so difficult to take in along with what's happening at home – all too close for comfort." They nodded. I wasn't the only one feeling it.

I still hadn't told them about my liaison with Seb and its impact on my life, but this wasn't the time. Tess continued, "Such dark times, and eventually the authorities admitted that the trials were a mistake. Unfortunately, that didn't bring back loved ones, or repair damaged reputations."

"Have either of you felt any bad vibes over here?" Laura wanted to know. "Sensed anything going on?" We shook our heads.

Tess laughed. "I don't think anyone around here is practising. Honestly, it all feels a bit more like Harry Potter, don't you think?" We agreed. For now, we felt quite safe. It was a good feeling. We may have spoken too soon.

CHAPTER 18

So back to the history lesson, we wanted to know more, and Tess was gagging to tell.

"How did it all start?" I asked. Tess lowered her voice to spooky. "Well it was all very strange, and revolved around a group of nine girls, known locally as 'the afflicted'. After playing a fortune-telling game they started to act weirdly. She paused for effect, and I had to admit I felt a chill up my spine. I could see that Laura was freaked out by this story but, like me, she wanted to know more.

"What sort of weird things were they doing?" Laura asked softly. Tess gave a wicked look. "The way they acted after this innocent game was frightening to watch from all accounts. They started doing bizarre things, acting as if they were possessed. A local doctor was brought in to check out all the girls, but he could find nothing physically wrong with them, there didn't seem to be any logical explanation."

"Go on," Laura and I said together, we were entranced.

"It was like some form of hysteria running through the girls. The doctor, with no logical explanation to hand, diagnosed that they had been bewitched."

We wanted to know what happened next, and Tess obliged. "The God-fearing villagers needed a scapegoat, someone to blame for bewitching the girls. The gossip and malicious rumours spread, and three names were put forward. Sarah Good, Sarah Osborne, and Tituba, by the girls themselves." Tess enunciated the names slowly. I frowned – how strange, I was sure I had heard these names before, they sounded so familiar. She continued, now on a roll, "The rumours that witches were living among them gained traction and this was the catalyst for the witch hunts in Salem, and the surrounding area. Other women also arrested as the witch hysteria took hold were Rebecca Nurse, Martha Corey, and Dorothy Good." Tess paused for breath, as we digested the horrendous history lesson we'd been told.

Laura said, "Wow, their names sound so ordinary, don't they? What about their families? Do you suppose descendants of the Nurses, Coreys, and Goods still live around here?"

Tess nodded, "Probably, those names are still quite common around here, those surnames are also quite common back home too." I couldn't think why the surnames rang a bell. I was positive I didn't know anyone back in England with those names.

As I lay exhausted on the bed, on the last but one night in this grotty place, I reflected on day one and the history lesson Tess had given us, she'd certainly given us food for thought, and I was transported right back to the seventeenth century. Our tour guides were endlessly knowledgeable too, and as well as covering witch hysteria around here, they brought the area alive in other ways as they took us from one place to another, describing what had happened and showcasing the unique architecture, which I so loved. Salem was still known as Witch City to this day, and on our walk, we were moved by quotes from some of the accused scripted onto the paving slabs, I am completely innocent of such wickedness. Such a heartfelt statement contrasted with the frivolous road sign we saw: No stopping or you will be toad. It certainly summed up the place, a mixture between real history and imagined.

Tired but happy, we'd had an awesome day with brilliant vibes. There was no doubt there was a unique atmosphere about the place, and the dodgy hotel room was already forgiven. As I glanced around at the peeling wallpaper, water stains and general neglect, I smiled. It just added to the spooky atmosphere. Maybe it was the right place to stay after all.

On our last day, Tess had booked tickets to visit the Witch House, dating back to 1678. We loved the colonial-style architecture created with local stone, and the clapboard exterior painted seaside colours. It was part of the Salem Village Historic District and had been sympathetically restored as a museum in 1909, before which it had been a private home. After lunch, we took in the Witch Museum, which looked like an old church. There had been many reported ghostly sightings here, and

I wondered if I'd feel a presence or two, but they must have been on vacation because neither I nor the other two felt anything.

Tess had only concentrated on the historic sights and, although we knew the movie Hocus Pocus was filmed in Salem, we didn't bother with their tour, sticking with the authentic, preferring to stay away from the main tourist attractions. The whole area seemed to be two halves of a whole with lots of spooky frivolities alongside more serious historic sites. We all smiled, though, at the statue in the town of Samantha Stephens from Bewitched, apparently she was a witch in a sitcom back in the nineteen sixties!

We couldn't resist visiting Wynatt's wand shop, where you could buy a hand-crafted wand. They'd apparently been making these since 1692, each with individual symbolism, depending on what you wanted to manifest. Some reviews said, "The wand felt like it was choosing you". As well as wands, they sold crystal balls, spell books, and anything a magical practitioner might need. Their shop now attracted a younger audience after the Harry Potter craze made owning a wand a must! It was tempting to buy our own wands, but it might attract some attention at customs if our bag was searched, especially with the laws on witchcraft in the UK, how could we explain it away? We were mindful that if we got arrested, we could get ourselves into some real trouble.

CHAPTER 19

An early start the following morning, we were heading for a breakfast stop on the way to our next location, Cape Cod, and our few days on the coast. Funny, I'd always thought of Cape Cod as an island but more accurately, it was a narrow peninsula famous for its wealth of historic lighthouses, which were beautiful in their own right, along with stunning beaches and spectacular mansions of the rich and famous. Tess had promised a visit to Herring Cove Beach, one of the most picturesque beaches – it sounded like my sort of place. She had also organised a visit to the Truro Vineyard, where we'd tour, taste, and pick up a few bottles to relish as we relaxed at our next stop. It was like being back in England looking at the map around here, so many familiar town names – Falmouth, Truro, and Chatham named by the original settlers who'd stepped off the Mayflower at Plymouth, ready for a whole new life. We'd be driving through Plymouth on our way to the Cape, although Tess didn't think we'd have time to stop at the famous Plimoth Patuxet Museum – the living history recreation of the original seventeenth-century settlement.

"Damn," I'd commented, half laughing, "such a shame, looks like we'll just have to have more holiday and less full-blown history trip!" Tess grinned, taking the teasing in good part. But even she agreed we'd had our fill of the Salem witches and hadn't felt any remotely witchy vibes from tourists or residents. Tess's history lessons had been impressive, but we probably now knew all we needed to, although she insisted the John F. Kennedy Museum, plus some other early American attractions, were still on the agenda.

Tess, who'd taken on her role with a vengeance, had to be dissuaded at several points from adding further to the itinerary. But there was no doubt it had been a fascinating trip so far, even if we hadn't had a great deal of time to kick back and relax. We'd been promised some fabulous views on the twenty-five-mile Rail Trail, a paved track that would take in six Cape Cod towns, but Tess was proposing bike hire for that, and I can't say I was keen. I'd never really been into bike riding and thought I might leave the girls to do that on their own while I chilled out with a good book, a glass of vino, and an ocean view. On the other hand, I was excited to see that the small town where we were staying had a riding stable, and they took groups for a hack on the beach – now that was much more my bag. I'd just have to see how I felt on the day. Something I was looking forward to later on the trip was the whale watching tour when we got to Nantucket, and I smiled to myself as I wondered if Tess was already brushing up on a David Attenborough-style commentary. She really had missed her vocation.

Joking apart, so far being on this trip with the girls had exceeded my expectations, even taking into account the dodgy Bates-style motel. Surely the house we were heading for would be better. At least we'd have more space and best of all there was a garden leading onto a private beach. It sounded divine. Time with the girls made me think back fondly to nights with Alice, Lizzie, and Sarah when we'd stayed up until the early hours singing and dancing to some banging tunes. I'd suggest a holiday house party, just the three of us, when we got there. We'd have plenty of local wine in and could pick up some tasty nibbles from the town, taking turns picking our favourite tracks, I already had a playlist in mind. I'd start with the twelve-inch version of Donna Summer's "I Feel Love" which always got the evening off to a good start. The girls already knew all about my obsession with music, especially the eighties alternative stuff – maybe I was more like my mother than I was willing to admit. I always preferred old-school and alternative tracks, especially since my North Yorkshire experience, they just had a better vibe.

Laura was driving, and we took the picturesque coastal road, a stunning, ninety-mile journey that passed swiftly because there was so much to look at along the way, and all I had to do was sit back and let it all drift past me. We were looking for a nice restaurant, and I reflected the sooner we found one, the better, I was hungry and was missing my morning coffee hit. But unexpectedly, and to our consternation, most shops and restaurants we passed didn't open until 12.00. We weren't happy, but we were starving, and thankfully found a service station where Tess filled the car with petrol while I filled a basket with snacks and other goodies. If we didn't eat them on the journey, they'd be a good start for stocking up the house.

"Glad to see you're open," I said to the guy behind the counter as I put my purchases by the till. "It's like a ghost town around here!"

He smiled. "Yup, that's about how I'd describe it. Not from around here, are you? Australian?"

I laughed. "Wrong, England. London." He wasn't the first person who'd identified our accents incorrectly.

"Ah right, well round here we still close on a Sunday – meant to be voluntary but most folk stick to it."

"Not you, though?"

"Always the rebel, ma'am, not one to follow the rules. Not that it does any good. Seems to me we're heading right back to the old doctrines, and those who don't follow the pack are scapegoated. There's people no longer come in here for their goods, you'd think I was a devil worshipper." I smiled politely, he was efficiently packing what I'd bought, but he was on a roll. "Your fault," he said, "You English settlers started it with your Puritan ways." He was smiling, just not as genuinely as before.

"Er, well, don't think I can take the blame personally," I said, "it was over 400 years ago. But is there somewhere you could direct me where we can get some breakfast –

another rebel business perhaps?" He gave me a dark look and lowered his tone. "Nope, you won't find anything here on the main drag. Need to get yourself off the beaten track, away from the coast and the tourists." He was no longer smiling as he passed over the brown paper bag packed with my goods. "Not many choose to flaunt the rules. Have a good day now." He turned away to fill up some of the shelves behind the counter and didn't respond when I wished him the same.

Back in the SUV, Tess had taken over and was in the driver's seat. They were now taking turns to keep me company in the back, and I passed on the dire reality of the situation along with a bag of potato chips, cookies, and a bottle of water. We wolfed down the snack as if we hadn't eaten for days, but even after another hour down the road, we still hadn't spotted anywhere to stop and eat properly, and we were all starting to feel hangry. Somehow on holiday, you always polish off far more than usual, and we loved our American breakfasts, I was salivating just thinking about what I'd like to order, and my stomach was making the most embarrassing growling noises. As I said to the girls, I was glad I wasn't in polite company.

It was a given that I had been put in charge of the music and had sorted cool playlists for every part of our journey, and one song came to mind that was perfect for our current predicament. At least it'd give the girls a giggle, that spooky guitar riff and two-tone beat, mixing Ska with new wave – "Ghost Town" by The Specials. It had to be played loud, and as it boomed through the speakers, Tess said, "What the hell, Ellie? Another of your weird, dark tunes!" Laura laughed. "It's certainly spooky enough!"

"Shut up and just listen to the words," I said, and they suddenly twigged, laughing out loud.

"The Specials, right?" Laura was certainly taking on board my teachings.

"Isn't it perfect?" I demanded. "It's like we're driving from one ghost town to another!" Not a soul in sight, we sang along with enthusiasm, the music way too loud, maybe we'd get arrested for flouting the rules, but we didn't care, the SUV was rocking! My eclectic music tastes were growing on them.

We'd followed the advice of my not-so-cheerful acquaintance at the service station and left the main road, and were on the point of giving up, heading back to the coastline, when Laura suddenly yelled,

"Look, sign on that door – it's open." Tess came to a screeching halt, scaring us half to death. I was glad I'd put my seatbelt on!

It was a slightly hippy, new wave-style cafe. Maybe they hadn't got the memo about the half-day closing? Or perhaps they'd got it but had chosen to ignore it, so far as they were off the beaten track, maybe they just did things their way. No point speculating. The sign said open. That was all that was important to us.

CHAPTER 20

We shouldn't have minded what the cafe looked like because we were starving. But as it happened, it was picture perfect, an archetypal New England style, with its tasteful seaside colours and weatherboard cladding – very much our sort of place – and best of all, it was open, although we'd have missed it had it not been for Laura's keen eye. But as we got out of the car, stretched our legs, and looked around, our hearts sank a little, there were no cars parked in the car park, which was odd as it seemed to be the only available place to eat for miles around.

"D'you think it is open?" I murmured. "Maybe they just forgot to turn the sign around."

"No other cars here," said Tess, pointing out the obvious. "Not looking good, girls."

"Come on," Laura took the lead, "look, the lights are on." We followed her to the door, which thankfully opened with a cheerfully tinkling bell, and we gratefully piled in. The place wasn't exactly buzzing, there was just one occupied table.

"Maybe everyone hibernates on half days?" I said to the girls under my breath. But despite the lack of customers, first impressions were favourable. It was lush inside and tastefully decorated with warm lighting and a cosy feel, although there didn't seem to be any front-of-house staff to offer a welcome. There appeared to be only one waitress on duty, and she was deep in conversation with the other diners, a group of three black-clad, formally dressed, middle-aged women. She glanced up as we came in, then went right back to her conversation. So much for customer service.

In the absence of anyone to show us to a table, we picked our own, just far enough away from the other group so it wouldn't appear obvious we were eavesdropping in on their conversation, which was clearly important enough to keep the waitress fully engaged. Giving them a surreptitious once over, I thought the women looked interesting and promptly decided I should listen in, if only to get a feel for local life.

As we settled ourselves, the three of us exchanged looks.

"Bit rude!" Tess said quietly. I don't know whether the other table thought we were commenting on them, but as we laughed, all three of them turned and gave us a glacial stare.

"Wow," said Laura, "think we're being given the evil eye." We were starting to feel uncomfortable. My sixth sense, that twitch in my bones, told me they didn't want us here. We were intruders, outsiders disturbing the peace, rippling the pond. In the near-empty restaurant, you could cut the atmosphere with a knife.

"If they're not witches, I'll eat my hat," said Tess. I smiled, then stopped as she reached behind her; holy crap, was she doing a spell? No! With relief, I saw she'd only plucked her hat from the back of the chair to put it back on. We giggled again.

"Should we introduce ourselves?" suggested Laura. I wasn't sure whether she was serious but I shook my head. "Not sure that's a good idea."

Despite the commotion at our table, the women had swiftly returned to their conversation as if nothing had happened, and it was obvious the waitress had more important issues to attend to than serving us. In normal circumstances, we would all have jumped up right there and then and left. But something was stopping me, other than the fact I was desperate for breakfast, and it wasn't as if we had our choice of eateries – miss this one and who knew when the next one would come up. I was intrigued, I wasn't sure what we'd stumbled into here, and for a moment, I felt dizzy. Maybe it was just because I was hungry, but I didn't think so.

By now, even normally passive Tess was getting annoyed, she was generally chilled, but having taken responsibility for the trip, she wanted everything perfect, although she already felt she'd messed up with the motel.

"Shall we go?" she said. "This is a bit silly, and I hate being ignored."

"Let's give it a couple more minutes," I whispered

back, "after all, where else are we going to go, and the aroma wafting from the kitchen is divine."

Laura agreed, "I say we stay put. She can't ignore us forever. If she carries on like this, Ellie, you can make a scene. You're the tough one." We all laughed again, but I noticed the women at the other table didn't even turn this time. I made up my mind to sit back, relax, relish the time out of the SUV, and enjoy each other's company, no real reason to get het up, maybe this was just the way things were done around here. And sure enough, a few minutes later, the waitress made her way over, although I noted she didn't hurry.

"Sorry to keep you. How are you all doing today? I thought I'd give you a chance to look at the menu."

"That would have been kind," I said, "if we'd had a menu to look at." I couldn't help myself.

She looked a little sheepish and went to retrieve three from the serving station behind her.

In explanation she said, "Well, here you go. It's the calm before the storm right now, I was grabbing myself a break. Gets really busy later on and I'll be rushed off my feet. Now, why don't I get you girls some hot coffee while you're deciding?"

Conscious of not being rude to the waitress, who might then ask the chef to spit in our food, I kept my mouth shut. "Just to let you know we're out of cinnamon rolls and bacon," she continued, "but check out our specials on the board."

"Thank you," I said politely, but I'd seen the full jug of coffee which had been sitting beneath the percolator since we came in, and if there's one thing I can't do, it's stewed coffee. "Rather than regular, can I get a latte with an extra shot of coffee and skimmed milk? How about you guys?" They both nodded and agreed that sounded good. A momentary annoyance crossed the face of our waitress, she'd obviously been heading for the ease of that jug.

"Sure thing," she said, "no problem." She filled the three water glasses she'd set out for us, and by the time she was back with the lattes, we'd made choices.

I could have happily scoffed a stack of pancakes, but two days in a row would have been pushing it, so I went for the healthier option of sourdough toast with smashed avocado and a poached egg. Tess didn't even try to resist and, without hesitation, asked for stacked pancakes, maple syrup, peanut butter, and fruit. I won't say I wasn't sorely tempted to change my order, but Laura, like me, was going for healthier today, granola with toasted almonds and berries. The food was delicious, but we were still hungry – must have been all that walking yesterday – so we each went for a blueberry muffin and another latte. Having brought these over and asking us if we were "All set?", the waitress returned to the other group, and they carried on talking.

I'd been covertly observing the women at the other table, a little frustrated because they hadn't stopped talking and gesturing, but only the odd word floated over to us. Call me nosey – I'd prefer interested – but I'm sure it's not just me? Who else loves listening to other people's conversations? In the past, I'd found one or two favourite places where the acoustics worked in a peculiar way and allowed you to hear the most intimate conversations. In Whitby, it was Sanders Yard, my favourite deli. London, it was a little more challenging. There was usually a quicker table turnaround, so more eating and less time for talking. Nevertheless, all sorts of secrets had reached my ears. It was an art to tune into tone and rhythm.

I could have done with being a little nearer to this lot to get the thread of their conversation. I was intrigued. I had one ear on what the girls were saying, the other on the mysterious ladies. One woman's voice was more dominant. She was holding court, another queen bee. I laughed inwardly. If I asked Tess and Laura, they'd say in our group it was me. A compliment, as I remember being intimidated when I first saw them at Pilates, the two perfect women at the front of the class.

"Ellie, you listening?" Laura clicked her fingers. "You realise you just keep saying yes, not answering anything properly. Are you with us or somewhere else?"

"Sorry, I was miles away. Back in the room now!" One thing I had noticed, the three women at the other table were way overdressed for breakfast, more like afternoon tea at the Ritz. Here, where everything was so much more casual and way out in the sticks, they looked totally out of place. I put them around my mother's age, in their sixties, but they could have got away as younger in a kind light. It was their formal dress that dated them, old-fashioned and over the top.

They paid us no further attention. We'd been assessed and dismissed; we were of no interest. I made a deliberate effort to zone back into the conversation I should have been involved in as opposed to the one I shouldn't. Tess was holding forth on the excitement she had planned for us, lighthouses we'd visit, the beaches, and museums. Because I made an effort to listen properly, it was only when I was swamped in a waft of expensively heady perfume that I looked up, as one of the black-clad women moved across the room. Maybe she'd decided we might be of interest after all.

Up close, she was even more intimidating. I couldn't make out the perfume, but it was overpowering, like Poison by Dior, a headache-inducing scent. The aroma was as overdone as her outfit. Theatrical and punky at the same time – think Helena Bonham-Carter. To this ensemble had been added a leather biker jacket. The weather was still warm enough for bare legs, but she had opaque black tights under black, high-heeled boots. It was clear she had a good and ongoing relationship with her plastic surgeon. Her face was almost completely unlined with that unmistakable tautness, her teeth bright white, and her makeup thick but flawless. She had on lacy, fingerless gloves, possibly, I thought bitchily, because the one thing the surgeon couldn't sort was the crepiness of ageing hands. Nevertheless, she oozed languid sex appeal, and I knew instinctively you wouldn't want to cross her. I had a weird feeling of foreboding; I couldn't explain it.

I felt extremely underdressed. I was wearing a simple white shirt, with a sleeveless knitted vest in a shade of cerise, jeggings and trainers. We'd all relaxed our style over here, no one to impress.

The vision in black spoke, "Hey ladies, are you from

England?" We all nodded, and although she had a wide smile on her perfect face, it didn't reach her eyes. Her focus was on me, so I answered for us. "London."

"Oh, whereabouts in London?"

"West London." For an undefinable reason, I didn't want to say Hampstead, I felt the girls' surprise but didn't look at them. They seemed temporarily mesmerised by this woman who was way ahead in the gothic glamour stakes, and I knew they were taking in all the details. She nodded slowly, unperturbed at my vague answer and the coolness of my tone. I wondered whether she was or had been an actress, now living a quieter rural life but unable to give up on some of the glitz and glamour, although the only movie I could see her in would be The Addams Family.

She was making some more small talk, this time about the weather, nothing serious, but I could feel adrenaline fizzing deep within me. My reaction was purely visceral, I couldn't explain it other than that I so clearly saw past the saccharine sweetness to the bitterness beneath. She surveyed our plates, scattered with only a few crumbs as evidence of the blueberry muffins.

"They do good breakfasts here," she said.

"Well, I couldn't resist," said Tess. "Not great for the waistline, but the pancakes were to die for."

Laura added, "Not our usual breakfast, but a nice treat!" I looked over at the table the woman had left. Both her friends were looking at us. I glanced quickly away and was pleased they didn't seem inclined to come and join her. The woman was nodding at Tess and Laura's comments but was looking at me with an unsettling intensity to her gaze, which I tried to meet but couldn't. I was first to avert my eyes.

"I'm Em Corey, my friends over there, Beatty Nurse and Blanche Good." I didn't want to exchange glances with the girls, but we all recognised those surnames we'd heard so recently. Could they be descendants of the Salem witches, or was it just as Tess had said, that these names were typical of the area? It was impossible not to respond to the introduction, but I kept it brief.

"I'm Ellie, and this is Tess and Laura."

"And how long are you over for?"

"Unfortunately, just two weeks," Tess said. "Not enough time to see all we want to."

"Where are you going next?" I saw Tess hesitate, maybe she was starting to sense the same intensity I was, but she could hardly ignore the question. The woman was still standing, we hadn't offered her a seat, so she towered over us.

"Staying on the Cape for a few days, visiting the islands, you know, usual tourist stuff."

"Awesome!" That smile again, one hundred per cent insincere. She turned her eyes back to me; I wasn't sure why this felt more like an interrogation than idle chit-chat.

"So you're Ellie? How odd." I raised my eyebrows, and she continued, "A coincidence, last time I was in London, a few years back, I was searching for an Ellie, an ad executive. She'd been talked up by several people, they said she was very good, I wanted her for a planned campaign, but I guess it's a common name in England?"

I tried not to let my shock show. I knew precisely who she was. Oli, my ex-colleague at the agency, had told me someone wanted to use me and had been disproportionately cross to find I no longer worked for the company. He'd described her – and he wasn't wrong – saying she'd have been at home in a goth band. Simon had commented, too, he'd said the woman was remarkably odd, and it was all a bit cloak and dagger. She wouldn't hear of talking to anyone else who could help her, and she'd left in a huff, trailing displeasure.

I didn't for one moment want to acknowledge it was me, what would be the point? I could no longer help her and certainly didn't want to prolong our contact. Which is why I absolutely can't explain what happened next. My head said: nod politely, smile, and move the conversation on – or better still, wind it up. But when I opened my mouth, something entirely different came out. I felt strands of my thoughts being plucked from my head as if words were being unstoppably sucked out of me.

"I am the Ellie you were looking for. I was an advertising executive in the city. What an extraordinary coincidence!"

She shook her head firmly, "No honey, it wasn't you; the woman I was after had a great headshot on the company website. You're nothing like her."

I should have left it there, with relief, but it seemed I couldn't stop myself. "It was me; you met my friend Oli and my boss Simon, both of them described you. You're from the Boston area; you own Tuttuba Cosmetics, right?" She didn't say anything, and I forestalled her.

"I do look very different from back then, it's a long

story, but I had to change my look," I said and could have kicked myself. What on earth was I doing oversharing like this? She didn't need to know. What the hell?

I shivered involuntarily. It wasn't cold in the cafe, but I was freezing. She was still staring at me, drilling, it seemed, through my eyes to my soul. I shivered again.

As I did, she inclined her head, "Ahh, now I see, yes it is, of course, you. I can see it in your eyes." I didn't want this, and I had no idea why I'd spoken up, I needed to put up a barrier of some kind, I needed to protect myself. I felt baffled and cold from the inside out. She must have read my mind. "Your picture on the site was unusually clear, and you nearly had me fooled, but your eyes – you can't change your eyes." I swallowed, a click in a dry throat I hoped nobody else could hear. What a peculiar thing for her to say.

When Oli had given me the name of the company, I'd googled it out of idle curiosity, Tuttuba Cosmetics was a global, highly successful brand. They were on shopping channels, supplied upmarket department stores and were lauded by makeup artists worldwide. I remember being curious as to why they'd been so keen on me. From what I could see, they were on top of their advertising, branding, and even PR. I wasn't sure I'd have had anything to add to what they were already so good at. I was aware, though, that many top-end established companies were upping their infomercial output, maybe it was that they were recruiting for.

She gave me that smile again, open mouth, whiter-than-white teeth, eyes still ice cold. "Well, what an incredible coincidence that this should have happened, that we should meet this way. And indeed, Ellie, your transformation is miraculous. I might even say, truly magical. I am so pleased to finally meet you, such a shame you weren't available to help back then, but I believe everything happens for a reason, and we were obviously destined to meet." I didn't know what to say. Both her friends were watching, maybe impatient at the time she was spending with us. She waved an arm in their direction. "Both Beatty and Blanche are Tuttuba board members."

Despite none of us asking her to, Em Corey pulled out a chair and perched on the edge as she went on to talk about the success of her company. "You'll have to subscribe to our new beauty channel, that was why I was looking for you back then; maybe it's not too late for you to cast a professional eye?"

I smiled politely as she talked, knowing no way would I be "casting a professional eye". I wasn't paying too much attention to what she was saying, I was thinking that Tuttuba was a play on Tituba, a slave of the Puritan minister Samuel Parris and the first convicted Salem witch. That surely was not pure chance. I was sure Glamour Girl and her friends were witches, they even had the surnames Corey, Good and Nurse.

I stopped smiling politely and interrupted her, I couldn't help myself. "So, are you descendants of the Salem witches?"

She barked a sharp laugh. "No, these are our married names. Sadly, we are now widows, our husbands all passed within a short time, and that was when we started the business." She didn't expand on this, and I didn't dare ask. In answer to my original question, she said, "My family didn't come to the States until the late eighteen hundreds. They were from England, a little place called Whitby. I don't suppose you've ever heard of it?"

"As a matter of fact, I have." I kept my tone neutral. I had no idea what was going on, but I wasn't a great believer in coincidences either, and all this was too close for comfort. "I lived in Whitby for a while. It's a lovely place."

"Really?" she said. "I've never made it as far north on any of my trips over there. Maybe one day."

I felt increasingly queasy. Was it the breakfast or the awkward situation that was becoming more uncomfortable by the minute, although she seemed unaware? If these women were witches, they weren't the sort I knew. I didn't know whether it was the overstrong perfume or the insincerity of her smile, but there was something decidedly unpleasant about her, it seeped through her pores. These women, all three of them, were giving off some powerful vibes, and I wondered whether we'd bitten off more than we could chew, and then I wondered where on earth that thought came from.

"You know, honey," she continued, "you could have made big bucks if you'd been around when I came looking, you really missed a trick."

"My bad timing then, wasn't it?" I said.

She continued as if I hadn't spoken, "However, we still have major plans for the company, we're prepared to throw massive amounts of money at new projects. We have bottomless funding at our disposal, we get anything we want ... anything." What she said next floored me. "Ellie, I know you are the mistress of the sublime message; we have an idea that will change the world of beauty and cosmetics forever. Maybe you could still get involved?"

This was the last thing I wanted to do right now, I just wanted to get the hell out of there. There was an awkward pause before I said coolly, and maybe a little rudely, "I'm afraid I no longer work in that sphere, you will need to find someone else." She didn't say anything, just nodded slowly. If I hoped that would wind up this odd encounter, I was wrong.

"Funny," she said, "we had another Brit pass through here just a couple of weeks back. Not that many tourists find their way here, and that's how we like it. She was part of a group, most were American, so she stood out. She was tall, like you, that's what reminded me."

Tess caught my eye; I could see she was as disconcerted as I was. She took up the last remark, "We wouldn't have driven this far," she said, "but everywhere else seemed shut. Although," she added, "glad we did, delicious breakfast."

Em continued as if Tess hadn't spoken. "Interesting woman, a model, originally from the UK, been working over here for a while, living in New York. I don't think she gave her name?" She turned to her friends at the other table for help, then turned back. "I just know she was a great fan of our cosmetics."

I stared at her – surely not, but I had to ask, "One of my best friends is a model, although we've lost touch over the last few years. Her name is Lizzie."

"That so? Tall, knockout looks, Nordic, I'd say."

I didn't want to reveal too much to this strange woman, but could it have been Lizzie, what a coincidence – was it possible I'd missed her by just a couple of weeks? She continued, "The group were travelling on, I heard them mention Goa. The English girl did say, though, she was glad she'd relocated, that things were starting to get very weird across the pond."

By force of will, I took control of my thoughts and didn't take the bait. I knew where she was leading and was aware I'd probably already said too much. I buttoned my lip and fastened the polite smile back on my face, I was finished with mind games. Until now, we hadn't sensed anything from anyone, and I didn't want to get involved in the local scene now. From the body language of the girls and their unusual silence, I knew they didn't want to either.

I didn't feel safe around here, the atmosphere was menacing; I knew I wasn't imagining it. We'd finished our breakfast, we'd drunk gallons of coffee, and I now urgently wanted to settle the bill and go.

"Tess, if we're following your schedule, we need to move on," I said. She nodded, seeing the look on my face, and she and Laura started gathering their things, getting up to put on their jackets. "I'll nip to the bathroom, and then we must rush." I looked over at the waitress and made the universal gesture of signing to get the bill. She was already looking our way, and it was clear from her body language that she had been secretly eavesdropping on the conversation. She nodded. I couldn't wait to escape, going with my instincts. Something was very wrong. I didn't understand what, but knew I had to act on my intuition.

Em had got the hint. What was that fleeting look on her face – satisfaction? Disappointment? I couldn't tell, as she reverted to the false smile. As I moved past her, I could smell the malevolence radiating from her skin, it was repulsive. I could understand the heavy hand with the perfume.

When I returned from a hurried trip to the bathroom, she was still talking to Tess, who, to my horror, was spilling the beans. I tried to send a warning look, but she was in full flow.

"Oh yes, that's our last stop, we're basing ourselves in Cape Cod, then over to Nantucket and Martha's Vineyard, then back to Boston for our last few days for sightseeing and retail therapy."

"Well, doesn't that just sound awesome? I hope you all have an amazing time." And with that, she gracefully glided back to her table.

I could feel the eyes of all three women on my back as we left the restaurant.

Piling back into the SUV, I was the first to voice it. "What the fuck happened in there? It felt like she was reading my mind."

Laura, who hadn't spoken for a while, said, "How bizarre was that? We got a lot more than just breakfast in there! She was interrogating you, less interested in me or Tess."

"Yes, and ..." I said slowly, "... that was even before she found out who I was." I looked at Tess. "You seemed to be getting on OK while I was in the bathroom, oversharing our plans?"

She nodded, shamefaced, "Oh God, I know, it was so weird, I didn't want to tell her, but didn't feel I had a choice, my brain got disconnected from my mouth, if that makes any sense?"

I nodded. "It does, it's exactly how I'd describe it, she was one intimidating woman." I shuddered. I felt violated, unbelievably glad to have made our escape from the supernatural weirdness in that room, although I wrinkled my nose, I couldn't get rid of that sour smell inadequately covered by the perfume. Oli hadn't mentioned her repulsive aroma, it's the sort of thing he'd have noticed, but then maybe only I could smell it? I'd ask the girls.

As we continued on our journey I checked out the online presence of the brand. Their social media was insane, they had over twenty million followers, like nothing else I'd seen before, all this for a makeup brand. What was going on? Had Em Corey really needed advertising assistance when she came to find me in London or was there another reason? And how crazy if Lizzie had been right here just a couple of weeks ago. What had happened to make her flee the UK? Was I becoming completely paranoid? Surely it wasn't Lizzie anyway, the idea was crazy.

CHAPTER 21

Happy to be safely away from that godforsaken place, we unanimously agreed that from now on we'd stick to the safer option, stay away from off the beaten track, mingle with the tourists, stay with the crowds. The last thing we wanted was to tangle with other witches, however intriguing they were. We were all a bit shell-shocked from our recent experience; what exactly *had* happened in that room? I'd met many witches in my time, and I was travelling with two of the best, but we all agreed the last hour had been way beyond anything we'd encountered before and more than we wanted to handle.

"Do you think they *are* descendants of the Salem witches?" I said. "I know she denied it, but I wouldn't trust anything that came out of her mouth."

"They could well be," Tess said thoughtfully. "Don't forget the accused women had children and families, and in this area, many people didn't leave, they continued to live a Puritan lifestyle and, in many cases, stayed within that insular society."

"That's all well and good," Laura put in, "and very interesting, but I never want to run into that lot again. I'm truly creeped out."

Apart from dropping into a convenience store to stock up on provisions (going heavy on chocolate cookies and wine), we didn't stop until we got to our rented house. I was still full from breakfast, but the uncomfortable feeling I had wasn't from eating too much. It was something else entirely.

We planned on finding a local restaurant for dinner that night and would leave exploring the area until the next day. Tess was filling us in on the cute little town we were heading for and had even more information on the eighteenth-century colonial-style house waiting for us. Apparently, the artist Edward Hopper stayed there in the 1950s. It gave him the perfect view and air quality and inspired many of his paintings, and was actually called Hopper's Rest, Tess had told us. I smiled to myself – or perhaps just a great marketing ploy by the owners. Anyone could say anything, and gullible Tess would believe it! My only concern was that artists' retreats were often shabby affairs.

By the time we turned into a private road, following Tess's written directions, we were all excited. It all looked promising as we passed pristine properties, shingled tiles painted in typically muted Cape Cod colours, pretty porches with sofas, swinging chairs, and an abundance of outdoor plants offering relaxing havens for reflections. I imagined us on ours with candles flickering around us and a glass of something in our hands. The neighbourhood itself looked immaculate, shipshape, you could say.

"Mmm, my sort of place, well done, Tess," I murmured. Tess was a romantic, and this place had been sold to her based on a romantic vision. She'd already told us about the influx of settlers at various times, the seventeenth-century Pilgrim settlers, the nineteenth-century whalers, and then, in the early twentieth century, the bohemian types and artists, arriving in droves for the stunning scenery and unique light, the perfect backdrop.

Revelling in my anticipation, I hadn't noticed that we'd stopped at the end of a road – a dead end. The satnav was firmly telling us that we'd reached our destination, but surely it was a mistake. Tess must have put the address in wrong. She'd promised us an artist's retreat, historically vintage with ocean views to die for, not this ramshackle dwelling. Or maybe she was just playing a joke?

"This doesn't look right," Tess sounded panicked. "The house looked different in the pictures. It wasn't yellow, I'm sure of it. But I'm positive I put the right address in."

"Don't panic, this can't be the right place, and who on this earth would paint their house that colour? Yuk, it's gross!"

Ever the diplomat trying to defuse the situation, Laura sensed Tess was tearing up. "I'm sure you'll find the key you have won't fit, so we can phone the agent right away and sort this out."

Tess got out of the SUV, reluctantly sliding through the gate, and climbed precariously up the steps to the dilapidated-looking porch. It didn't look inviting. She knocked on the front door. I hoped that whoever lived in this shack would open up, and then we could be off, laughing with relief and find the right property. After waiting a few moments, she knocked again, harder this time, while Laura and I studiously avoided looking at each other. Still there was no answer. Tess disappeared around the back of the house, returning to the front a few minutes later, shaking her head. It was obvious there was no one in.

She glanced back at us and then reluctantly tried the key to the front door. Our hopes were well and truly dashed as it opened, and she entered the house. A few minutes later, grim-faced, she emerged. Her expression said it all. This place was obviously as awful inside as it was from the front. "I'm so sorry, guys, this is the house," she pointed to a dirt-caked sign next to the door, if you squinted, you could just make out what it said: Hopper's Rest.

"Wow, it really is Hopper's Rest," said the normally diplomatic Laura, "and it doesn't look as if anyone's decorated since he did the place up! Is it better inside?" If the situation wasn't as dire, I might have smirked, didn't she realise that Hopper painted pictures of houses, not decorated them? I decided to keep my mirth to myself.

Tess grimaced. "You'd better see for yourselves." That didn't bode well. I took a few covert pictures before I followed Tess and Laura inside. I wasn't optimistic. This was taking historically vintage, shabby chic to new levels. "Way too much shabby and not nearly enough chic," I muttered to myself. I felt that if Hopper had really been here, he would have certainly hopped straight off. The exterior paint, a vile shade of duster-yellow, was peeling, as were the bottle-green shutters and the brick-red door. It would seem to have been decorated by someone who'd never heard of the colour wheel because there was a lot more clashing than complementing. This place needed more than a little TLC. The rickety picket fence was weathered and worn and, although still standing, looked ready to collapse at any time. The wooden gate was hanging lopsidedly off its hinges, and the porch looked like the last place you'd go to relax – no soft furnishings in sight, just a lone wooden rocking chair. I was surprised not to see a toothless, banjo-playing guy, rocking and grinning manically at us. Following Tess back into the house, we were knocked back by a putrid smell, not the newly cleaned aroma you'd expect from a holiday rental. Historically vintage, my arse, marketing-speak for old and decrepit more like – 10/10 for getting it wrong! I was more than irritated, I was thoroughly pissed off!

What the hell was Tess thinking when she booked? Surely she'd checked the reviews? Was it the thought of the ocean view that seduced her, along with the bargain price? I knew budget considerations were high on her list, as evidenced by the creepy motel she'd organised, but this is what happens when you scrimp and save. I wished they'd left it to me. Maybe I was a spoilt little rich girl, I knew they couldn't magic money – a spell too far – and the money tree at the bottom of my garden was mercifully more fruitful than theirs. But I would have been more than happy to pay the difference. Maybe it was pride, even though they were both magical, kick-ass women, sometimes common sense was lacking in both of them, and Tess was gullible, always willing to think the best, while I was far more cynical.

I had to bite my tongue so hard it hurt. I was seething. We could have easily fallen out over this; things gone sour. Then I saw her dejected expression.

"I'm so sorry, girls," she said quietly. "I think I've been conned. It honestly looked so different in the pictures. This is not what I expected, it was a total misrepresentation." I was wracking my brain for something both tactful and positive to say to ease the situation until I decided what to do practically. I wasn't usually known for my peace-making qualities, but I could feel her mortification, and after our near miss with the witches, I couldn't cope with any more histrionics.

"The weather forecast for the next few days is meant to be glorious, so we'll be spending most of our time out and about, and we do have the ocean on our doorstep." I didn't dare look at that point, hoping that, too, wasn't a misrepresentation and we weren't, in fact, looking out over a car park or similar.

Laura quickly read the situation, too, trying to lighten the mood, "OK, the place may look a bit weird and creepy, but the location is fabulous, a great base for exploring." Tess gave a weak, grateful smile. She knew we were trying to put a positive spin on the situation, but our words didn't convince her, and she didn't reply. She was deeply disappointed, with herself as much as feeling terrible at having let us down so badly.

She led the way through the hall while I held back a little – I won't lie, I put space between us so I didn't say something I'd regret. We followed her into an open-plan space, a kitchen, dining, and living area. The curtains were drawn across the patio door, and blinds were down, so it was difficult to see too much, which may have been for the best.

"It's spacious, isn't it?" Laura said brightly. Game girl! I was holding my nose as the whiff was getting worse. It smelt as if something had died in here, and not recently.

Tess pulled up the blinds, coughing as she took in a mouthful of dust, and opened the patio door, which gave a protesting squeal. At least I hoped it was that and not an injured mouse. A strong sea breeze swept in and billowed the drawn-aside curtains, the salty air wafting away a little of the foul smell. Thank God for some fresh air.

"I can see the sea!" Tess announced with relief. Well, at least that was one redeeming factor. And the living space wasn't cramped. What a waste of such a perfect position and footprint, it was crying out for some high-end interior design – if only I could get my hands on it. But it wasn't mine, and we were only here for a few days, so we had to make the best of it, and we couldn't just stand around and grumble. Tess had already tried to get through to the agent she'd booked with to demand they organise cleaners, but she was only able to leave an indignant message in response to their out-of-office assurance that they'd get back to us within forty-eight hours, so that was no good. We weren't going to hold our breath; they hadn't excelled themselves so far.

With the light flooding in, we could assess the living area's true state. It needed a thorough cleaning, and we had to find the source of the smell, but to be fair, the furniture didn't look too bad, good quality at least. A brown leather sofa with an assortment of cushions looked as if it would be comfy, once we'd beaten the dust out of the cushions. The dining table and chairs looked sturdy. Maybe it just hadn't been cleaned after the previous guests, who must have had one hell of a party. Wine and beer bottles, cigarette butts on the table, and the kitchen counter cluttered with detritus. First things first, I picked up my phone and started taking pictures. Little did I know how important these pictures would be.

First of all, we needed bin bags. I found a roll and an unopened pack of rubber gloves, enough for us all. I was taking charge, my bossy side. "OK, nobody gets so much as a cup of coffee until we find where that smell is coming from." Neither of the girls protested as I handed out cleaning equipment. I think they assessed my mood and decided this was a time when it was best to say nothing at all. "Tess, you start in the bathroom, Laura in the kitchen, and I'll whizz round the bedrooms. Now, don't forget, you must take pictures of each area before you clean, please." They both nodded obediently. I'm rather ashamed to admit I'd allocated areas to be cleaned on the basis that they were more likely to find something gruesome in those rooms, while the bedrooms might be safer for me. Call me vindictive! "Chop, chop, no time to waste!" I commanded. And like women possessed, we set to.

I surveyed the three bedrooms, which weren't quite as bad as expected, not so much of a stink, just a musty, damp smell. I pulled up the blinds and flung open the windows as far as they would go. There was discarded rubbish in each room and overflowing bins into which I deliberately didn't look too closely before upturning into bin bags which I swiftly sealed. Unsurprisingly, beds hadn't been made, but there was fresh linen in drawers under each bed, so I stripped them, thankful for the rubber gloves, and left clean bedding on each bed, ready for the girls to make their own beds later. I wasn't doing that as well!

I could hear retching noises from the bathroom; it must be gross in there. "You OK, Tess?"

She opened the door looking green. "I've cleared the rubbish and just tackled the loo! I've thrown some bleach down. I'll let that do its stuff and get back to it. Luckily, they left cleaning products."

"Did you take pictures?"

She looked flustered. "Yep, don't worry!"

"Send them to me, so I've got them all together. I'll be making a massive complaint and demanding our money back. And not only that, I'm going to insist on recompense for the cleaning job we're doing – and our hourly rate is not cheap, trust me."

She was tearing up now and started sobbing, "I'm so sorry, Ellie, this wasn't what I was expecting."

I relented a little. Maybe I was being too hard on her, it wasn't really her fault. "It's OK, babes, no point crying over spilt milk, we'll sort it out between us." And then it suddenly occurred to me I had the magic to deal with this, but I needed the girls out of the house.

Tess had finished what she was doing for now, and we went in search of Laura. She was tying up yet another bulging bin bag.

"What did you find?" I asked, with apprehension. She looked like she was about to retch too and screwed her nose up in disgust.

"I don't think anything died in here; the stink was from all the rotten food. You wouldn't think it possible for there to be so much mould on so many things. And the fridge! I'm not even going to talk about that!"

"Who on earth would leave it in this state?" I said. "And where the hell were the people managing the place? They knew we were booked in." Tess was quiet, I don't think she knew what to say. "But there's something else you have to do." I grabbed my bag, opened it, pulled out a wad of dollars, and peeled off a handful of notes, stuffing them into Tess's hand.

"What on earth—" she started.

"Go into town, find a florist, and buy as many flowers as possible, but they must be white."

"OK, but—"

I didn't let her finish. "There's more. Get fragranced candles and diffusers, nothing too fussy, maybe some candles for outside too." I was really in charge now, letting my diva take over. "We must get this place smelling divine, or I'm off!" They knew I meant it, so they didn't hang around, which was just what I needed.

CHAPTER 22

I had to act quickly. I gathered up the bin bags, made sure they were tied securely and dumped them all in the large bin at the side of the house, making sure the lid was well and truly down on the noxious contents.

The house was already smelling better with the removal of the rotting food, and I had a clearer space to work my magic.

Some years ago, I'd learnt a cleaning spell from the wonderful Diana, one of the Mystical Ladies who used to work miracles for me at the cottage. She'd shared her deep-cleaning spell, and I was honoured. She was risking doing herself out of a job, but we'd established a friendship and enjoyed each other's company. Every week she'd cast her spell, which only took a few minutes, Lavender Cottage would be squeaky clean, and then she and I could settle down for a chat over a cuppa. She taught me on the condition that I cross my heart and hope to die rather than reveal it to anyone else. After everything that happened after I left Yorkshire, I'd completely forgotten about it, but it was never more needed than now. It did also occur to me that I could have used it in Salem at the Bates-style motel, but as the cleaner there did put in a daily appearance, even if there was little evidence of it, it would have been too risky. Mind you, we had seen the funny side and took the opportunity for some great shots. Me putting fingers through the holes in the threadbare towels, Laura posing with the tacky plastic plants, and Tess admiring the shabby 70s style decor, that sort of thing.

While reminiscing, I'd been working the spell, and the living area was now sparkling and clean. I couldn't do anything about the shabbiness, but this was a hundred times better. I went into each bedroom, and then finally the bathroom, and sprinkled my cleaning magic around. This spell was a genuine deep clean with the benefit of not having to scrub, vacuum, or damage my manicured nails; I still had my standards, darlings! One thing was for sure, I'd be giving this place a scathing review, but it would have to do for now.

Knowing how bad Tess felt, perhaps I'd rubbed too much salt into the wound. I needed to find some empathy for when she returned. She'd been conned, there was no doubt about that. But I did know from experience that when you book budget, you don't get quality. It would have been different if I'd been booking, but it was now at least bearable. I thought guiltily how keen they both were to get away from me and I hoped I'd gone part way to redeem my bad temper with the results of my spell. I retrieved my phone and went round the rooms taking the after pictures. The change was astonishing. The previously stained and dirty kitchen worktop was spotless, and the stainless-steel sink reflected the sun shining through the open window. Even the bathroom looked good. I'd physically made the beds myself, as I wasn't sure how to do that spell. I did plan, though, to tease the girls for a while. It would be satisfying to make them think I'd sweated over such a thorough clean. I looked around for some vases and found a few that weren't too badly marked and chipped. I filled them with water to await the expected flowers.

The girls were taking their time, avoiding me, or perhaps I was getting paranoid. I boiled some water, made a cup of coffee, and moved out into the garden. It was the redeeming factor of our temporary residence, and it was beautiful. The borders were a little ragged, they needed a good prune, but the stunning flowers and shrubs against the ocean backdrop were delightful. It was better described as a courtyard than a garden. There was no lawn, just a wooden decked patio area and then paving with a picket fence and gate leading onto the beach, as promised. A round, wooden table and four chairs were on the decking, so at least we could sit out here. I'd bring out some cushions and throws from the sofas to make it more comfortable. There were some large pots dotted around, the plants withered from lack of watering and hanging on for dear life. I made a note to water them when I next got up. Meanwhile, the stunning view of the ocean, the sound of the crashing waves and the scent of the salty sea air more than made up for the shabbiness indoors.

They found me still out in the garden, soaking up the atmosphere, my mood agreeable by now, and listening to the sublime "At the River" by Groove Armada, an old-school chill-out classic. Tess, in a much more upbeat mood, announced their presence with a shout. "Ellie, you little devil, you've worked wonders! What the hell? You must have been down on your hands and knees! We didn't expect you to do that."

I nodded, wiping my brow for added effect, "Phew, it was hard work!"

Laura gave me a quizzical look. She'd twigged. "She doesn't look that sweaty to me, Tess. Stop playing the martyr, Ellie. You've worked some magic, haven't you?"

I chuckled. "OK, I fess up. It's a clever but simple deep-cleaning spell."

They both giggled, and it hit the spot, diffusing the bad feelings, and we were back on track. They begged me for the spell. "Why didn't we know you could do this!"

I laughed. "I'd forgotten, to be honest; I get a service clean at my apartment, so I haven't had to use it in a long time. Anyway, never mind that, come and sit down. The view is divine – but before we do, show me what you've bought. I'll make some coffee, or do you fancy something stronger? We have that Cape wine. Not sure about you guys, but I'm a little peckish. Maybe some olives and crisps to tide us over before dinner." Silly question, they both agreed with the peckish and opted for the wine!

"The town's awesome," Tess was excited.

"So many fabulous shops, we were spoilt for choice," Laura chimed in. "We got some sublime-smelling candles, diffusers and matching room sprays, and – wait for it – the scent's called *Calm*; I think that'd be good for all of us!" That was a not-so-subtle hint to me. Nobody had died, after all, and I needed to chill.

"They were quite expensive," Tess said. "Can we contribute?"

I shook my head, "Not at all, my way of saying sorry for throwing my toys out of the pram, and don't worry, they won't go to waste, we can take them on to Boston with us."

We didn't hang about; Tess ran through the house strategically positioning diffusers and spraying *Calm* which certainly hit the spot with its earthy tones. As a finishing touch, she lit two large candles in the kitchen area and one in the lounge. Laura, in the meantime, was doing an expert job with the flowers in the vases I'd found, she was cleverly mixing the divine-smelling white lilies – taking care to cut out any stain-making stamens – with gloriously full blooming white roses. The girls had done well!

I supplied the finishing touch, retrieving the bottle of local Truro wine from the now-pristine fridge.

As I did, I blessed Diana, everything was sparkling. Even the glasses I retrieved from the cupboard looked as if they'd been buffed to within an inch of their life. That was a spell I wouldn't forget again. I don't think the house knew what had hit it, but we were all now viewing it in a completely different light, thank goodness. Settled outside in the garden, which had acquired a sublime candle-lit glow, we filled our lungs with fresh sea air, and as the light faded and the temperature dropped, we huddled together for warmth, pulling throws around us. It was lovely to relax before clearing up and heading out to the seafood restaurant the girls had booked for dinner.

CHAPTER 23

The girls were not wrong. They had found us the coolest restaurant, specialising in locally caught shellfish. The fact it was full of locals was testament to the excellent online reviews. As Tess and Laura had reported, the town was delightful, with lots of upmarket boutiques and eateries. There was a buzzy atmosphere and an air of understated luxury. Everywhere was super-busy, people milling around like worker ants. Tess had booked us window seats, a great position for people-watching, and the next best thing to sitting outside as we'd reached the time of the year when the evening temperature drop was noticeable.

Tess was forgiven, and the restaurant was wonderful. I feasted on mussels cooked in white wine, sopping up the broth with crusty granary bread, then grilled line-caught tuna steak with a divine butter sauce and fresh asparagus. Laura and Tess shared a shellfish platter, North Atlantic crab, lobster, whole prawns, and mussels, and I watched with amusement as they dealt with all that – a bit too messy and fiddly for me. We finished off with affogato – the latest craze consisting of a scoop of ice cream with espresso – and a shot of amaretto, and I didn't even try to resist a Tia Maria coffee topped with extra thick cream. I'm not proud to admit I surreptitiously undid a button on my trousers.

It's amazing how a few glasses – or more than a few in our case – put everything in a better light, and through rose-tinted lenses we saw the funny side of things we'd nearly fallen out over earlier; we couldn't stop giggling. Obviously, we didn't discuss magic in public, but as soon as we were out of the restaurant, Tess tugged at my arm.

"I know there are things you haven't told us, Ellie. What other spells do you have under your hat?"

"I'll show you the cleaning spell, but if I told you all my secrets, I'd have to kill you!" That sparked a memory. I'd said this to Alice, Sarah, and Lizzie somewhere, sometime, a lifetime ago, and a wave of sadness passed over me.

"Ellie?" Laura had seen the change in my expression. "You OK?" I shrugged it off and looked across the road, my attention caught by the loud music coming from a gorgeous house a similar size to ours but a world away in looks. The sofas and egg chairs on the porch called out to us, maybe we could gatecrash the party, but we'd been travelling all day, had some disconcerting experiences, and now just needed to keep moving. I, for one, was dying to get out of tight trousers and into something more forgiving. Luckily our house was within walking distance, but we were all holding on tightly to each other as it was now fully dark and none of us wanted to break an ankle. Reaching our porch, Laura gained a second wind and threw herself into the sad old rocking chair on the porch, rocking manically. Just looking at her made me feel a little nauseous. I had no idea how she could do it on a full stomach. I wasn't going to risk it.

With relief, we found the putrid smell had vanished. A delicious mix of candles and spray had taken its place, blending with the heady scents of the lilies and roses. We dispersed to our rooms to change into comfy clothing, meeting up again for a last nightcap. Tess had planned for the next day to be full of stunning scenery, with lighthouses, cute shops, and somewhere good for lunch. We were all a bit over-historied for now, so this was going to be pure pleasure – no lectures, said Tess – well, perhaps just the odd fact here and there where called for. The forecast was perfect for driving around, not too hot, and no rain. A short time later I said goodnight to the girls, deciding I was ready for bed and a book and took myself off. Tess had recommended The Lying Life of Adults by Elena Ferrante, and although I hadn't made much of an inroad, I was enjoying it so far. Despite that, as soon as I relaxed against the pillows, my eyes refused to stay open.

Then I was back in the restaurant, looking at the women in black sitting at the table. I saw, with no surprise, that there were no other diners. The waitress appeared, now not in uniform. She was dressed in black, in the same striking style as the other women – she was one of them. Two of them moved aside a little as she pulled up a chair and took her place at the table with familiarity. I knew beyond a shadow of a doubt they'd sat this way many times before.

The table was piled high with an obscene amount of food, and the waft of strong coffee was intense. It blended with the mouth-watering scent of the pastries stacked unrealistically high, a stack that didn't diminish however often the women helped themselves. I watched them eating in slow motion. I was so hungry, I really wanted a bite of a pastry, especially the pain au chocolat. They were savouring each mouthful, taking care to waste no crumbs, sipping coffee between mouthfuls. My stomach ached with wanting.

As I crept nearer to the table, I recognised their faces, but couldn't remember their names. They looked familiar, but just then, the floorboards creaked, and they jumped out of their skin. The tower of pastries and pancakes went flying, and coffee surged over the table and dripped onto the floor. It was utter chaos, Mad Hatter's tea party time. I looked around for a white rabbit. I hadn't noticed the women moving towards me, obviously angry. I had ruined their party, but the look on their faces was a crazy overreaction; their eyes bored, chilling me to the bone, radiating pure evil. The ringleader was the woman who had come to our table, I was sure, but for the life of me I couldn't recall her name. Now she hissed, "She's back. I knew she wouldn't fucking stay away for long. Ladies, we have a problem; we need her gone!" Surely I wasn't a problem? Why would I be? I knew I had to flee, leave the restaurant, get back to the SUV and my friends. Where were they? Had they already left, were they waiting for me? My mind was completely befuddled trying to understand what was going on, but there was no doubt these women meant harm, or worse.

But try as I might, I couldn't move, my feet seemingly encased in concrete, sealed to the floor. I couldn't open my mouth either, and my legs and arms were lead-weighted. As I stared helplessly a stricken statue, the women changed, a ghastly metamorphosis, their features melting. Smooth, unlined – botoxed to the hilt – faces were now wizened, lined, with yellow, rotting, tombstone teeth. The leader spoke again, venom dripping from every word, "I knew you were the meddling sort. I saw it in your eyes, knew you'd disturb our peace, bring trouble." What was she talking about? I'd brought no trouble. Her eyes, malignant with hate, lasered into mine. My mind was feeling foggier by the minute.

I woke abruptly to the shrilling of the alarm. I should have been excited about our day's activities, but my head was banging, and I was still in the shadow of the nightmare. I sat up, trying to pull myself together and shrug it off. It was just my overactive imagination and far too much wine the previous night. As I reassured myself, beneath the common-sense explanation, there lurked an unnamed fear – was my dream a message? A sign? A warning?

CHAPTER 24

Despite the hangover from hell and the remnants of the nightmare hanging over me, we'd set off at the crack of dawn (Tess was a tough taskmaster) to fit in a jam-packed itinerary, Laura and I were just thankful to get back to the house with a few hours to spare before we had to get ready to go out for dinner. I'd craved a rare fillet steak, but the girls wanted to return to the seafood restaurant tonight, two against one, I was fine with that. I might even risk sharing the platter with them, it could be messy, but it had looked sublime.

In our couple of spare hours, Tess suggested we watch In the Heart of the Sea, a DVD she'd found earlier. It was based on a book by Nantucket author Nathaniel Philbrick, inspired by the horrific sinking of the Essex, a nineteenth century whaling ship. Another of Tess's historical snippets, dropped in as she slipped the DVD into the machine, was that Herman Melville, the author of the classic Moby

Dick, had met the captain of the Essex, a broken man after his experience at sea, and that was his spur to write his book. Laura and I groaned in unison.

"No, shut up," Tess laughed. "It's relevant to our trip, and you might fancy the actors in this one, Tom Holland and Cillian Murphy!" Now she was talking. I didn't much care for the subject matter, but I did have a thing about Cillian Murphy, one of my favourite actors. I loved him in Peaky Blinders.

"OK, I'm hooked," I said.

"I'm not sure," said Laura, "that it's a great idea to watch a whale sinking a boat just before we head off on a trip of our own."

"Don't be daft," said Tess, "nothing's going to happen on a modern ship, not with all the 'elf and safety stuff in place."

I laughed, too. "Don't worry, the film won't put me off. "

Later, as the credits rolled, I yawned, stretched, and said, "Now we have to find the energy to get ready to go out and eat."

Tess and Laura were getting up even earlier than usual in the morning, so tonight promised to be a more sober affair than our previous dinner at the restaurant. I'd declined tomorrow's cycling trip. The girls were set on joining the Cape Cod Rail Trail, and I hadn't cycled since I was a child. I know they say you never forget, I just wasn't sure that applied to me. Instead, I'd made a booking at the local stable for a hack along the beach later in the morning. Unlike the others, I saw no point in getting up at sunrise.

We enjoyed another delicious meal – I'd opted for clam chowder and lobster linguine – in what had fast become our favourite restaurant of the whole trip. We agreed to forgo a rich dessert and return to the house to finish off the plump strawberries and blueberries we had in the fridge, at the same time as doing some packing for departure the next day, although our ferry to Nantucket didn't leave until five. Tess and I fancied one last glass of wine, Laura said she'd have a coffee as she was driving tomorrow and didn't want to risk it, but we all agreed we'd take our drinks outside to savour our last night with the fabulous view.

As we strolled home beneath a clear, inky black sky, it steadily got chillier. Laura confessed to her inner geek and admitted she had a planet app on her phone.

"Tonight, ladies," she announced, "is stargazers' heaven, we can see Mars, Jupiter, and Saturn." Oh my God, I reflected, first Tess with her history, and now Laura giving us a stargazer's guide to the galaxy, you couldn't make it up!

"Such a shame we haven't got a telescope," she said.

Tess and I giggled. "What, so you can perve on the neighbours across the road?" I said.

"Weirdos," Laura countered under her breath.

Tess was still laughing as she went to unlock the patio door, then stopped, puzzled. "Funny, "I'm sure I locked it." We went in cautiously, but a quick look around showed nothing untoward; everything looked just as we left it.

"Don't worry, babe," I said, "it's so easy to overlook,

but everything seems fine, and anyway, this appears to be a pretty safe place, a zero-crime sort of area. Relax. I'll get the glasses, you bring the wine, Laura, you making your own coffee?"

"Yep, and I'll put on a playlist. We need a chill-out vibe," she said and, as if on cue, "Slip Into Something More Comfortable" by Kinobe came on. It totally suited our mood.

Tess was like a dog with a bone, not prepared to let it go. "I know I locked it," she insisted. "You have to fiddle a bit with the key to get it to turn, and I remember doing that."

"You go on outside," said Laura. "I'll just have another check around to put your mind at rest." She was holding a pair of scissors she'd picked up in the kitchen and looked quite menacing. "Just in case," she said, and we laughed. It didn't take her long to go thoroughly through all the rooms. It wasn't that big a place. "It's fine," she reported. "Nothing disturbed. Stop worrying."

Tess poured a glass of wine and murmured, almost to herself, "Maybe I am just losing it!"

I picked up the bottle of wine in one hand and another glass in the other, and Tess grabbed the punnets of strawberries and blueberries, not bothering with bowls or spoons, we'd just dig in. Laura brought a steaming cup out, not such a good idea before bedtime, but probably neither was the wine. As we settled ourselves outside with our drinks, snuggled into the furry throws we'd taken from the sofa, we dropped the locked door subject and simply enjoyed the beauty of the night sky, unmarred by light pollution. Combined with the salty air and crash of waves breaking on the beach below us, it was mesmerising, and I could feel my eyelids getting heavy. It wasn't that long before we decided to turn in.

I was careful to lock and double-check the patio door after us. "Locked, Tess," I called out teasingly. Paranoid now, she gave me a mock glare, went to check herself, and then made sure of the front door, too, as I headed upstairs. I was so exhausted I didn't even put my alarm on. It might mean missing the horse riding, but right now, sleep seemed more important. Before I drifted off, I remember hoping for a smooth journey to Nantucket. It was only about thirty miles off the coast, but the ferry took a couple of hours. I also hoped that when we arrived, we wouldn't have a repeat of the unpleasant experience we'd had at this place. At least, I thought with an inward smile, wherever we ended up next, it would smell divine. We were taking all our gorgeous smellies with us!

CHAPTER 25

I heard the clatter of the girls getting ready to go out, they weren't quiet about it, but I was still half asleep, not bothered and certainly not ready to make any moves myself. Luxuriating in the warmth, I vaguely heard them shout goodbye and was firmly back in dreamworld by the time they shut the door behind them.

I have no idea how much time passed before I gradually became aware of a familiar smell: smoke. Was I back at Lavender Cottage? The smoke I'd smelt in the garden had been so strong, yet I'd never been able to find its source. I felt my nose twitch, if this was a dream, it was extremely realistic, but I couldn't focus on where I was, why I was wherever I was, or who I was with. Was it Alice, Sarah, and Lizzie, or Laura and Tess? My mind wasn't processing properly. I knew something was wrong but couldn't get a grip on it. The smell of smoke was creeping down my throat, restricting my breathing. I needed to cough but couldn't seem to summon the breath to do that. I could feel what sense remained slipping away. Distantly but definitely, I knew I was in danger but could do nothing; I was helpless, mind woozy, slowing down, switching off.

Then there was an almighty crash of shattering glass, and someone was lifting me, trickling water into my mouth. I started retching, eyes stinging, acrid, pungent smoke deep in my lungs, I was choking, suffocating, and couldn't take in even a single breath. There was a hive of activity around me, more water dribbled into my mouth. Was it a dream? Or more of a nightmare? Why couldn't I wake? Then movement as I was lifted again, rain on my face mixing with tears. I was in a vehicle, then blackness.

Someone was gently washing my face. I tried to open swollen eyelids. My head was both spinning and splitting. "… Water …" My voice sounded gravelly, even that one word hurt.

"She's coming round." Someone was leaning over me. "Hey honey, it's OK, you're safe." Behind that voice was another. "Only just in time." Had someone saved my life? Blackness claimed me again, and the next time I opened my eyes, Tess and Laura were sitting, anguished, by my bed.

The emergency services had called Tess, as she was registered at the property, and she and Laura had come rushing to the local hospital, terrified of what they'd find, they explained, interrupting and talking over each other in their distress. It seemed I'd emerged almost totally unscathed from what had been a dreadful fire, the timber-built house had been an inferno. The doctor checked my lungs again and shook his head.

"Smoke inhalation usually kills well before the flames take hold. I can't understand it, you must have a guardian angel. There's no trace of damage to your lungs. You'll have a persistent cough and a bad head for several days. Lots of water will help. I've given you a batch of painkillers." He shook his head again, he had a dilemma. "I should keep you here overnight for observation," he patted my shoulder "but I'm discharging you against my better judgement, you are one lucky lady to get out of a fire like that." He nodded at Tess and Laura, "You two, keep an eye on her. If you're worried, bring her right back, she's gotten off lightly, but she will have after-effects."

I got the full story from the girls as they helped me dress. It seemed a vigilant neighbour had noticed smoke coming from the house and instantly called the emergency services. I owed her my life. From what the girls had found out, there had been an electrical fault with a plugged-in phone charger in my bedroom, they reassured me I wasn't to blame, the wiring was past its sell-by. I'd had a lucky escape, but it was way too close for comfort.

I insisted the girls take me back to the house, and as we gawped in horror at what was left of it, I couldn't believe I'd got out of this charred wreck. As for all our stuff – clothes, cosmetics, toiletries – we'd have to replace everything, all on the insurance of course. We'd planned some major retail therapy on this trip, but not in this way and not quite so urgently. The girls only had what they stood up in, and I was dressed in a set of scrubs the hospital had given me – not my best look. I shivered, I wasn't cold, just shocked into silence. I'd had a lucky escape.

Tess was distraught, blaming herself for what had happened. "Ellie, you could have been killed! We should have left the minute we saw the horrendous state of the place."

I refrained from saying, "Told you so". I didn't want to give Tess a hard time, she already felt remorseful enough. But of one thing I was sure – no more budget properties. I was taking over, the next two stops were luxury, or I was off. I should have insisted the minute we walked in the door of our Cape Cod haven. I'd fund any additional costs, but I wasn't risking our lives again.

As if she'd read my mind, Laura put an arm around me. "You must have used one of your nine lives today, Ellie." I thought back to drowning in the Thames, where I'd technically died, and nodded. They didn't need to know that I was now down to seven!

The fire service had told Tess that although they hadn't had time to do a proper inspection yet, the wiring at the property looked as if it hadn't been updated since the place was built. They were also appalled that two smoke detectors seemed to have been dismantled and, so far, they hadn't come across a fire extinguisher, which was required by law. I frowned when Tess mentioned that, I was sure I'd seen one in the kitchen, but my head was still so foggy, maybe I was mistaken. It seemed, though, that the owners and, indeed, the letting agents, could be facing criminal charges.

All three of us were in such a state of shock after seeing what was left of the house, it was maybe not such a good idea of mine. The sympathetic taxi driver who had picked us up from the hospital and driven us to the house, against his better judgement, had insisted on taking us to a nearby coffee shop, one his friend owned. He ushered us inside, explaining the situation to the owner, who gave a concerned look when she saw the state of me, and said that sweetened coffee and a big slice of cake was in order. She led us to a booth at the back and told us to take as long as we needed, bringing over a welcome jug of iced water and glasses.

First things first, Tess and Laura hastened out to a local store tasked with getting some basics for me, underwear, a few toiletries, and a leisure suit or similar. While they were gone, there was no time to lose. I consulted the helpful owner. I didn't mess around, just asked for a top-notch recommendation, borrowed her mobile and booked luxurious rooms in a boutique hotel on Nantucket. Thankfully, and despite my foggy head, I remembered enough passwords and security questions to access my bank account. On a roll, I also took the precaution of booking ahead for Boston, I wasn't sure what Tess had already arranged, but I wasn't taking any chances and went for the Boston Harbour Hotel. It sold itself as luxury on the water, which was exactly what I was looking for.

When the girls returned with some essentials and a leisure suit and trainers, which would at least do until we got to Nantucket, they were relieved to see I was much recovered after coffee and cake. Back to my feisty self I put my foot down firmly, I said it was my way or the highway from now on. If they didn't want me on the next flight back to Heathrow, they'd accept our changed bookings without argument, we'd sort out refunds and insurance later. This was the only time since we'd become friends that there was a serious risk of falling out, but after my near-death experience, they knew I wasn't joking. Call me paranoid, but I'd already checked reviews and the health and safety standards of both of our new destinations. Narrowly escaping being burnt alive hadn't been fun and I wasn't prepared to do it again. I needn't have worried; they were both so distressed at what had happened that they put up only the faintest of protests, and even those were smothered later that day at first sight of our Nantucket hotel.

CHAPTER 26

The only excursion we were doing from Nantucket was a whale watching tour, and after the trauma at our last stop, we were just happy to take it easy, luxuriate in the hotel, the natural beauty of our surroundings, and chill out over lazy lunches and dinners. We needed to relax before our final stop in Boston. That was always going to be a busy one, but now, after recent events, it would require some extremely focused retail therapy.

So mortified were the girls that they'd left me alone to go on the Rail Trail that they now didn't want to let me out of their sight. I was more than delighted that I'd booked us separate rooms, which gave me the breathing space I needed. Since I'd never made it to that hack along the beach, I found us a stable on the island, happy to take beginners, although I wasn't going to let the girls cramp my style. They had to keep to the back while I cantered ahead. It was amazing, crashing through the waves along with other riders, salt spray cooling my face. For me, this was one of the shining highlights of the holiday. I made a determined effort to put the fire to the back of my mind and managed most of the time, but it had left a horrible feeling of unease. I know the receptionists at our hotel were surprised by how often I asked whether they were certain all fire alarms and sprinkler systems were in full working order. They eased my mind by showing me the inspection logs they had to complete by law.

We all loved Nantucket, still bustling in the early autumn. Although only fourteen miles long, there was plenty to see and do and an abundance of sea birds and seals, both harbour and grey.

In another life, in other circumstances, I felt this might have been a place I would have settled in. It had an ethereal feel and the perfect vibe, although we were told the best time to visit was late June to late September, as winters were cold, getting as low as minus twenty-four, and storms could hit with powerful winds. That explained why the rich and famous flocked here in the summer and departed at the same time as the sun. In our meanderings, we'd come across some divine boutiques. They were eye-wateringly expensive, but we had insurance coming and enjoyed picking up chic items to pack into our newly purchased cases.

Before our whale watching trip, we wanted to visit the Maria Mitchell Aquarium downtown to gen up on local marine life. The main street's cobbled paving and waterfront views reminded me painfully of Whitby. A home from home, I thought, then reflected with sadness that it wasn't my home any more. I could have happily stayed here, living the American Dream, especially as it was getting so weird across the pond with the Purge, which, like the fire, I'd tried to put to the back of my mind. But then I reflected that I wasn't keen on freezing conditions and storms, so maybe not. When we left the museum, after an enjoyable couple of hours, we stopped at a delightful bistro for a light lunch. Tess had regained her good spirits and slipped back into bossy tour guide mode. She informed us we'd need to find an outdoor store for waterproofs, binoculars, water bottles, and rucksacks – she sounded just like Alice. In the tour information, they also recommend having some seasickness pills to hand because it could get a little choppy. We grimaced and laughed. I didn't know then that seasickness was the least of my worries.

Our nautical adventure was on our last full day on the island, and the tour was small, taking a maximum of thirty tourists. Tess had woken us at dawn, countering our protests because she wanted to ensure we arrived early to get the best places on the boat. We were greeted by a God-like creature with a million-watt smile, tousled, naturally highlighted hair, green eyes, and sun-weathered skin. His arms and neck were adorned with surf dude leather jewellery, and he wore cut-off shorts, a Led Zeppelin T-shirt, and flip-flops on his feet. He made me feel cold; we had followed instructions from Tess and dressed in many layers. He looked like he'd be at home on a surfboard, riding the waves, or headbanging at a rock concert.

He introduced himself in a lazy drawl. He seemed a bit

out of it; head in the clouds, or maybe a late one last night? Or maybe it was just his natural Nantucket style, a chilled-out, charmed life, searching for whales for a living. "Hey guys, welcome to our tour. I need to tick you off the list. I'm Jacques, your tour guide. Sit and relax for a minute, and I'll do my spiel when everyone's here. I'm a marine biologist, so I should be able to answer all your questions as we head out." Laura gave me a look, and I had to stifle a giggle. A dreamy, intelligent guy with a French name, what more could you want? As everyone else piled onto the deck and settled themselves noisily, we exchanged smug glances, we'd bagged the best seats. Jacques recited the statutory health and safety information, which he could probably do in his sleep. Then he ran through the other tours available from the company. Unfortunately, we wouldn't be here long enough, but the cocktail cruise certainly sounded like something we'd love. The captain and crew of two were briefly introduced as they readied the boat to depart, and they all nodded politely before returning to their tasks.

Tess and Laura couldn't contain their excitement as we cautiously moved out of the harbour, heading out into the Atlantic. I couldn't deny I was full of anticipation as well. Jacques explained that the reason the captain was going so slowly was that he needed to navigate around the Nantucket Shoals, a nightmare for seafarers. The water in some places is less than a metre in depth but constantly changing due to the strong Atlantic currents. Jacques then moved on to whaling history, Nantucket being the global centre for the whaling trade in the nineteenth century. He had a mesmerising voice that should be reading a bedtime story, that sort of slow drawl that had an effortless charm.

"These magnificent creatures, the right whales, were so called because they were the most valuable. Nearly every part of the carcass was used, for oil, food, and more." From behind us, someone called out, "Are they still hunted here?"

Jacques shook his head. "Not since 1869, the last whaler to sail out from Nantucket was the Bark Oak, although the trade had been going for nearly two hundred years at that stage. Nowadays, here in the US, they're a protected species, although sadly, that's not the case in other parts of the world."

"Surely," someone else said, "they're not still hunted for food?"

"Still used in pharmaceuticals and health supplements, I'm afraid, and in some countries, whale meat is served as a local delicacy." There was a silence before Jacques lightened the mood. "So, you wanna take a Nantucket sleigh ride?"

"The song by Mountain?" asked a man sitting near us.

Jacques laughed. "Hey, dude, before my time, what was that, the seventies? No, at the height of the whaling era, sailors would sail out in small open boats and harpoon the whales who naturally thrashed around in pain, desperate to get away." A woman on the other side of the boat made small noises of distress. "But the harpoons were attached to ropes, and the traumatised whale would drag the boats along at high speeds – and sometimes it wasn't only the whale who lost its life. Between 1724 and 1896, more than 1,000 sailors lost theirs."

A woman muttered, "Serve 'em right," and received assent from people nearby.

"So, you see," Jacques continued, "why they called it what they did."

"How fast can a whale go?" asked someone. "Are some faster than others?"

"Humpbacks could drag the boats at around twenty-three miles an hour. The sperm whale was slower but kept going longer, taking the boats further away from their ships. Most dangerous, though, were the fin and blue whales." He paused for us to think about that, then added, "Hope none of you are squeamish, but you did ask. Anyway, eventually, when it ran out of energy, the whale would be dragged back to the ship, killed, and then butchered. The blubber was removed, and the oil rendered." There were a few green faces, whether from the boat's movement or his vivid recounting of hunting practices in the not-so-distant past. He caught my eye. "Don't worry," he said, "I promise not to put you out in an open boat, and I've not lost anyone ... yet." Everyone laughed.

We were now around thirty miles out, and our luck was in; the captain slowed the engine, and Jacques immediately pointed out a couple of minke and, a little further away, a group of fin whales. There were a lot of oohs and aahs as everyone raised their phones for shots. And then, most thrilling, we spotted two clustered groups of humpbacks accompanied by calves.

"We're coming up to a feeding ground, that's why we're seeing so many," said Jacques. I was holding my breath in awe as the majestic, magnificent creatures breached; impossible to imagine the strength needed to lift themselves out of the water. It was exhilarating, breathtaking, and overwhelming, everything I'd been looking forward to and more. What a memory to treasure.

"They gather to feed on schooling fish – mackerel, herring, and krill," Jacques said and added with a grin, "And they like nothing more than performing for an audience."

"How long do the calves stay with their mothers?" a cute, gap-toothed girl of around seven asked.

"Well, honey, humpbacks are pretty great moms; they don't leave their calf, who's dependent on them for everything. When the time comes, it's the calf who decides he or she is off – a bit like all kids." We laughed. "Look over there," he pointed, and heads swung in that direction. "There's a mom and calf. When they're born, they're brought straight to the surface to take their first breath."

"So, they breach to breathe?" someone asked.

"Yes, but that's not all. Research, my own included, shows they slap fins and tail flukes because sound travels further and quicker underwater, and they may well be communicating with other whales some miles away." Jacques looked over to where other sightseeing boats were drawing closer and signalled to the captain. "We need to move," he explained. "Too many boats rocking up is irresponsible and stressful for the animals. Overcrowding totally freaks them out. They have been known to strike a ship, not on purpose, just to get away." I gulped, it was not something I wanted to hear, especially after seeing that movie. I think Jacques mistook my expression for disappointment because he added, "Don't worry, we're going further out; you'll see more." And he was right. In fact, we saw more of these incredibly graceful giants of the deep than we'd allowed ourselves to even hope for.

So entranced was I that it wasn't until we were on our way back that I reluctantly gave in to the fact that I needed the loo and decided that even if it meant missing some sightings, I dare not leave it any later, or I'd have a marine incident of my own. The ladies' toilet was on the lower deck, and before I made my way back, I took the opportunity for a few shots from this different position on the boat. There was no one around, everyone being clustered above for a better view, and I took some deep breaths of the fresh air, leaning closer to the water, relishing the salty spray on my tongue. I thought I heard something, maybe someone else from the deck above descending for a comfort break. I looked around to say hi, but I must have been mistaken, no one was there. I shivered, my imagination must be in overdrive, and then, for just a moment, I thought I sensed malevolence all around me, that hyped-up imagination again. And then, suddenly and shockingly, I felt myself being lifted. My feet left the deck, and before I could even draw breath to scream, I was propelled over the side of the boat.

I desperately struggled to find a fingerhold, but there was nothing to grab on to, and I was falling, falling, hitting the water. I screamed, but even as I did, I knew the sound would be lost below the engine noise. Was this, then, my fate? Had it always been an inevitability? As the cold invaded my body, it wasn't an unfamiliar feeling, I'd experienced it so many times before in my nightmares. The waves were lashing and crashing around the boat. No one could have seen or heard me; no one would know what had happened. There was nothing I could do to keep my head above water, and the Atlantic was merciless, spitefully choppy, devastatingly icy. The ship had picked up speed, and I knew I would lose sight of it in a second. They say your life flashes before you, but alone, and struggling to take a breath as the chill tightened its grip, cold and fear had paralysed my mind to only one loop, over and over. Would the protection spell save me this time? I didn't think it could or would, and it was dangerously tempting to let the familiarity of drowning, the nightmare of so many years, follow its well-run pattern. The numbing cold, the brain fog, the seduction of sleep, the ease of simply closing my eyes and surrendering to the peace of the deep … and then there was nothing.

Until I was lying on the deck, surrounded by horrified faces. I had been turned on my side and was retching violently as my body expelled seawater. Something or someone had saved me. After what seemed an age, they seemed satisfied I'd voided all the water. My eyes stung, seawater saturated, and for a moment, I was lost, with no idea who or where I was, or why I was there, until a familiar voice, Tess, sobbed, "Ellie, thank God, we thought we'd lost you … again!"

"What the hell happened?" Laura shrieked. I came to check on you, and you were nowhere to be seen. Next thing, the captain's yelling man overboard." She was interrupted and moved gently aside by Brad, the first mate.

"Give her some space guys, there can be a danger of secondary drowning, and she was in the water a while; we have to warm her up. She needs time to recover and get warm." Speech was beyond me, so I tried a weak smile, but the water was still slowly trickling from my mouth. When I was finally deemed fit enough to move, they maintained my modesty by swamping me in emergency silver blankets, warming my body, as they took off my sodden clothing, bringing over some spare items they kept on board.

Humiliatingly I wasn't even allowed to walk to a cabin, and Jacques and Brad carried me to where I'd have some privacy until we docked. I suspected it was important for Jacques to continue his narration so no one could complain and ask for their money back, acting as normal as possible so as not to panic the other passengers. Although I certainly felt entitled to mine, I couldn't swear exactly what had happened, but I was pretty sure I hadn't just tripped and fallen. I couldn't prove it, but I was pretty certain there'd been helping hands tipping me over the safety rail.

When we docked, they wouldn't let me leave the harbour office until a doctor had been called to check me over. Covering their backs? Or was that just me being cynical? He declared himself satisfied there was no lasting damage and signed me off. He was amazed at how quickly I'd recovered and was more or less well enough to walk out of there. "One of the lucky ones," he commented. "It doesn't always end this way, the ocean's a force to be reckoned with. It must have been your lucky day." Strange thing to say, was this a regular occurrence?

After the doctor left and Brad had completed all the forms necessary after such an event, he turned to look at me. "Sure you don't remember anything else?"

I shook my head. "I've already said. I remember falling, trying to tread water, then nothing." I'd decided not to mention the possibility of being pushed, it sounded too crazy. He paused and then obviously made up his mind. "I think you should watch something." He exchanged a look with Tess and Laura, then went on, "There are two cameras, one on the top deck, one on the lower. Both automatically run throughout the trip. I'm going to play the video from when we see you on the lower deck until you are rescued."

"Is this really necessary? I'm not sure I want to see it." I looked at the girls, but they shook their heads and indicated I should look at the screen. The picture was in black and white, grainy to start but my eyes adjusted. We saw me leave the bathroom, take some shots, look out to sea, pause, and turn back as if looking for something behind me. I watched in silence as there seemed to be a fractional hitch in the video before it continued, and then the next shot showed me shooting over the rail and falling.

"That's weird," I said, "it looks as if there's a break, it couldn't have been edited, could it?"

Brad shook his head. "Sometimes there's a fractional lapse in the power. Coincidence that it happened to be right at that point, but that's not what I want you to see, keep watching." He switched to the top deck camera view, which showed the sea in front of the boat. And what I saw next was unbelievable.

A humpback whale was circling the boat, gently nudging the side, certainly not aggressively, as if it was trying to tell Jacques something. It looked like it had a calf tucked under its fin. I heard him reassure the tourists, "It's OK, she's not aggressive, looks as if she's just coming to say hello or show off her calf – can you see, tucked under her pectoral fin, you'll see that—" and then he stopped abruptly as everything kicked off. I heard screams, people were pointing and leaning over to see. And it wasn't a calf she was protecting – it was me. I watched incredulously as the slowly moving whale carefully kept my head clear of the water. That mighty fin could have crushed my bones in an instant, but she held me safe and sure, with incredible gentleness, until the crew reached me, and only then did she slowly move away. She remained for a few minutes, apparently waiting until she saw I was back on the boat again and then she dived, surfacing again as she reached the rest of the pod. As I watched the video, I had a strange feeling, the faintest of memories like the edge of a dream, a sense of being nurtured and protected, a force for good. I only wished I could remember more.

There was silence for a moment when the video finished, and then Brad's phone rang, and he excused himself to go and take the call. As he did, Laura said, "Jacques told us there have been many accounts of other species being rescued by whales, but he said he never dreamt he'd ever witness it himself."

"It was amazing," Tess added, "although I'm afraid he

wasn't so much interested in you as in what the whale was doing. And, of course, everyone was filming." I grimaced. The last thing I needed was to go viral, although, luckily, you couldn't make out my face. Beneath our conversation, my mind was whirling. Had I been saved once again from my legacy, instead of following in Hettie's footsteps, in the sea this time rather than a river?

"You still haven't told us how it happened," said Tess.

I shook my head. "I honestly don't understand it myself." Then, keeping my voice low, making sure no one else was around, I added, "It felt like someone lifted me up and threw me over." They exchanged looks, and Laura protested, "But Ellie, you could see for yourself, there was no one there."

CHAPTER 27

They say bad luck comes in threes, but by the time we'd reached our last full day in Boston, I thought maybe that wasn't going to be the case. I was in two minds about our flight home tomorrow. I was looking forward to getting home – at least there I'd know what I was up against. Here, at the end of our stay in the US, I was still sensing a malevolence I couldn't shake off, and every time I thought about it, the strange women we'd met came to mind. I just wished I could put them completely out of my head, they freaked me out. I didn't speak about it to the girls, they'd think I was imagining things, and after all, they were of the view that two unfortunate accidents didn't make a full-scale disaster, simply a couple of times I'd been in the wrong place at the wrong time. And I think any worries went right out of their minds when they saw the hotel I'd booked us into.

I was pleased to check in there too. I hadn't relished

the ferry trip back from Nantucket, and I suspected it would be a long time before I'd feel at ease anywhere near deep water. For now, though, the mood was lightened by the amount of shopping taking place. Our new cases were fast becoming filled with gorgeous new outfits. We'd especially enjoyed the One Seaport area in Boston, a vibrant shopping area with all the brands we loved, and that certainly went a long way to lifting my dark mood, as did a glass or two of pinot over a seafood lunch in a divine rooftop restaurant with a sublime view. I was looking at Boston through rosier-coloured glasses.

It was only on our last full day in the city we'd all grown to love that I had the feeling of being followed. It was nothing I could put my finger on, just a change in the air, a weirdness I couldn't identify. I mentioned it to the girls, keeping it casual.

"Do you get the feeling someone's been following us?"

They both shook their heads. "Ellie, you need to chill out," Tess said. "I know you've had more than your share of shocks this trip, but there's no one there."

She looked at Laura for confirmation, who nodded and added, "You know, when you get back, it wouldn't be a bad idea to book in for some counselling that might help you put all this behind you." Then accurately assessing my response to that suggestion, she quickly changed direction. "But hey, look on the bright side, if it hadn't been for the fire, we wouldn't be wearing brand-new outfits right now." She wasn't wrong, I had on some skinny leather trousers, Chelsea boots, a smart blazer and shirt, finished off with a gorgeous silk scarf that had taken my fancy –

ridiculously expensive but an irresistible colour match. I'd already been into Cartier and a replacement watch was now on my wrist, and I was still able to wear my Tiffany jewellery, mercifully unscathed by the fire.

We were walking off another delicious lunch, making our way along the South Waterfront, one of the coolest places and a great place for people-watching. I'd lagged behind the girls a little, busy taking pictures, when I suddenly felt a tug at my neck. My scarf was being pulled from behind so hard that I couldn't even turn around to see what was happening. I tried to shout to the girls, but they didn't look back, and the scarf tightened further, the fine material thinning and cutting painfully into me. I was being garrotted in public; there were people all around but nobody seemed to be paying any attention. Just before I lost consciousness, I felt that familiar shift in time and the sudden release of the pressure on my throat.

I was in exactly the same spot, on the Boston waterfront, but now it looked entirely different. The boardwalk, seafront cafes, and smart restaurants had disappeared. There was no beach in sight either. No longer a tourist hotspot, there were the sights, sounds, and smells of a busy working port, and the ground was slippery with food, rotting where it lay, irretrievably damaged as it dropped from carts or boxes. From the unmistakable whaling ships in the port, I hazarded a guess I was back in the nineteenth century and, from the number of vessels, at the height of the whaling trade. I'd never smelt a dead whale before but instinctively recognised the overwhelming stench of blubber and whale carcasses.

Milling around the docks was an endlessly moving stream of labourers, along with children and opportunists who seemed to be taking their chances and grabbing anything that fell or could be pulled from what was being carried by careless workers from ships to shore and shore to ships, ready for onward trade. The noise was intense, and I turned my eyes away from the decks of the whalers, where massive bodies were being slashed open, and blood flowed freely over the planking of the deck. As I did so, the sign on one of the ships caught my attention, the Whitby Whaling Company. I saw the Union Jack it was flying, so it must have been from my Whitby, not Whitby, Ontario. What was it doing so far from home? Why not simply hunt in the North Sea – or had whaling been banned in England?

As on my previous time trips, nobody could see or hear me. I tried to shout out several times but gained no reaction. I was curious as to who would disembark from the Whitby ship. Workers on the dock were already bloodied to the elbow, and I knew nothing would be wasted, even the bones would be used as stays in corsets. But then my attention was caught by a bedraggled group of women, some bent with age, others younger, all sharing the same look of ragged exhaustion as they shuffled, unable to move faster because they were shackled together. They must have been on the ship for weeks; judging by their state they were barely alive, suffering from malnutrition and dehydration, clothing in tatters, and I could smell unwashed bodies from where I stood. One by one, they were being roughly unshackled by a burly seaman. Their hands went instantly to their hair to scratch desperately, flaking skin falling away. Had they come from Whitby? But why on a whaler, and what was their crime?

The crew member who had removed their chains didn't hang about. "Go," he said with a well-aimed kick at the backside of one of the younger women. "Get yourselves off, go cause mischief in Boston. We're well rid!" As I watched, some of the women cupped their hands and drank desperately from the horse troughs on the docks. This seemed to give them a new lease of life, and one of them turned and, with all the strength she could muster, spat at the retreating back of the man now climbing back on board.

"You're all cursed," she hissed, her voice carrying the strength of her venom. "May your ship sink, may you drift for hours waiting for rescue that never comes. Water all around you but not a drop to drink, a time of torture before you finally drown." Her words reverberated chillingly in the air and for a moment, there was silence before the crewman joined his shipmates in raucous laughter, and he made a crude gesture and swore roundly before turning his back on her.

The other women paid little attention as they began moving away from the ship that had dumped them on this foreign shore. I caught the eye of an older woman who looked at me directly – though surely she couldn't have seen me? What little colour she had in her face drained away as our gazes locked for what felt like an age but was only a few seconds. She broke the gaze first, looked away and, shaking her head slightly as if to clear it, continued shuffling behind the rest of the ragtag group. They hadn't slowed to wait for her but were frantically foraging, grabbing bruised apples and any other dropped fruit from the ground, biting into their spoils greedily, juice running down their chins. They looked as if they hadn't eaten for weeks. I followed them as far as I could along the waterside, no longer the beautiful tourist trap of my own time but a foul-smelling hive of rough activity.

I wondered who the women were. I knew criminals were deported from England to Australia, but I didn't think to America. I may need to brush up on my history. It wasn't long before I lost sight of the small group, swallowed up in the hustle and bustle and unceasing cacophony of scavengers, traders, and purchasing agents. I was still trying to break free of the crowd when I was hit with that unpleasantly familiar feeling as the scene began to swirl ever faster before fading, and then I was on the sidewalk, my neck aching, and Tess and Laura, who you'd think would be getting used to drama by now, were looking horrified and trying to help me sit up. For once, they were both struck silent. There were a couple of men in uniform, one a policeman, the other a security guard, and another man, who must have been a doctor because he was asking me to follow his finger. He then examined my eyes with an instrument taken from a bag next to him. Someone gave me a bottle of water to sip from.

"Ma'am, can you tell me what happened?" the cop asked. "Did you see your attacker? Can you give me a description?"

I shook my head, putting my hand to where my neck

felt raw and swollen. "I remember my scarf being pulled, that's all."

He grunted. "Your friends tell me you had some high-end jewellery on, not sensible in the city. It's asking for trouble. I'll file a report, but you say you didn't see anyone?"

"I did think someone might have been following me," I said and glared at the girls who'd been so dismissive. My jewellery was gone – my new Cartier watch, my Tiffany diamond band, necklace, and matching bracelet and, I realised as I looked around, my new Mulberry bag. I could have wept. At least I still had my phone, which had been in my pocket. Bloody hell, enough was enough. The sooner I was on the plane home, the more thankful I'd be.

Laura said, "We were only a few steps ahead of you, Ellie, then we turned around, and you were on the floor, with your scarf tight around your neck, we loosened it right away but you were already unconscious."

I didn't want any fuss, which was a bit rich, as I was still on the ground and an interested crowd had gathered. I didn't feel I was properly back in my body, although I wasn't even sure whether this had been another time travel episode or simply my brain playing tricks as my oxygen was cut off. Luckily, we weren't far from our hotel, and the doctor who'd been passing when I collapsed said I was good to go, although my throat was badly bruised. He didn't think I needed the emergency room. The cop gave me a report number for insurance purposes – yet another claim – and shook his head again at a foolish tourist with too much money and too little common sense. I'd been garrotted with my own brand-new silk scarf, and it was probably only because I'd had it knotted around my neck that I hadn't lost that too. On the surface, it seemed I'd simply been the unlucky target of an opportunistic mugger.

As the girls kept saying, valuables can be replaced. Thank goodness I hadn't been injured badly. I didn't say much as they hurried me up to my room, plied me with hot sweet tea, and insisted I put my feet up. They knew my throat was painful, I sounded hoarse, so they didn't expect me to talk too much, which was a good thing because I was thinking a lot. I was sure it wasn't just bad luck, even if I was due a third disaster. But somehow, I didn't think it was random. Burning, drowning, and death by strangulation were the three most common ways of executing a witch. Was I reading more into it than I should, or was there a darker plan, someone or something trying to eliminate me?

CHAPTER 28

Boy, was I glad when we touched down at Heathrow Airport, it had been the most memorable holiday I'd ever had for more reasons than one, and had shaken me more than I wanted to admit. But once back home in Hampstead, as I slowly came out of the intense shock induced by the three separate but equally horrific incidents, I cried copious amounts of tears, with Tess and Laura comforting me as I realised just how close I'd come to breathing my last.

I didn't have the answers to all the questions. Why me? What would they achieve by bumping me off? But I felt happier in the relative safety of London, a place I called home, and I just wanted to put my head down and live a normal life, no high drama, just everyday stuff. Boring banality was the name of the game, life under the radar. But was it too much of a coincidence that I had survived three attempts on my life? I wasn't even sure that Carol had successfully re-administered the protection spell, she'd got me out of a tight spot by releasing me from the spell, but was I also protected? I didn't know. After the horrific experiences of the last couple of weeks, I certainly wasn't planning on testing it any time soon. Both Tess and Laura had commented at different times that I must have my own full-time guardian angel. In my own mind, I wondered whether she may or may not have been called Carol.

Some of what happened in the States was starting to make sense, and I was now convinced that each incident was indeed foul play. I'd received the report from the fire service in Cape Cod and, although they were originally convinced it was an electrical fault, after further investigation they'd revised their report as they apparently found evidence that the blaze had been started deliberately. It was confirmed that the smoke alarms had been tampered with. They'd previously asked us for any shots we'd taken during our stay, and as it happened, we'd taken quite a few in the kitchen, preparing meals in the grotty workspace, cracking up after a few glasses of vino. Piecing those together, the forensic team had spotted that the required firefighting equipment – blanket and extinguisher – were in place, just as we'd said they were. However, amidst the ruins, no trace of them had been found, and the irrefutable conclusion was that they'd been removed while we were out. Tess felt exonerated as the report said she was almost certainly correct in her conviction that she'd locked the door. They thought someone had used their own key to enter and had forgotten or simply hadn't bothered to lock up again when they left.

It made my hair stand on end; someone had been in the house. Tess had been right all along.

That chilling report gave me cause to look at the other incidents in a grimmer light. I'd been convinced someone had pushed me overboard, and the fact that the blip on the video occurred at the precise moment I went over the rail convinced me even more. That wasn't just a coincidence but someone or something covering their tracks.

I was also convinced now that the mugging in Boston wasn't just an opportunist, robbing me for my expensive jewellery. Someone had tried to kill me utilising my own scarf, the theft was just a cover and, according to the Boston police department, where I was attacked happened to be a blind spot between two CCTV points. Another coincidence? I didn't think so.

All of these facts added up to an extremely disturbing conclusion, and even the girls agreed it wasn't just my vivid, overactive imagination. I couldn't help but cast my mind back to the meeting with the strange women on the way from Salem to the Cape. I couldn't prove anything, but there was no denying that it was after the odd confrontation that things had turned decidedly weird, not to mention life-threatening. I made up my mind that I'd revert to my original plan and keep my head down, stay within my tight-knit group and under the radar, although the puzzle remained: why me?

Once we were back, we said little else about the trip. What happened in the States, stayed in the States. Life continued for us in as normal a way possible. We were all conscious that something dark had happened, to me especially. I'd been targeted for whatever reason, so we were more cautious back home, not drawing attention to ourselves, or giving anyone an inkling of what we were up to behind closed doors, which wasn't very much, to be honest. It had shaken us all up, and I couldn't afford to be complacent. Even though I'd settled back down to normality and a relatively peaceful life, if I had to flee again, I would have no qualms.

And then my peace was shattered again. He walked into the exercise studio. Before I realised who exactly he was – no uniform to give me a clue – I'd already admired his slender frame and handsome looks. I wasn't sure where I'd seen him before; he wasn't one of the regulars, I'd have noticed him. Not my usual type, though, and a little too young, maybe? Then ... oh my God, it was Matt, the policeman who helped drag me out of the Thames and guarded me at the morgue. Holy crap, would he recognise me? So what if he did? Kat only let the magical or sympathisers anywhere near us, didn't she? Surely he was one of us? He caught my eye, but there was no sign of recognition, he just gave me a friendly smile. Wow, that warm fuzzy feeling, like a steaming cup of hot chocolate with all the trimmings, chocolate flake, marshmallows, hundreds and thousands and squirty cream – you get the picture. He was hot!

How idiotic, I thought. Of course he didn't recognise me. The last time he saw me, my body was blue, battered and bruised. With a sprinkle of magic here and there, I certainly hoped I looked different. I still felt unnerved, but if he did recognise me, I'd laugh politely, say it was mistaken identity; of course I hadn't been dragged out of the Thames. What a bizarre idea.

I couldn't deny, though, that it was fabulous to see a familiar face, and over the next few weeks, Matt came to classes sporadically. I looked forward to seeing him in a weird way and was a little disappointed when he didn't turn up. I presumed he was doing different shifts at work. The odd times our glances met, he would always direct a sweet shy smile at me, although it seemed, to my relief, he hadn't recognised me. He finally mustered up the courage to come over at the end of a class one day, when I was rolling up my mat and ready to head home. I was thinking of a quiet chill-out evening, the girls were busy with their work stuff, so weren't out to play tonight. For no particular reason, I was feeling a little down tonight, I'd planned a night in with something cheery on Netflix and a G&T to lift my mood, and was anxious to get going, when Matt appeared at my shoulder.

"Hey, it's Ellie, isn't it? You're looking a bit sad tonight, d'you fancy cheering up over a glass of wine?" I gave him an apprehensive look, had he or hadn't he recognised me? "Not to worry if you have something else planned."

"No," I smiled at him, "nothing, other than a date with the TV. A glass of wine would be lovely."

"Do you usually eat before class?" he asked.

I shook my head. "Generally just snack afterwards."

"OK, let's start with the glass of wine and see where we go from there."

We were both in our sweaty sports gear, so we decided to nip home, change, and meet up at Jones Bistro, a casual place in town.

He dropped me off at my place, and I jumped into the shower and changed into black leather jeans and a floaty chiffon blouse with a big bow. As I rushed around, I realised I was looking forward to the date, although he could not know how much I knew about him. Jones Bistro was popular with us witches, and although there were loads of regular diners, we could always be assured of a good table, a discreet distance away.

I felt good, sipping from my glass of wine. Sitting across the table from this gorgeous guy had certainly lifted my mood, he was very pleasing on the eye. To a casual observer, Matt and I looked like just another couple whispering sweet nothings to each other on a first date. In reality, we were more interested in finding out about each other's magical journey, what we had in common. I felt comfortable with him right away. The word safe came into my head. I wouldn't call it love at first sight or anything mind-blowing like that, but we certainly got on well with no shortage of things to talk about. I gave him a stripped-down version of my story. I still didn't trust anyone, not even this fabulous guy. After Seb, it was hardly surprising, was it?

He was, however, more than happy to unload his back story on me, telling me he wasn't magical himself but had a strong family background. "We call our mother the White Witch, didn't take her too seriously growing up, although she had a cream or a potion for everything, and our scrapes and bruises would disappear. But she mostly kept everything under wraps. My sister Lily is a worry, though. She's inherited the magical gene, and she's a completely different kettle of fish. She's eighteen now and a real risk-taker."

"That's not great," I said. "Nowadays, you can't be too careful."

He nodded grimly. "I see what's going on day in and day out, believe me."

"Well," I suggested, "maybe I could get together with her and see if I can get her to see sense – it's always easier to take advice from people who aren't family, isn't it?"

"Ellie, that would be great, if you don't mind. I admit I'm worried, not just for Lily, but for everyone. Witches have always been victims of rumour, and even worse in our times with social media out of control, nobody can be sure what's happening online."

I nodded gravely. I'd help his sister in any way I could. He stopped, drank a little wine, and then briefly touched my hand. "Tell me about you. Brothers or sisters?" I decided it was too complicated to go into details about Lottie and my birth mother.

"No, an only child."

He laughed. "The problems I have with Lily, maybe that's not a bad thing. But back to you, have you lived in this area for long?"

"I used to live in London," I said vaguely, "but then moved north." I didn't want to continue this conversation, so I used a little magic to knock over a glass of water which splashed onto my outfit. "Damn, how did that happen. I won't be a minute, I just need to nip to the bathroom." I left him looking puzzled as to how the water had spilt; neither of us had touched the glass. In the bathroom, I took a few deep breaths, the conversation was getting a bit beyond my comfort zone. I needed to steer it away from anything I didn't want broadcast. Returning to the table, I asked many questions about his upbringing, and he was surprisingly forthcoming before moving back on to the subject that was a huge worry to our community – the Purge.

Matt didn't think it would be long before our area became caught up in what was happening. We'd been lucky so far, but while there was an underground movement of sympathisers, of which he was a part, many more people believed the propaganda of the witch hunters and were petrified of the witches. He added that the reality of the situation was far worse than that being relayed by the media. I nodded grimly. I, of all people, could confirm that.

His reasons for joining the Pilates group were pretty straightforward; like the other guys, he wanted to do what he could to protect us. His bosses knew nothing about this – he would get the sack if they knew. I thought he could be a great undercover agent. Apart from liking him enormously, he could also be a brilliant ally for me in the future. Our delightful evening out finished when he gave me a lift home, and we had our first delicious kiss, the icing on the cake. He was a complete gentleman and didn't ask to come in for a coffee, which I appreciated; I was pretty shattered. The kiss was more than enough for a first date. But as I left the car, he said, "I'll message you when I've checked my rota to arrange another night out, that's if you would like to go out again?"

I smiled and nodded. I was pleased there would be more than one date, "That would be lovely, thanks for a great evening. It was fun! Send me Lily's number."

CHAPTER 29

One year later

I was drawn to Matt from the start; he suited my quest for normality and was an amazingly nice guy. I'd assessed his character as empathic from the beginning, and he came along just at the right time, a complete antidote to what had happened before, and just when I felt I needed protecting.

Matt and I soon became an item; before I knew it, I'd surpassed my normal six months deadline, and we were still going strong. We'd fallen into an easy relationship pretty quickly, no passionate love affair, no massive spark but I felt I knew him so well, I needed no warm-up. The right thing at the right time, I convinced myself. Of course, I couldn't explain it to Matt, but he was convinced it was because we'd somehow met before, although I always laughed that off.

I'd seen him unguarded and knew deep down what a

kind soul he was, it felt good being in his company. It was also a novelty dating a policeman; he gained useful information, and I'd just about got used to his shift pattern. In return for his innate kindness, I'd tried to help as much as possible with his sister Lily, she was such a sweet girl, and I'd grown really fond of her. He'd been correct, she could be a loose cannon, a danger to herself, although I thought I was finally getting through to her. She and I had several magic nights at my place where she could let loose in a safe environment. Practising her magic helped her reign it in at other times. Matt was our radar, assuring us he'd warn us at the first sign of trouble in the area. He was just as surprised as the rest of us that he never had to do a shift in Hampstead, that his grisly work took place further down the river.

He was a special guy, kind, courteous, the perfect gentleman. One of his lovely gestures was buying me a house cat, a beautiful ragdoll kitten, Mia. Beautiful, wise blue eyes, and grey fur, I was thrilled – well, not so thrilled with the odd accident during house-training, fur balls were disgusting. Thankfully my cleaner took care of any accidents, so I couldn't be cross with her for long. Matt made me feel that nothing was too much trouble. He was the absolute opposite of Seb. Where had that popped up from? They were incomparable, like chalk and cheese. Matt made me feel safe and secure, but it gnawed away at me that something was missing – the dark and dangerous chemistry I had with Seb, my inner voice confirmed. Laura and Tess adored him and were delighted things were going so well. I just needed to convince myself I was head over heels.

Things had moved on for Laura and Tess too. I was so happy for them. They were totally loved up with two guys they'd met at Pilates, Jack and Eddie. It seemed the safest option of dating these days, no Tinder or other dating apps for us witchy ladies. It wasn't so much stranger danger, but what if we came face-to-face with a hunter? Hard to trust anyone, and we'd all heard the horror stories. Jack and Eddie were amazing, I was fond of them both, and they were good for the girls. Not only were they sympathetic to the cause, but they were also magical themselves, not wizards or warlocks, they explained, but male witches, despite the female stereotype. Check the history books for a long line of men tried for witchcraft. In countries like Estonia, Russia, and Iceland, there were far more men persecuted, prosecuted, and sentenced to death than women. Our beaus acted as lookouts. Eyes open and ears to the ground, they picked up all sorts of information.

One evening we three girls had a night in, a rarity nowadays. We were relaxing on my roof garden, admiring the fabulous night-time view.

Laura was the first to break the reverie, "You know, I'm the happiest I've ever been. I've fallen hook, line and sinker. Help!"

"Jack's awesome, and I know he adores you," Tess said, laughing. "I'm the same about Eddie, he could genuinely be Mr Right and the fact they're both magical is the icing on the cake, isn't it?"

I felt I had to comment, or they'd think something was up. "Matty's amazing too. He doesn't have a magical bone in his body, but even so, he's cast a spell on me."

They both gave me a weird look – what was that for? Had they caught on that I was saying it for effect, just joining in the conversation? Did they suspect my words weren't enthusiastic enough? Perhaps they knew me too well by now?

"You know I could see myself having babies with Jack." Laura leaned over and refilled her wine glass – was she drunk? She looked over at Tess. "Strong magical genes, just imagine what power our babies would have!"

I woke up now. Babies? When had we ever talked about babies before?

Tess agreed. "Me too – with Eddie, I mean, not Jack! Ellie, everything OK? You're quiet tonight."

I shook my head. "I'm fine, just chilling. Yes, I could see a future with Matt, but kids?"

"Well, that biological clock's ticking." Laura grinned as she said it but added, "Better not leave it too long, or it might be too late." I just smiled. I honestly couldn't see a future with children. I wasn't even sure I could see it with Matt if I was being honest. Thankfully the subject changed then, and Laura started telling us about a brilliant Netflix series someone had told her about.

I didn't want to rock the boat. I'd see the girls on their own occasionally, and Matt when he wasn't working or exhausted from working. When we could all get together, the six of us would grab a quick drink at the pub, or one of us would cook for the others. Matt, Jack, and Eddie had become good mates in their own right, and it was lovely to let my social life be organised by everyone else rather than as a single girl, having to be my own organiser. The guys were brilliant cooks, too, so they'd all chip in when we had nights in. I wasn't the best in the kitchen, but on one occasion had treated us all to a personal chef to come in and cook for us. The meal was delicious, but I could tell the others found it a bit embarrassing, splashing my cash in that way. So, after that, I stuck to buffet-style from the local deli. I knew none of the others was in my financial league and, although they weren't in the least bit jealous, I didn't want to overstep the mark again and embarrass them.

Matt hadn't yet officially moved in, I couldn't quite take that step, but he stayed over often when he wasn't working unsociable hours. I needed a good seven hours of sleep, and he knew how grumpy I got when that was disturbed. We spent more time at mine because it was more luxurious and comfortable, while his was a bit whiffy and messy, like student digs. I was also a bit precious, and he'd learnt from experience to tidy up after himself, especially in the bathroom, otherwise I'd show my displeasure. I'd given him a bit of space in a wardrobe, and he left a wash bag in the bathroom, but even those small concessions felt like an invasion of my personal space. Maybe I was destined to live alone, be a spinster of the parish.

Although my friendship with the girls wasn't as intense as before, we did get together just the three of us for our magical sessions, which we all needed every now and then to let off steam. We kept them low-key, nothing too wild. Purge news from all over the country was dire and getting worse. I felt despair, reading about the poor souls losing their lives, yet for reasons no one could explain, there was still no persecution in Hampstead, almost like we'd been forgotten, erased from the witch-hunter map. I wasn't complaining. Maybe we were good at hiding our magical legacy in plain sight. But change was in the air, I could feel it, and we had to be extra vigilant. Matt had warned of the suicide contagion spreading, more women were being dragged from the Thames, and there were other gruesome deaths that he had been unfortunate enough to attend. Thankfully, we all agreed at Pilates, it had never been anyone we knew, but Kat felt that we needed to be careful, even the class was under threat now.

So I kept telling myself I was happy; my relationship with Matt felt safer, kinder, more comfortable, like an old pair of comfy slippers. And now we'd passed the year mark, a record in my dating book. But I couldn't deny I was getting restless and had started to have intrusive thoughts of Seb, which were becoming ever more frequent and much harder to ignore. I was shit-scared of him, yet he was the only man I'd truly fallen in love with. It was more than lust, it was an obsession. My relationship with Matt was a watered-down version. I'd hoped his nurturing nature would override everything but feared in my heart that wasn't the case, or maybe it was my pattern of behaviour, perhaps I was just self-sabotaging my chances of long-term happiness. I wasn't being totally honest to Matt either, there were things about my past that I hadn't told him – and Seb was one of my darkest secrets.

Matt was a comfortable lover; he didn't have any hard edges. But then another word popped into my head: boring. No – where on earth had that sprung from? Did I want a destructive relationship again? Matt was funny and considerate; Seb had been moody and disagreeable most of the time. There was no comparison between the two. Matt was a dream boy, and he cared for me, didn't he? He was my protector. I was a lost soul. But another thought intruded, Seb was my soulmate, so was it inevitable I would be drawn back to him? Maybe now was the time to sell Lavender Cottage and draw a firm line under that part of my past. Matt was starting to hint at a future for us; at the same time, I felt guilty that I'd dream not of him but Seb, I hoped to God I never spoke in my sleep. Little did I know that fate was about to take the decision away from me. Life was about to change … again.

The news Matt was bringing home grew ever worse, and he didn't stop warning me to stay focused and discreet. He would be working long shifts for a few days, and I felt bored and restless, so I decided to go a bit further afield and have a mooch around Camden market. Casually dressed, with a book, sunglasses, and water bottle in my bag, I looked just like any other tourist, blending in. I made my way out of the apartment. I could have got a taxi I suppose but it was healthier to walk. I never used the tube; it was always such a dirty, sweaty experience that I felt happier getting cabs.

I had a coffee when I got to Camden, in a cute coffee shop overlooking the canal, and a quick pit stop before moving off. I passed the Amy Winehouse statue which always saddened me. Deep in sombre thought, I wandered from stall to stall. Maybe I'd get Matt some tasty morsels, pick up some chocolates for myself, improve my mood. I glanced across at the stall opposite that sold vinyl; in another life, I'd have dashed straight over, but I had no record player in London. Note to self: add to my list, maybe when I bought another place? The stall wasn't as busy as it usually was, there was just one tall, lone male, bent over studiously looking through the stacks of second-hand vinyl, he looked like a man on a mission. Then with a shock that ran through me from head to toe, I realised who it was. It was Seb.

I was rooted to the spot. He was opening sleeves to inspect the record inside, checking for scratches on both sides, completely focused on what he was doing, and had no idea I was staring at him. Fear and temptation raged through me. I knew him so well, his stance, his concentration, his shoulder-length hair, dressed in dramatic black. I felt a taut wire quivering between us, an unbreakable connection. I knew that at any minute, he'd be able to sense my eyes lasering into him, and turn and see me. Did I have a death wish? Another bolt passed through me as I realised I was still passionately in love with this man. Matt had been a mere distraction from the intensity of those feelings for Seb. What an absolute nightmare. What was I to do? I couldn't let him see me. But I couldn't move either.

He was deep in conversation with the stallholder – not surprising, music was always a passion of his – but what the fuck was he doing around here, just a few miles from Hampstead? Was his visit coincidental? It was much too close for comfort. Perhaps he was on a break from his undercover government business. After all, he had been on his way to London after that fateful last night at the cottage. Or was there a more sinister reason. Was he after me? Maybe I was flattering myself. Perhaps I was just one of many he was hunting, having a love affair with me was just part of his undercover work, getting to really know me. But somehow, I didn't think so; we were soulmates. Did he know I was living around here? Could it be he was biding his time, ready to pounce when the time was right?

I'm not sure how I prevented myself from fainting or going into a full-on panic attack. My heart felt as if it would beat itself out of my chest. Trying to stay as calm as I could, under the circumstances, I turned and walked away slowly, not wanting to draw attention to myself until I reached the perimeter of the market and was back on the high street. I didn't dare turn around just in case. Could he be following me? I needed to get back to my apartment. With urgency, I flagged down an empty cab. I was in a high state of anxiety.

"You OK love?" the cabbie asked.

"Fine," I managed, and then, "Hampstead High Street, please, as quick as you can." Finally able to look back, could I see Seb? Was he following me? I shuddered. I put my sunglasses on, looked out the back window to see if I was being followed, and kept my head down. The driver could see I didn't want to talk and put his foot down as much as he could. I wanted desperately to be safe, back in my apartment. When he stopped outside my apartment, I had the money ready. I rushed inside, up in the lift, double-locked the door, and then my legs wouldn't hold me any more, and I sank to the floor.

What a bittersweet moment – my heart was telling me I was still helplessly in love with this man, while my head was reminding me of the lethal danger I was in. My mind was in overdrive, and I shakily rose to my feet to set the security system, cutting-edge technology no one could bypass. He hadn't seen me. My theory about him sniffing me out was simply panic and paranoia. I looked different too, and he hadn't turned around, so why was I so worried. I needed to get on with enjoying my life and write this off. Matt was here to protect me, although I wouldn't mention the sighting, I couldn't run away all my life – in fact, I was running out of places to run to. I'd just be a little more vigilant, ensuring I always had my shades and a book. I needed to carry on as normal and shake off the uneasy feelings.

My anxiety kept me imprisoned at home for the next few days, and I put off my friends by saying I felt a little off-colour, some sort of bug. Matt, thankfully, was working extra shifts, so I didn't need an explanation for him. I knew for sure now that what I had with Matt was bland compared to my feelings for Seb, and I had no idea what to do. The thing that bothered me the most was that even though I was disguised, if I bumped into Seb again and he were to look into my eyes, the windows of my soul, he would know.

CHAPTER 30

Three months later

I'd gradually calmed down after seeing Seb in Camden, I told myself it was just a coincidence, and decided the most rational and safest thing was to stay put. After all, where else would I run too? I'd built a network around here. I remembered that Seb had a strong dislike of London, and I was sure he wouldn't have come here to live, he hated big cities. Or was that what he had led me to believe, another lie? But in this vast city, what was the chance of seeing him again? I was certain he hadn't seen me. I was worrying myself silly for nothing.

On the other hand, the news I was getting from Matt wasn't good. "Ellie, things are hotting up, literally. There's a vicious undercurrent, and accidental deaths of women are starting to increase round here. Our friends in the fire service are attending more house fires, and women are dying from smoke inhalation." I cast my thoughts back to the house fire in Cape Cod. Matt continued, "Going back to the old ways of getting rid of the problem, history repeating …" He sighed. "I will do anything to keep you and the family safe, Ellie."

One night he came home after a particularly bad shift. "I think going to Pilates is too risky. It's not safe for us all to get together, things are changing, and danger's getting closer."

I didn't want to believe him. "Surely, they won't know what's going on? I'm a powerful witch, and even I didn't sniff out the group until I saw it with my own eyes. Is there anything you're not telling me?"

"Not really," he said. "But think, it would only take one of the group to mention something, however innocently, and we'd be hunted down. Imagine a raid in the middle of one of our magical evenings. Maybe we should have a break, just for the time being, from the group, keep our distance?"

I nodded reluctantly. "But I can still see my friends, at home?"

"Yes, but I'd suggest no magic, it would take just one nosy neighbour to blow everything wide open!"

I had to admit that I was worried that Matt and I were starting to act like an old married couple, and now he was bursting my bubble by bringing his work home with him, raising his concerns. There was part of me that would feel happier burying my head in the sand about what was happening. As long as I kept my magic in the confines of my own home, and kept wary of Seb on the warpath, I would be OK. Where was the spark though? I understood and tried to be sympathetic, as surely it wasn't easy dealing with the things he had to deal with on a daily basis. But when he did have time off, he was so exhausted that he'd simply flake out, and that wasn't what I wanted. I was still in my thirties, after all, not my fifties!

Lily always managed to cheer me up. Matt was on a gruelling shift pattern, so we'd agreed to see each other again when he finished. Today I was sitting at the table of one of my favourite bistros on the high street, waiting for Lily to meet me for lunch – my treat. I felt a maternal protectivity over this young woman, she was a cross between a younger sister and a goddaughter. They'd managed to squeeze us in last minute, and Lily joined me at our table, only a few moments late for a change. When we were together at my apartment, she was like an excitable puppy, but I'd say she was perfectly behaved today, even subdued. I knew this was an act for the outside world, and I was pleased with myself, my tuition was helping. We never discussed magic when we were out, so the next best subject was fashion, a subject close to both our hearts. Her degree at university was in fashion, and she hoped to be a designer one day. She was brilliant at adapting her charity shop finds and had created some pretty unique outfits. One thing was for sure, you wouldn't see the same thing on anyone else.

We ordered smashed avocado on sourdough, topped with a poached egg, a nice healthy lunch. By now she had shaken her subdued mood and was on to her favourite subject – fashion – showing me her latest buys, while I nodded my head absentmindedly, saying the right thing

automatically to everything she showed me. It was
definitely the Lily show when we got together, and it didn't
take much concentration. I must admit she'd bought some
real bargains, other people's cast-offs, but precious to
Lily. I knew she'd love them to death once she'd put her
stamp on them, getting the wear out of them until they
gave up the ghost. She had her own style, but she'd look
amazing in a bin bag. Stick thin, her nervous energy burnt
away those calories, and she ate whatever she wanted to.
Matt said she ate like a horse but didn't put a pound on.
I did wonder if she secretly retched it out over a toilet
bowl afterwards, but I didn't share my concerns with him,
I'd look out for her myself. I'd see the signs, having had
problems myself in the past. Today she wore distressed
jeans, a cropped top, a khaki jacket, and trainers. Her
style was a little on the grungy side, and she was certainly
not manicured. I cringed when she wore a vest top as I
could see she didn't shave her armpits, God forbid. I really
couldn't follow this craze, however fashionable! She had a
short bob with severe fringe, which she'd cut herself, but
somehow it worked, and her makeup was quite heavy, and
I'd say a bit sixties-style – think Twiggy. She was totally
oblivious to her natural beauty, though, I sometimes
thought it would be good to give her a beauty session, but
as she was young and carefree, I left well alone. It wasn't
my place after all. Part of her course was to make or adapt
her own clothing, so she always had new stuff to show
me. I did, however, decline her offer to make me a new
wardrobe, I was getting too old, not my thing!

While Lily was talking, I cast my eye around the

restaurant to see if there were any familiar faces. I'd got to know a fair few people in the neighbourhood. At a round table not too far from us was a group of men, smart in grey suits, having a meeting over lunch. Nothing unusual about that; they were deep in conversation, discussing something important – and apparently confidential, from their lowered tones. Something pulled my attention back to them as it clicked that these weren't the normal diners seen here. They looked too uniform, too official. Focusing, I felt it in the air, a dark vibe, a sixth sense, and I shuddered. This was no ordinary meeting. I knew instinctively they were witch hunters and right on our doorstep. These were our persecutors; had they finally realised what was happening in Hampstead, and had to come to see for themselves?

One man stood out from the rest, the only one not dressed in the same manner as the others. Much less formal, shoulder-length hair, and that's when he caught my eye. A chill went down my spine, it was Seb, and I'm sure he recognised me too. He was on official business with these older men, part of the establishment, and this was ominous. What were they all doing in my neighbourhood? This was much too close for comfort. He hated London, but here he was again, or had he never gone away? Was he living around here somewhere, maybe right here in Hampstead?

I couldn't look away. I was barely conscious of Lily's excitable voice saying, "Ellie, are you OK?" Unable to answer, I was drinking him in, but I was in such a dangerous situation. He looked straight through me, deep into my eyes, through to my soul, the true me ... soulmates, I'd never truly escaped from his clutches. I was a fly in a spider's web. In an instant, the re-fabricated Ellie, my disguise, fell away. How stupid I'd been, thinking that he wouldn't find me. As I stared back at him, everything around me disappeared. Back to earth, he gave a half-smile and turned back to his fellow diners. We'd only been staring at each other for seconds but it seemed like an eternity. For whatever reason, he didn't leave the table and he didn't look around again. Maybe I was mistaken?

Then self-preservation kicked in, and it was like waking from a dream. I needed to protect Lily. It didn't look like he was immediately going to get up from the table, so I knew we had a little time before they finished their important meeting. We had to leave, get the hell out of here, and I had to leave Hampstead right now. Whether fate or design, the decision had been taken out of my hands, and I had to leave Matt. He'd have to protect Lily, somehow, but I had to let him know the danger they were both in. Or should I take Lily with me? I might be taking her out of the frying pan into the fire. Where else was safe anyway? I quickly shook off the idea, she would be a liability. Matt would have to protect her as much as he could. I'd be very sad to leave the area and my friends, but I didn't have a choice. I didn't want to stick around to see if the spell protected me or not, I still felt vulnerable. Truth be told, I didn't want to see what would happen to my friends either. It felt like déjà vu, Whitby all over again.

I leaned over, "Lily, we have to leave, right now." She looked baffled, then smiled; she thought I was joking.

"I'm serious," I hissed. She looked at my face, and the smile left hers. "Follow me, don't look back." And I stood up quickly, almost knocking over my chair. People were looking, which was exactly what I didn't want. But then we were at the door. I didn't give her a chance to question, just grabbed her arm and hustled her to the end of the street. As we turned the corner, I said, "Lily. Go. Promise me you won't stop running until you get back to your place. And message me when you're there." By now, she was looking petrified, as well she might. "No time to explain, just do it. You need to change your look when you get back home." I gave her a shove in the right direction, and, good girl, she took off.

I turned with dread, but there was no one following. Seb was nowhere to be seen. He hadn't followed us. Was that because he knew exactly where to find me when he was ready? Then I heeded my own advice and ran back to my apartment's relative safety as fast as possible, trying not to think how deliciously handsome he'd looked. I couldn't tell Matt about my relationship with Seb, just that I knew that the witch hunters were in the area, that they were meeting locally. I didn't need to explain more than that, did I?

Difficult though I knew it would be, I couldn't stay here. I needed to contact Matt to give him time to warn everyone to protect themselves.

Once back home, the doors double-locked, I checked the CCTV for the last forty-eight hours but saw no sign of anyone loitering. And then I breathed a sigh of relief to get a message from Lily to say she was safe at her place, and had changed her look, she sent me a picture. But she wanted to know what the hell had happened. I ignored her questions. From necessity, I'd become an expert at packing quickly. I raced around, pulling out jumpers, jeans, shoes, and underwear from the wardrobe and drawers. I had bought a few more things as time passed, but I had little time to sort out what I wanted to take. I just had to throw in as much as possible into the cases and leave the rest, it wasn't the end of the world.

When the intercom buzzed, I nearly had a heart attack before seeing it was Matt in his uniform; as I let him in, I realised I had some serious explaining. He was deathly pale. Poor guy, Lily had told him what had happened. He took in the scene around me because what was clear was that I was leaving my apartment, leaving him.

"Matt, I don't have time to explain. I have to get away as quickly as I can. I spotted someone bad from my past, one of the reasons I left Yorkshire."

"Who— and where are you going? You know you might be in more danger somewhere else?"

I had to tell him a white lie. "I'm heading to my parents for a while, I'll message you when I get there. Don't worry, I'll change my look again. I'll do it right now." I didn't want to say that Seb had recognised me, regardless of my appearance. I did a quick transformation. "Better?"

"Yes, but why take all your clothes, and what about Mia? You're not coming back, are you?"

"Matt, you know me, I'm not sure what to take, so I'm just throwing in everything, give me a minute, and anything that doesn't fit Lily can have."

He shook his head. "Is this it for us?"

I had to tell him the truth, I owed it to him. "I'm sorry,

you're right, I don't think I'll be back. I'm scared, it's not safe. It's not safe for anyone else either if I'm around."

"But you're the love of my life, let's at least keep it going – a long-distance relationship for a while. I could even transfer to another area. Let me come over to your parents, I should meet them."

I was starting to feel sick, he was such an amazing guy, I didn't want to hurt him, but now I could only stick with the truth. "Matt, believe me, you don't know my parents, they wouldn't appreciate you coming over, we didn't part on the best of terms. I've got some bridges to build."

He sighed. "I know there's so much you haven't told me."

I shrugged; I was starting to feel a little irritable. However guilty I felt, I didn't need a clingy boyfriend. "Look, all I want right now is to get away. I'm so sorry, Matt, I've got to go." As he enveloped me in a bear hug, I felt remorse. I knew he loved me, but after seeing Seb again, I knew I wasn't in love with him.

"And don't worry about Mia," he said, "I'll take her to Lily, and I'll take your cases down to the car. Now have you got all you need?" I nodded, doing a quick double-check, making sure I had everything for my quick getaway. He gave me a final hug, I could see tears in his eyes, but he knew there was no point saying another word. Practical matters such as breaking my tenancy and sending the agent the keys could all be dealt with once I was settled elsewhere. I had to make my escape and I knew in my heart of hearts the sad truth was that this relationship had run its course for me. Matt stood and watched me until I turned the corner out of his sight.

CHAPTER 31

With relief, I was in my car, leaving all my complications behind, just two cases of possessions, and that was it. At breakneck speed, I tried to put as much distance between myself and Hampstead. I felt I'd wasted too much time already. I was so relieved when I was finally out of London. I didn't know where I was heading. I just had to disappear for a while. I only hoped I wouldn't spend the rest of my life on the run. I felt bad about how I broke up with Matt, he didn't deserve that, but he needed to know there was no hope. I also had concerns for Lily, but I had to pass these back to Matt. She was his sister. I knew it was unlikely I would see her again. Such a shame, I'd grown fond of her.

Finding the Funny, the hilarious podcast featuring James Corden's sisters, was just the right tone for my journey. I needed to zone out and listen to something light-hearted. I found it hard to ignore beeps from my phone so I turned it off. I needed some space before I stopped to reply. I was running low on fuel, so I'd have to stop soon to fill up. A few miles down the road, I saw the sign for a service station, just in time. The shock of leaving and the fight or flight reaction was catching up with me, and I gave myself a little time to calm down with a few deep breaths before I got out of the car to fill up. I used the Rescue Remedy I always carried in my bag – always good in times of stress, and this was certainly one of those times.

I filled the car with as much fuel as possible; I didn't want to stop again for a good while. I nipped to the loo, then back to the shop, where I filled a basket full of things I'd need. Turning my phone back on, I saw I'd missed a mass of messages and several calls from Matt. I messaged him back swiftly and then thought about what to say to Laura and Tess. I knew Matt would have contacted them to warn them and the rest of the group of the need to be super-vigilant. In the end, I said, Sorry girls, I have to go away for a while, speak soon. I sent it with a heavy heart because, in all honesty, I wasn't sure if I would be in touch. Then I turned my phone off again.

An hour or so later, I passed a secluded country hotel surrounded by beautiful countryside. I hadn't a clue where I was, but that didn't matter, it would be suitable for a couple of days, if they had any rooms. I had thought my days of skulking around hotels were over. Thankfully, they were not too busy and had a luxury room available for a few nights. As I settled into the room, the concierge brought up my cases, and I finally started to feel safer. I didn't have the energy to unpack, I relaxed on the bed and must have immediately fallen asleep.

And then I was running as fast as I could from something or someone. I was racing through a dark forest. There was a bright light ahead of me, I had to reach it. It was autumn, my favourite season, the telltale crunch of the leaves under my pounding feet, but the faster I tried to run, the slower I seemed to be going, my legs becoming heavier and heavier, leaden. Panic shot through me, bile rising in my throat. I heard a droning noise behind me but couldn't turn to see where the sound was coming from. All too soon, I saw I was surrounded by a swarm of part-human, part-zombie-like creatures, dressed like city workers in dark grey suits, white shirts, black ties, bowler-hats, and each with a large, black folded umbrella. Their faces filled me with horror. Their features looked like they'd partially melted. The noise I'd heard was chanting. "Kill the witch, kill the witch, kill the witch," over and over. Suddenly, as if on cue, they all began to prod me viciously with their umbrellas. A laughable weapon in murderous hands.

Then everything paused, and silence fell. A figure approached, and they parted to let him through. He was all in black, but his eyes were bright with delight and shining devil-red. It was Seb. I realised he'd finally found me, and he laughed, "Oh Ellie, you knew there was no point in running." Then he transformed into an enormous spider, black, furry body and legs, fangs gleaming, the shining red eyes unchanged and boring into me. Something wet and sticky was covering me, more and more of it, until finally I couldn't move at all. I was a human fly in a spider's web. Then he pounced …

Waking, I was shaking and sweating, feeling sick. My

heart was pumping, but it was just a nightmare. I'd slept for a couple of hours. I drank some water and popped a couple of painkillers for a fast-advancing headache, but I couldn't shake the feeling of dread. I wasn't sure I could bear the prospect of living out of a suitcase again, but what were the options? Looking around my room, like so many others I'd stayed in, I knew I was pining for Lavender Cottage and its cosy decor. What I'd give to live back there. I still owned it but moving there seemed to be a pipe dream.

In the midst of my apprehension and sadness, I suddenly remembered the numbers Carol had given me. Two numbers for emergency use, a lifeline. I'd totally forgotten about the phone she had given me, not given it any thought until now. I scrambled to the bottom of my case, and grabbed the phone. There were only two numbers, named Contact One and Contact Two; Carol hadn't left hers. If this wasn't a crisis, I don't know what was. Nervous, I wondered who would be on the other end of the phone – or maybe they wouldn't answer, that would be worse. What if they had changed their number? Had I left it too long?

CHAPTER 32

The phone rang at the other end. A woman answered. "Hello, Ellie," she said. I was struck dumb, wondering if I'd finally cracked and gone mad, I'd recognise that voice anywhere.

"Alice?"

She laughed. "Yes, it's me; I've been waiting so long for you to call, my sweetie. You took your time!"

I sat down abruptly on the bed. This was more than I could take in.

"Have a drink of water. We haven't got time for dramatics."

I took a few gulps from the bottle beside the bed, then screamed, "What is going on?"

"Feeling better?" she asked, then, "I know you've been in real trouble."

"You knew I was alive? You know Carol? How the heck do you know Carol?"

"Ellie, I know patience isn't your strong suit. All your questions will be answered. Things have moved on in all sorts of ways since we were last together. Do you trust me?"

"With my life."

"Right then, here's what's going to happen, my darling girl."

I was in a daze. Alice wasn't in Scotland but living in the Cotswolds. "A long and complicated story," she said, "but plenty of time to catch up." I made arrangements to go and stay with her, driving down on Friday. There was so much I didn't know, including how Lizzie and Sarah were. Alice had already told me I wouldn't be seeing them, it was "too dangerous". She'd also indicated that Robbie wouldn't be there, away with work maybe? But she flatly refused to answer any of my questions. My mind was in overdrive.

Before setting off, I kept a low profile, using room service and catching up on movies. Needless to say, I was packed and itching to go when I checked out of the hotel. I was both anxious and excited. She'd given me an address outside Chipping Norton, and her directions led me onto a farm track. Alice's cottage, the Old Coach House, was the first building I came to at the end of the track. It was lovely, nice and secluded, and looked Victorian, with gothic turrets smaller than Alice was used to, but the view was to die for, with open fields for miles around. There were sheep and cows dotted around, chewing the cud. Maybe this had been the draw for Alice and Robbie, but I was still puzzled. I rang the old-fashioned bell and the door immediately swung wide open. Just as wide was the grin on Alice's face. Apart from some fine lines on her pretty face, crow's feet at the edge of her eyes, and a change of hair colour – I think you'd call it truffle – she looked the same, although there was a distinct absence of freckles, then I smiled as I remembered that spell. Maybe I could work a beauty spell or two to help with those fine lines, that's if she'd let me. When she saw me, the look on her face made me realise I'd forgotten I'd had a transformation myself.

"Ellie?"

I laughed. "Yes, it's me!"

"What have you done? You look like a Stepford Wife with that hairband." I smiled wryly. She hadn't mellowed.

"It might have saved my life. There's so much to tell you," I said and ran into her arms. I didn't care that she didn't do hugs, she was going to get a hell of a one now, after all this time.

"Well, you still look beautiful, just not the same, Ellie. We'll have to do something about your clothes too." She was still bossy. "I had heard that you may look a little different, but I wasn't expecting this. It will take a bit of getting used to." She grinned. "I'll show you up to your room in a moment, but first, I'll show you around, it won't take long." She was right, it was tiny, but cosy. A lounge with a log fire led into a dining room and tiny kitchen area. Following her up narrow stairs, there were two bedrooms, a bathroom with a claw-foot bath, and a shower. No sign of Robbie. I decided to wait a bit before asking questions. The decor was beautiful, although there was only one wardrobe in the bedroom. That wasn't like Alice, and I gave her a questioning look.

"I'm living a much simpler life," she said. "Look, freshen up, then I have your favourite white wine chilling. And I've cooked my signature dish."

I hugged her. "Thank you, my lovely, and I won't be long." I changed into blush-pink loungewear with an elasticated waist, which I was sure would be needed, and hurried back downstairs.

I hugged her again when I came down, and could feel how much weight she'd lost, skin and bones.

She sensed my reaction. "I know what you're thinking, missy, but I'm getting my appetite back, and I'm ravenous right now. Let's eat."

The kitchen table was set for two, with white roses as a centrepiece. There were gold-rimmed glasses and her best cutlery and china. But just two settings?

"Robbie and I split up two years ago. We're divorced now."

"No! But you two were made for each other."

She nodded, tears in her eyes. "I thought so too. Never saw it coming. It was another guy, one of the lawyers we'd taken on. We spent a lot of time with him and his partner."

"Oh Alice," I interrupted. "What an idiot!"

"Well, water under the bridge now, but yes, I'd thought we were for life. Pip, Sam's partner, didn't suspect a thing either. But I suppose, in hindsight, there were red flags. They started having lots of boys' evenings. Pip and I were excluded, and they'd stay out incredibly late on a school night. But it was an incredible shock when they declared their undying love. Of course, we couldn't carry on working together, we sold the business, and I took time out. I wasn't in any fit state to work for a while."

"I'm so sorry I wasn't around for you. You'd worked so hard to build the business up together."

She shrugged. "I'm coming out of it now, moving on, as they say. Let's not dampen the mood, it's amazing to see you, so much to share, but it can wait." She reached over and poured us another glass of wine. I was starting to feel hazy, but it was a good feeling, one we had shared too many times to mention. We'd dropped right back into our beautiful friendship.

Like a dog with a bone, I had to ask again, "What about Lizzie and Sarah?"

She answered guardedly, "They are fine."

That sounded ominous; what exactly had been happening? Did she know that Lizzie had been travelling in the US? "So let's ring them now!"

The timer buzzed, and she rose. "Not right now, you don't want dinner burnt to a crisp." She returned with beef bourguignon and went back to get crusty bread and butter, greens, and creamy mashed potato, true comfort food. "Get stuck in," she ordered and changed the subject. This was as delicious as it was posh, seventies-dinner-party fare, and I discovered I was starving.

Now I'd found Alice, I wasn't letting her go again. I still hadn't fathomed how she knew Carol, and after that, there was a host of other questions, but I knew not to push her. Full of food, we flopped onto her comfy leather sofa.

"I've put together a playlist for us," she said, but before long she was nudging me. I'd nodded off. "Go on up," she said. "We can talk tomorrow."

"Wait," I said urgently, "I haven't told you everything that has happened with me, don't you want to know?"

She smiled. "Silly girl, do you honestly think I don't know?" I just looked at her, I think my mouth might have fallen open a little, but by that stage, I was beyond feeling surprised at anything. Alice wasn't a witch, was she? Once again I thought, how did she know Carol? It didn't make sense. This opened up another can of worms, but I didn't think I'd get an immediate explanation.

I slept like a log. The spare room wasn't massive but it was beautifully decorated, and the bed and pillows were perfect – Alice knew I hated soft ones that your head sunk into. I woke up to the sun shining through the wooden blinds.

She knocked on the door. "Heard you moving around. Still having to pinch myself that you're here."

"Me too," I said with feeling.

"Rise and shine then, we'll have breakfast, then there are some people I'd like you to meet."

"Lizzie and Sarah?"

She shook her head. "Sorry, not possible at the moment, I told you, but all will become clear, just relax and go with the flow."

I dressed quickly and went downstairs to find Alice setting the table. I couldn't believe it was already eleven, I never lie in that late, I must have been shattered. It was going to be more brunch than breakfast.

"You look great," she said, looking up. "Thank goodness that headband's gone, it doesn't suit you – so twee!" I laughed as she continued, "Sit down, we need to head out as soon as we've finished breakfast. They'll be waiting." The suspense was killing me.

CHAPTER 33

My patience was running out by this stage, and I grabbed her by the shoulders and turned her to face me, "Alice, you have to tell me, do you know where Sarah and Lizzie are?" She nodded.

"And?"

"And they're perfectly fine, but there's too much going on for us to be in touch right now."

"At least tell me if Sarah's still living locally?"

Alice shook her head. "No, both of them are out of the country." I opened my mouth to ask more, but she said, "Ellie, that is all I can tell you at the moment. Now, do you still take your coffee the same?" Maybe it was Lizzie that the weird witches in Salem had seen. I hoped she was OK.

We ate quickly, I could tell there was a lot more to come, but Alice would always do things to her timing. I couldn't put my finger on it, but I was certain of it in my bones; something pretty major was going to happen –

and it might not be great. Why the secrecy about my best friends? She was on her feet as soon as I'd demolished my last piece of toast. She was in such a hurry she didn't even stop to clear the table, that was very unlike Alice. Something wasn't right.

"Come on," she said. "Time to go. Have you got some boots? We're not going far, just up to the farmhouse, but it can be muddy."

We still didn't have a chance to talk because she rushed me out the door and then marched briskly along the narrow path. I followed, feeling a sense of foreboding.

The main farmhouse was built of beautiful Cotswold stone but had gone through a 'Grand Designs' style, full restoration project. Black wrought-iron balconies at the top windows and a massive, contemporary orangery had been added to the side of the property. Light grey paintwork was on the window frames, and the front door was painted on-trend pink. I recognised the signs from my work at Lavender Cottage – this was a recent project, still lots of builders' rubble and equipment strewn around, and derelict-looking barns, stables, and farm buildings were waiting their turn for beautification. An enormous pond had been dug out, ready to be filled with water, and a grey stone patio dotted with exotic-looking potted trees wrapped around the house, with groups of luxurious outdoor seating and umbrellas. A manicured garden was also taking shape. Whoever had taken on the project must have bags of money to have purchased in such an exclusive area, and there looked to be acres of land too. I felt like I was participating in an episode of *Through the Keyhole*. Maybe it was someone famous, the area was known for celebrities. Was it a famous celebrity who I was about to be introduced to?

We were now near the front door, and I must have been daydreaming as Alice grabbed my arm quite forcibly, "Come on, and you're not to freak out when you see who it is. Things are not as they seem, so hear us out. You trust me, don't you?" I nodded but couldn't deny how perturbed I felt. There was a welcoming floral wreath on the door, Alice tugged a bell pull and a few moments later the door opened slowly, and I nearly died.

The face of my adoptive mother, Sandy, was as impassive as ever. I wanted to turn on my heel and run, but I couldn't keep running. The last time I'd seen my mother we had not parted on good terms. In truth, she'd been pretty vile – but what was the connection with Alice? Had she taken over my position in the family? It wouldn't have surprised me; Alice was, after all, the daughter my mother always wished she'd had. As my face paled and I thought I might faint, I couldn't help but take in the fact that Sandy was as graceful and immaculate as ever, and in the time since I'd seen her, she hadn't aged one bit, if anything she looked younger. Good genes or an expensive cosmetic surgeon?

"Hello Ellie," she said as if she'd only seen me yesterday. "I'll give you a few minutes to compose yourself; join me in the kitchen when you're ready. I'll get coffee on." This didn't come close to warm, as welcomes went, and effusive wasn't even in the picture.

"Alice, what the fuck is going on? How could you

do this? You know about the argument. If this is a reconciliation effort, forget it!" I kept my voice low, even though my mother had disappeared back into the house.

I was frozen to the spot on the doorstep. Alice put an arm around me. "There's so much you don't know. Keep an open mind, it will all make sense, I promise." I shook my head; my heart was pounding, and a panic attack wasn't far off. I took a couple of deep breaths.

"You know my parents never supported me when I moved to Yorkshire," I said. "They didn't even come to see me."

She nodded. "I also know why they weren't keen for you to make that move. There's more to it. Come on, let's go, your mother has a lot to say to you."

"Leopards don't change their spots," I muttered, as I followed her inside.

Composing myself, I went through the farmhouse door like a lamb to the slaughter, but I had to put my trust in Alice, there was no one else, and surely she wouldn't stab me in the back? I pushed my dark thoughts and doubts to the back of my mind. I'd face this head-on. The least I could do was give them a chance to explain what was happening instead of being my usual hotheaded, defensive self.

Looking around, I could see no sign of the chintz my mother once loved. The hallway and a couple of the other rooms I peeked into as we passed were minimalist and very cool. Where were all the collectables my mother had spent years accumulating? Expensive tat, I called it. This place was so far removed from our family home. Alice led the way into the kitchen at the back of the house where Sandy was busying herself with drinks. It was a large, beautifully contemporary room with little clutter, two inviting, brown leather sofas with a selection of tasteful cushions and a long dining table with brown, padded leather chairs were at the other end of the space. There was an island with bar stools in the kitchen area and a large TV tuned to a music station, my mother's favourite, Classic FM. While I was looking around, Alice slipped onto one of the bar stools and was silent for once.

It was all so odd. There was no mention of the argument or my disappearance over the past few years. They were behaving as if I'd never been away. My mother put three cups of coffee down, then stepped back and looked me up and down.

"Darling Ellie, Alice told me you looked different. What an amazing transformation, you look stunning." I glanced over at Alice, but she seemed intent on her coffee and a biscuit she'd taken from the plate set out by my mother – if it was my mother and not just a clever impersonator. I don't think she'd ever paid me a compliment before.

"I can see it's you, but with improvements." That was more like it. "You look fitter than when I last saw you, and I see you've kept your weight down." Then, before I had a chance to ask her what the hell was going on, she swept me into her arms, squeezing the breath out of me, and certainly taking the wind out of my sails. She was never demonstrative – this was wrong, totally out of character, and I was truly freaked out by now. As she let me go, I realised someone was missing: my father should have come bounding in by now. I know we parted on bad terms, but my mother's attitude showed that time heals. I turned, smiling, as I heard footsteps, but it wasn't my father, it was a taller, thinner man with a familiar face. Oh my God, it was Mike, my old driver from my city-working days.

I turned to Sandy. "So where's Geoff hiding?" I asked. A look passed between the other three.

"Darling, I'm afraid I have some bad news. Your father passed away a couple of years ago."

I didn't say anything for a moment as shock drained blood from my head. "I can't believe it. Was he ill?" I looked at Alice. "You knew? How could you not tell me?" She shook her head, and my mother took my hand.

"Look," she said, "this is a little delicate." She gave a slight smile. "You must know we had an open marriage?"

"Thanks for the rundown on your love life," I snapped, "but that doesn't explain how my father died." "You remember Kylie, his masseuse?" she took my silence for assent. "Well, your father was having a fling with her." I bit my lip. I remembered them getting embarrassingly cosy in the summer house on one of my last visits.

"I'm afraid your father's heart gave out after a" – she paused – "rather energetic session."

I wished she hadn't said that. I didn't like the picture it put in my mind. "I did have my suspicions," I said hastily, "I didn't want to say anything though."

She smiled. "It's OK, Ellie; we had an open relationship although we loved each other dearly, as you know. It was very quick, he didn't suffer. Kylie had first aid training, but nothing could be done."

And then it hit me. "But we never made up," I wailed and started crying deep, raw sobs. I truly did love my father despite everything that had gone on, and what an undignified way to go. He'd have been mortified.

"Your love was never in any doubt," said my mother. "And we always had unconditional love for you, despite everything." I blew my nose with a tissue Alice handed me, I honestly didn't know how to handle the news, nor the show of affection, never mind the word love. I don't think it had ever been spoken before in our house.

"Here, have some coffee." Alice pushed my cup forward.

"I'm so sorry to drop this on you after all you've been through. I didn't know where you were, you just disappeared, even Alice didn't know. We finally found you through Carol." I closed my eyes, yet another revelation. I wasn't sure I could take any more. But I was wrong.

Until that moment, I hadn't thought much about Mike, but he now had his arm draped over my mother's shoulders.

"This may be difficult for you to hear, darling," she said anxiously, "but you need to know I have moved on. Mike and I are together as a couple; we sold our properties and moved away from the area. We wanted more privacy, and this farmhouse was perfect, especially with our sensitive work."

"Sensitive work?" Then I echoed, "You and Mike. I can't believe it."

"Mike has always been there for me, and he's been my rock." She smiled up at him.

"Well, Mike," I said, "who would have thought, while you were working for me, you were also screwing my mother." He was familiar with my humour, but Sandy was shocked. "Ellie, no need to be so vulgar!"

Mike laughed. "I'd expect nothing less."

Sandy continued, "It was heart-wrenching, selling the family home, so many memories. But then this came up with all the land, the privacy, and a lovely property for Alice to live in too, especially after what was happening."

"But how long have you and Mike known each other?"

"A very long time, going back to when I was in London. Since your father died, Mike has been very supportive." My first cynical thought was, I bet he has, he's bagged a wealthy widow, but I knew it was ungenerous. Mike, after all, was one of the good guys.

"But neither of you said anything to me about the coincidence."

She shook her head. "It wasn't a coincidence. He was hired to make sure you'd be OK."

I looked at her, completely baffled. "I don't understand."

She smiled. "I think we've given you enough to think about today, plenty to digest. I'm so sorry some of it was such terrible news. But there's much more to tell you. Why don't you hang out this afternoon then join us for dinner later? You are welcome to stay over, I have aired a room for you, save you walking back down the lane in the dark, it can be creepy." I was beyond puzzled, but it was obvious that Alice was completely involved in whatever was happening. Sandy continued, "Why don't you have a break? Alice, you can show Ellie around the house, and then both of you should go and get some fresh air and explore the farm."

I nodded; I needed time alone with Alice to digest what I'd heard.

"Alice," said Sandy, "I've put Ellie in the room next to yours."

I blinked, her own room. Jealousy kicked in. "Why does Alice stay here if she only lives down the lane?"

"When we have a heavy day it's easier for her to crash out here." She turned to collect the coffee cups.

Alice slipped off the barstool. "Come on Ellie, let's do a quick tour."

It was the most exquisite house, with expert, high-end interior design. As well as a cinema room, there was a fully equipped gym, a steam room, Jacuzzi, and sauna. "They have done an incredible job with this place," Alice said. I nodded. That was all very well, but I wanted to know more, and Alice proved frustratingly tight-lipped. "It's not my place to tell you more, Sandy wants to fill you in. You know what she's like, she wants to be in control where you're concerned." I knew it was futile to argue, but I wondered what else had been going on, what other secrets they were hiding.

Having explored the rest of the house, we came to a well-equipped music room, which I loved. There was an old-fashioned music system, although apparently, internally it was bang up to date. There was shelving for vinyl and CDs and a full bookcase. "Mike's the musical one," Alice said, indicating guitars and a piano. "He plays those. Come on, let's sit for a while. What record do you fancy?"

She put on Sade, a mellow throwback to the eighties,

and we sat quietly listening. I felt shattered and emotionally drained. I couldn't stop yawning, and after a short while, I said would she mind if I went up for a nap. "I can't keep my eyes open." I went to the room she'd shown me and almost immediately passed out.

Waking up some time later, I wiped the sleep out of my eyes and headed downstairs.

"Feeling better?" said Sandy as I walked into the kitchen. "Mike's preparing food for later this evening. He's a brilliant chef." Alice was at the breakfast bar, flicking through a magazine, and lifted a hand in greeting.

"Much better, thank you. I needed that nap. The food smells delectable, and I'm starving." Besides my outburst, I'd hardly said anything to Mike, and he'd kept a dignified silence, supporting my mother, hovering in the background. I know it was rude, but I had so much to take in, and I was unsure what to say to him. She knew what I was thinking. "I'll leave you two to catch up." She breezed out of the room, and Alice followed her.

Mike gave me a concerned look. "It must have been a terrible shock for you to hear about your father. I'm so sorry. I want you to know I truly love Sandy, and Alice has become like a daughter to me." Happy families, I thought wryly. He must have read my mind. "It's so amazing to see you, Ellie. Your mother and Alice were beside themselves worrying about you. Especially when we heard what was happening in Yorkshire."

We continued with small talk as he busied himself getting the food ready. I asked him about the music room, and he admitted he played a few other instruments but so far had only kitted the room out with the piano and guitar. Like cooking, he said, he found it relaxing. He didn't play sports, so these were his hobbies. He didn't ride horses like my mother, either. "Don't forget I'm originally an East End boy," he said. I laughed, but then I thought that was also Sandy's upbringing; she had dragged herself up by her bootstraps. We continued to chat amiably, reminiscing about my time in London and how life had changed since leaving there. Nothing too deep and meaningful. I still didn't have the faintest idea what Mike knew or didn't know.

Later that evening, Sandy cracked open the prosecco and Mike set out a variety of delicious looking tapas and put an expertly made Mediterranean salad topped with feta cheese into the centre of the table. Remembering my mother's formal dinners of the past, I was delighted to see how laid-back things were now. I drowned my sorrows with a first glass which went down well, the second I raised to my father 'Geoff," and we all clinked glasses. There was a moment's silence then Sandy said, "I don't know about you, Ellie and Alice, but I'm ravenous. Tuck in." Over the meal, the conversation was about the house and other random, mundane matters. There were so many unanswered questions and I was dying to ask more. But I knew what she was like, there would be no budging her if she said tomorrow.

I concentrated on the delicious food. Mike was a creative chef and enjoyed cooking for us. I hadn't known he enjoyed cooking or had musical interests, but ours had been only a superficial relationship. Supper finished, Mike cleared the table, and Sandy went to a well-stocked drinks cupboard. If she was trying to get me drunk before I could ask too many questions, she'd succeeded.

The room started spinning, and I tried and failed to suppress an enormous yawn.

"I think that's enough for today, don't you, young lady? You look shattered," said Sandy, "and a little the worse for wear, I may add." I was surprised to see it was now 10.00 pm, the hours had flown by, and I knew I'd have the hangover from hell to look forward to tomorrow. Alice was as composed as usual, knowing just when to stop, but maybe she didn't have so much bafflement to deal with as I did.

In bed, my alcohol-befuddled head tried to make sense of what had gone on today, but my thoughts mingled with sadness and remorse about my father. I tried reading to take my mind off things, but I couldn't concentrate. Then just when I thought I'd probably toss and turn all night, I must have dropped into a deep sleep and a strange dream.

I was back at Lavender Cottage, though it didn't look like it was in my time or Hettie's. Whoever lived here now kept it spick and span. The kitchen's green, brown, and red geometric-patterned lino was spotless. Walls had been plastered and painted a rich, dark green, with no exposed Yorkshire stone to be seen in this era. There was no electricity, just flickering oil lamps and candles, the table set ready for a meal. Firelight gave a cosy glow to a room I'd gladly spend time in.

I felt that someone was watching from the shadows. It was unnerving, but no one was there. On the wall were black and white photographs that looked as if they were moving in the flickering firelight, and as I realised what they were, I took a step back. Death pictures, the ones I'd found in my time there. Now they were neatly framed, dead subjects were preserved by the camera. Children with flower wreaths, adults in their Sunday best. Most of their eyes were closed, although eyes had been painted on the eyelids in a few particularly unnerving examples. It seemed I'd dropped in on the Victorian era, but where, I asked myself, were the people who lived here?

I shuddered and moved away into the room I'd called the snug. It, too, had a lit fire, its cast iron fireplace smaller than in the kitchen, but nevertheless giving off warmth. There was a full bookshelf on one wall, a piano against another, and enough room for a small sofa. It reminded me of the drawing room at the Brontës' parsonage in Haworth. Upstairs there were three bedrooms; I imagined they must use the outside toilet. I still couldn't shake the feeling of being followed by an evil presence, yet no one was there whenever I turned.

In the bedroom that had been mine, there was floral wallpaper and a large, triple-mirrored, mahogany dressing table. I sat down and looked in the mirror, and a figure, a man, in a long dark cloak moved behind me, although try as I might, I couldn't focus on his face. "Ellie," he said. Did I recognise the voice? I thought I did in the dark recesses of my mind but couldn't place it. "Ellie, welcome home."

I woke up with an urgent need to pee and puke simultaneously and, as the contents of last night's tapas left my stomach, I felt slightly more human, although you wouldn't know from my reflection in the bathroom mirror. My head thudding with a self-inflicted hangover, I threw cold water over my face, found a couple of paracetamol tablets and swallowed them swiftly. I couldn't recall where I'd heard that voice, it was just out of reach. Who had been at the cottage? What did the message mean? I had hoped that the dread of those days was in the past.

CHAPTER 34

As I slowly came back into the real world, which right now was almost as bizarre as my dream life, I shuddered to think what further revelations were in store. The grief surrounding my father's death quickly followed this like a hammer to the head. It seemed strange, the lack of emotion on my mother's part; maybe she'd already done her mourning, as she said, she'd moved on with Mike some time ago.

I hadn't brought a change of clothes from Alice's cottage, but my mother had thoughtfully left me a simple lounging suit and brand-new underwear, with labels still on. Taking another long glug of water, I tied my hair back, used some moisturiser I found in the en suite, and headed downstairs. I was gagging for a coffee.

Mike was busy in the kitchen again. My mother and Alice were nowhere to be seen.

"Coffee?" he asked, and I nodded gratefully. "How did you sleep?"

"Well, thanks, the bed was so comfy. You have a house to die for," I added.

"Not what you expected, though?"

I shrugged. "None of this is what I expected, and I'm learning a lot about you, Mike. I didn't know you were musical or that you could cook. The tapas were delicious last night."

He laughed. "I'm learning a thing or two about you. You're a different person from the Ellie I knew. She wouldn't have been interested in my cooking or music."

"Ouch!" Was I that selfish and uninterested in those around me? But he was right, I'd never bothered to ask Mike about himself. He was just an employee as far as I was concerned. It had been all about me at that time.

He was busy at a high-tech coffee machine. "What coffee would you like, Ellie?"

"Skinny latte, extra hot with an extra shot of coffee, please."

"Wow, this isn't Starbucks, but I'll do my best." After a few minutes, he placed a steaming mug in front of me.

I took a few grateful sips. "Just what I need, thank you." He'd also brought me a glass of water, knowing I was nursing a hangover.

"Hungry?" he asked.

"No, it's OK, I'll have something when Sandy and Alice appear, no hurry." I realised he wanted to talk, maybe he found it easier when the other two weren't there. He poured himself a coffee and joined me at the breakfast bar but was interrupted as Sandy and Alice arrived, looking disgustingly refreshed.

They'd been over the fields for a brisk walk and to see the horses, although I couldn't see my mother mucking out the stables and said so. She laughed and assured me she had help, so she didn't have to undertake any dirty work herself, although the farmyard aromas had clung to their clothing as they came in. Neither seemed to be in the least hungover but, unlike me, they always knew exactly when to stop.

Mike brought them coffee.

"I thought you might like a continental breakfast this morning," Sandy said. "I had croissants delivered from the local bakery and we have eggs from the chickens if you fancy." I knew I ought to get something in my stomach, but the thought of an egg made me heave.

"Just a croissant for me, please." Breakfast was a quiet affair, and then Alice and I took a coffee outside onto the patio. After a while, Sandy joined us, continuing the conversation.

"So, Ellie, a lot for you to digest? I'm sorry you're being bombarded, but it might explain a few things from your childhood. One thing I want you to know is that everything I've ever done has always been to protect you." I nodded. "I expect you have a lot of questions," she said. "Fire away."

"Right," I said. "First of all, what are you doing working with Alice?" I didn't mean it to come out in such an accusatory tone, but all this had been going on behind my back, and I deliberately chose to ignore the fact that I hadn't been around and, as far as they knew, could have been dead. The close relationship between my mother and my best friend, the daughter she always wanted, made me so jealous.

Alice smiled at Sandy, giving her a get-out. "Shall I ...?" Sandy nodded thankfully, and Alice turned to me. "When Robbie and I split, we knew it wouldn't be possible to have an amicable working relationship, and the environment became toxic, so he bought me out. It was such a relief. Sandy and I had kept in touch after you disappeared. We knew we could contact the other if either of us heard anything about you."

Sandy interrupted, "You know I always thought highly of Alice as a lawyer. So it seemed logical."

"Logical?" I enquired.

"Yes, when she told me about Robbie and selling the business, I asked her to join my firm." She smiled fondly at Alice. "Robbie's loss was my gain."

Well, that made sense, I thought, pushing away a jab of envy at their working situation. "So you're still doing family law, mediation, that sort of thing?"

"Yes and no," my mother said, and held up her hand as I made to speak. "Before I tell you about our work, I need to explain a few things. As you know, I deeply regret you weren't told about your adoption." I grimaced; that's what our huge row had been about. I'd felt they'd let me live a lie, but now I was apprehensive. "Are you saying there's more you've been hiding from me?"

She nodded. "I'm not sure where to start."

"Try the beginning," I said.

Sandy nodded. "My early life in London—"

"I know all that, poverty, alcoholic mother, yadda, yadda, yadda."

"What you don't know is that I was aware I was a witch from a very young age."

"Oh, please! You're the least witch-like person I know."

"Things aren't always what they seem, Ellie, you of all people should know that by now. I could do things other children couldn't. I was a timid child, no one paid much attention, and all the time, I was developing my spells and expanding my magical knowledge. It was what helped me survive." Unsure how to respond to this mind-blowing news, I could only think of the dumbest questions.

"So, what spells can you do?" I said and looked up. My mother was no longer there. I looked at Alice and she smiled, then my mother's voice said, "I'm still here, Ellie!" She started taking objects off the patio table. A teaspoon, napkin, and coaster hurtled to the floor.

"What the fuck is going on, Sandy?" Then she reappeared, laughing. "No need to swear, but does that answer some of your questions?"

I shook my head; I couldn't believe what I'd seen with my own two eyes, it was spellbinding. She whispered something under her breath and disappeared again into thin air.

I thought back to my childhood, how my mum seemed to know everything as if she had eyes in the back of her head. I was mortified, as I thought, with her abilities, what might she have seen and heard? I shuddered, was nothing sacred? As she reappeared, I opened my mouth, but she forestalled me.

"Did I spy on you? I suppose so," she said. "But I wouldn't call it spying, more looking out for you." I put my head in my hands.

"Oh God," I exclaimed, "this explains so much."

"I only used it in an emergency, and when you reached eighteen, I respected your privacy."

"Eighteen?"

She ignored me and carried on speaking. "When Carol found you, obviously I had to identify you, make sure it was you. As it turned out, I recognised the scar left by the mole you had removed."

I gazed at her, mouth open in shock. "You mean you were there, at the hospital? Why didn't you say something? Save me?" But I think I already knew the answer; it had been about my learning curve, how to survive, to accept that nowhere was safe. I'd certainly learnt a lot about myself during that time. But right now, I needed to concentrate and find out what else my mother had been up to, and there was something else too. I turned to look at my friend,

"Alice, have you also been keeping secrets from me? Don't tell me you're a witch too?" I thought back to the magical evening we had at Lavender Cottage, when I made her freckles disappear. She had been very wary of me disclosing my magic, was this the reason?

She laughed, shaking her head. "Not a magical bone in my body; let's just say for now I'm a sympathiser." I'm sure there was more to come and knew it would, but only when Alice was ready. And I had my secrets too, not sure yet when I'd tell them about Seb and Hettie and my past life experiences.

Sandy said, "It's getting a little cold out here now. Let's go back inside. I think that's enough discussion for now, you'll have brain overload!"

"You mean there's more to come?" I'd said it rather sarcastically, but she'd not taken the bait. "Yes, but for now, why don't you go and watch a movie or something, ladies?"

That was a good idea and meant we wouldn't have to talk for a while. I had too much whizzing through my mind to make intelligent conversation. We made our way into the cinema room. Alice found one of our favourites, Love Actually, and it was just like old times as we sat watching a movie together in companionable silence.

Once the credits rolled, I had a question for Alice. "Does Mike know all about this too?"

She nodded. "Yes, he knows the whole story."

"You're not going to tell me he's a witch too?"

She laughed, shaking her head. "He has his own back story, and I'll leave that for him to tell you. He's not a witch, just a sympathiser like me."

Something I hadn't yet asked, "What's it like around here for the witches?"

"I'm sure it's like anywhere around the country. We just put our heads down and don't get too involved with the local community. We are fortunate to have all these acres of space."

"But are there others around here?"

"Well, Sandy's pretty sure there are, but we haven't got involved locally; it's too much of a risk. With our sensitive work, it's not advisable."

"Sensitive?" I raised an inquiring eyebrow, but she seemed to feel she'd said too much.

"Leave it, for now, Ellie. I told you a great deal has

changed since I last saw you. I've said enough already." I knew better than to push it.

As we joined Sandy and Mike, it was obvious from her demeanour that the subject was closed for the day. We took the opportunity to go to the gym and do a workout. I knew there was more to come, but I couldn't force it.

CHAPTER 35

Sandy had made it clear I could stay as long as I wanted, and I wasn't going anywhere until I had more information. But as always, she wanted to do it her way. Alice returned to her place, and after we'd waved her off down the path, Sandy made us coffee, and we sat on either side of the breakfast bar.

"I know you're impatient, Ellie, and there is more to tell you, but I feel it's best if we do it in bite-sized chunks, it gives you more time to digest things. Biscuit?" After years of her drumming into me about my weight, I knew it was best to decline. I shook my head, and she resumed her seat. "Right, well, I knew you were a witch from the moment I set eyes on you."

"You knew?" I exclaimed in shock.

"Hear me out. Let me explain," she said. "I heard on the witch grapevine there was a young witch going through the care system. She'd fallen for a boy in the same situation – he was also, incidentally, another witch. This young couple were strong-willed and disruptive, their foster families couldn't cope with their behaviour and, as well as that, both of them were having a hard time suppressing their magic." I remained silent, but I knew immediately who she was talking about.

"When your biological mother fell pregnant, she wasn't in any position to bring up a child, but she was adamant she didn't want an abortion ..." She paused.

"Go on," I said.

"Well, I knew she'd been living at Lavender Cottage then, so you can imagine my horror when I found out you'd bought it all those years later." I nodded slowly. That certainly explained her reaction when I told her.

This was a time for laying cards on the table without holding back, so I took a deep breath and said,

"Look, Sandy, I probably should tell you. I've met her, Anna, my birth mother." I don't know what I'd expected, but her look of relief was a surprise; she straightened, it was as if a weight had been lifted from her shoulders.

"I wasn't looking for her," I continued – it seemed important to make that point. "I just found her connection to the cottage, so you see, buying it wasn't a terrible mistake – maybe it was fate taking a hand?" Sandy didn't say anything, just nodded and gave the faintest of smiles, indicating I should go on, so I did.

I didn't stop talking for about ten or fifteen minutes. I recounted my dream, the picture I'd drawn, and my friendship with Lottie. I explained how it was that Anna, Lottie's mother, came to help at the shop and our developing friendship, which led to my invitation to supper at the cottage. I explained how affected she'd been once she was there, what she told me and how all the past pieces started fitting together. I finished, "and in the process, I also found out my best friend in Yorkshire was, in fact, my half-sister. You couldn't make it up!" I paused then for breath and sipped some coffee for a throat that was now dry.

There were some things I just couldn't share yet, not even with Sandy and Alice. I didn't want to go into why I'd left Yorkshire, nor the truth about Seb – that was my deepest, darkest secret. But I did explain that after I'd left Yorkshire, I hadn't been able to contact Anna and Lottie. "I don't know whether they're lying low and keeping safe, or ..." Tearing up, I didn't want to go on, but Sandy knew what I meant. She put her hand briefly on mine – this was a day full of the unexpected – and began to tell her side of the story.

"I only met Anna once, and that was in difficult circumstances, a sullen teenager carrying a baby she didn't have the means to look after. Geoff and I were desperate for a baby after several miscarriages, so as you can imagine, it was an intensely emotional meeting. But I fell in love with you at first sight. I couldn't say a thing to Geoff, but I saw another side to this moody young woman, and I knew beyond doubt she was one of us, a witch; she didn't need to say a word. I suppose I was hoping that you would be just like any other baby, but after only a few months, I could see your power. It shone from you like an aura. I thought I could contain your magic, but my goodness, my girl, you tested my patience over the years." She wasn't wrong – I knew how difficult I'd been, sometimes unintentionally, at other times deliberately.

"There were days," she said, "when you scared me nearly to death. I knew I had to protect you at all costs. It would have put you in mortal danger if you learnt about your legacy."

"Why wouldn't you have shared that knowledge with Geoff, a problem shared and all that?"

"How could I? It wasn't the right climate, and I'm not sure how he'd have reacted. You know what he was like. It would have opened a can of worms. And as you got older, you know how he worried about you – your dreams, the night terrors. It was a dilemma because I knew they weren't just dreams. I was certain your soul was leaving your body. You were dream travelling."

I stared at her. "How could you know that?"

She shrugged. "I just knew, knew your soul was elsewhere, sensed it when I came to soothe you. In the early days when I picked you up from your cot, held you close and paced up and down to quiet your crying, then later, through the years when you screamed out in terror." She stopped while I took in what she was saying. Had I been travelling out of my body? My dreams had felt so real, but then dreams often do. How could I be sure what was real and what was imagined? Yet Sandy seemed so certain, and I was suddenly indignant.

"My dreams weren't just disturbing; they were terrifying! I didn't understand them, but you could have explained what was happening. It might have helped." My voice had risen.

Sandy stayed cool. "I did what I thought was best, and I felt the wisest course of action was to suppress what was going on. That's why I kept you so busy. I thought boarding school would instil some discipline in your life and give you less time to brood on your thoughts. Your father insisted we take you to a child psychologist," she smiled, "but obviously, they never found anything particularly wrong with you. He was against sending you away to school too, but ..." She didn't need to explain that part, I was always aware within our household that what Sandy wanted to do, she usually did, regardless of anyone else's view. "As you grew up," she went on, "it became much tougher, more difficult than I'd anticipated, but I was desperate the darkness didn't get in the way of you enjoying a carefree childhood."

I sighed, looking at the woman I knew so well but, it seemed, didn't know at all. She'd carried a burden, kept a dark secret to herself.

"I just always felt you wanted me out of the way," I was disconcerted to hear my voice wobble. "I thought you didn't love me; that I was a cuckoo in the nest." With sadness, I thought back over the years of my childhood, my confusion about my feelings, and then boarding school, which only served to make me more isolated than ever. Right now, I didn't know if sorrow outweighed my anger or whether it was the other way around. "You could have helped me, developed my skills safely."

She shrugged again. "Ellie, we're all wiser with hindsight. Maybe that's what I should have done, but I didn't want you to feel you were different. I knew too well how that felt. Protecting you was my sole intention. I thought I was right, but maybe I wasn't. I'm not perfect, but everything I did was for the right reasons."

"I get that, but if I'd known, we'd have had a completely different relationship. I wouldn't have been fighting against something invisible I didn't understand, although I am aware I wasn't the perfect daughter most of the time." We exchanged a wry smile.

"You nearly finished me off on many occasions." She sighed. "I did want to tell you about your adoption and legacy, but it never seemed the right time, and before I knew it, you were a stroppy, moody teenager, so there was no chance. Then you were off to university, left home, and never returned properly."

It was my turn to touch her hand. Honestly, this had to be the most physical contact we'd had in years.

"It wasn't a complete mess, though, was it? I did have a pretty normal childhood, to be fair to you and Geoff."

"Until you upped sticks and moved to the Yorkshire moors, throwing everything you had worked so hard for away," she retorted sharply. "Then it all went pear-shaped. The pull was far too strong for you. I saw it, I knew you'd find out the truth, discover your calling." It was clear now why she'd been so violently against my decision. She knew I'd be giving up more than just my career. But I did understand and I wondered what I might have done with my child had I been in Sandy's shoes. Mike stirred on the sofa where he'd been sitting so quietly that I'd forgotten he was there. He nodded once at Sandy, acknowledging how difficult telling me had been.

"So, Mike," I said, "I presume none of this is a surprise to you?"

"Your mother had to confide in someone, and she knew I was safe, I've always been a sympathiser." In answer to my raised eyebrow, he added briefly, "Family stuff." And went on, "Your mother wanted me to help ensure you were as safe as possible. That's why I was hired. We go back a long way, your mother and I. We met when we were teenagers."

I wondered how different my life would have been had I known my mother was a witch. I'd always instinctively known she was hiding something. I did feel, though, that I'd missed out on so much. She'd lived a reasonably normal life, bland and vanilla, within the confines of an upwardly mobile society, concealing her magic, her power. Now it was as if she was coming alive before my eyes, able to be her true self.

Thinking of home, I realised she could have transformed the house regularly, but then how would she have explained that to my father? I was intrigued by what else she could do. She easily followed my thoughts and grinned. "I'll let you into another secret. I was good at getting rid of unsuitable boyfriends."

"Oh my God. Who? How? No, wait, I don't even want to know."

"Your first boyfriend, Ricky, I think he was called, remember?"

"Er, yeah?" I remembered she had said he came from the wrong side of town and she didn't approve.

"But he dumped me. I was heartbroken."

She gave me a wide-eyed look. "Ever heard of an anti-love potion?"

"You didn't! I did think it was a bit sudden, he was really into me, and then it was like he had an instant aversion."

"Which might have had something to do with a little something I slipped into his drink."

I was speechless for a moment, and when I opened my mouth to have my say, she interrupted. "You needed to be protected, Ellie. I didn't want you to make the same mistakes as Anna." I closed my mouth. She wasn't wrong; I was too young for a sexual relationship, and he had been persistent, not to mention the ridiculous amount of peer pressure at the time, and at such a young age. Even so, I wasn't sure I appreciated the high-handed interference.

She dismissed that with a wave of the hand and smiled, "It was the right thing to do, and you turned out fine, didn't you? Until you gave it all up and went to Yorkshire. But maybe I was wrong, and it wasn't such a bad thing after all. I can see now that you're whole and radiant, a true witch. And you understand what I tried to do, and I wanted normality for you; anything else would have wrought havoc in your life." Watching her as she spoke was like seeing a different woman, not the moody, rules-and-regulations Sandy I was used to, and all because she no longer had to worry about me. Looking back through different lenses, I felt a kinship I'd never had before. All she'd done was try to protect me. With the understanding came the melting of the grudges I'd held against her. Now I felt excitement as we moved towards a completely different relationship.

As I settled into the house and its routines, Sandy and Alice went back to work, about which I still wanted to find out more, I was sure they weren't telling me the whole story. But I knew there was no point persisting, they'd tell me when they were good and ready. Mike was involved in the building work that was about to start, and I was left to my own devices during the day, which gave me much-needed unwinding time, although I'd often join them for an early breakfast, and then for an evening meal. I'd started to ride again, going for a hack with the stablehands, exercising the horses, and getting some fresh country air. I'd also taken advantage of the well-equipped home gym and afterwards would relax in the Jacuzzi.

Life was good, and I was determined to enjoy it even though I knew in my heart that there would be more, probably a lot more, to come, things I still didn't know yet and maybe didn't even want to know. Did I really want to disturb this cushy life?

A week later, Sandy sat down and I saw she was preparing to tell me more. Alice was sitting quietly in the background.

"In the witching hierarchy, Ellie," she began, "I'm pretty powerful. I'm an intuitive. And so are you. Unlike most of our kind, we don't always have to have a spell in front of us, we know how to put things together. That's something not every witch can do."

"Such as?"

"Well, for a start, I can fly."

"You can fly?"

"I can," she said.

I giggled; I think it might have been a bit of hysteria setting in. "Well, that's pretty damn impressive, where've you parked your broomstick?"

"Cheeky! I also work with invisibility as I think I demonstrated the other day."

"Yes, but hang on – I'm still coming to terms with the flying." And then a thought hit. "So can I—?"

She interrupted me, she wasn't planning on going down that path today. "What about you, Ellie, tell me what you can do." So I told her about Hampstead, the friends I'd made and the fun I'd had developing my magical repertoire. Alice and Mike had taken a back seat most of the time, but now they joined in the laughter, and I told them about the Mystical Ladies and the forest faeries illusion, where it had all started.

"And most of this all came to you?" Sandy wanted to know.

I nodded. "Sort of, I suppose."

She smiled. "As you get older, you'll find your intuition and all your instincts will become stronger." Despite our growing closeness, I still hadn't told them about Hettie and her magical Book of Knowledge, and I felt now wasn't the right time. Sandy was already moving on. "Your apartment in Richmond."

"What about it?"

"Did it ever cross your mind who had bought it?"

I frowned at her. "No," then, "don't tell me—"

She nodded, "I felt Yorkshire was a terrible mistake. I thought you might change your mind, I wanted to make sure you had a home to go back to in London."

"I don't know what to say."

She chuckled at my dumbstruck expression. I wanted to know more, but my mother was an expert at changing a subject with which she was now bored. She tried to tell me something about what she and Alice had been working on and their conservation goals. They were both passionate about saving the planet. "I cast replenishment spells," she said. "Alice and I are constantly researching, and we have contacts all over the world doing the same. When there are issues, whether with plant or animal life, what we call an Extinction Alarm goes off. It alerts me and others like me. We then work our spells to save, strengthen, replenish, and revive so that the particular line can continue."

I was quiet for a moment, looking at the two women I had thought I knew so well. "I honestly don't know what to say," I murmured. "That's ... that's just insane!"

Alice nodded. "It is indeed, but it will always be a work in progress. The more successes we have, the more we seem to find that harm is done elsewhere. It's a constant battle against time, but," she smiled at Sandy, "it is a wonderful feeling, an exceptional thing to be doing. But we still manage to keep up with the day job, that grounds us." I still felt they were keeping something back, though – not sure what, just a feeling – but no wonder they were so crazily busy.

Then Sandy dropped the real bombshell. "More importantly, you should know that right now, Alice, Mike, and I are all covered by the protection spell, the one that went so horribly wrong for you. We know all about it from Cassie."

I was confused on all sorts of levels. "Who's Cassie? How did you know about the spell? And if you knew, why didn't you come and get me?" I could hear my voice rising.

She went for question two: "You should know it's a spell only the most powerful witches can interpret. That's why you struggled with it, I don't think you were quite ready." I nodded slowly as I remembered how, at first sight of the spell, I'd made no sense of it.

"But if only I'd known that you could have helped me, things would have been so different," I said. I knew that finding the book in the first place was due to Hettie, but I wasn't sure if adding her to the information mix right now would help or hinder. After all, my mother had kept her secrets, no reason I shouldn't keep mine, and there was something else. I couldn't quite put my finger on it but just knew it would be best to keep Hettie to myself for the moment.

My mother continued, "The old text is notoriously difficult to interpret, and this is a spell that goes back further than anyone can remember. It only takes one small mistake for things to go wrong."

I nodded ruefully, didn't I know it! "But if the spell is known and can be cast," I said, "why isn't it being used more widely, saving people from the witch hunt?" Sandy exchanged glances with Alice and Mike, then shook her head. "Ellie, you're missing the point, it's not as simple as that, only a chosen few can interpret the text, and the majority of people aren't even able to read it at all. Even I didn't know about it until Cassie told me."

"Cassie, again. Who is she?"

"Sorry, forgot, you know her as Carol, but her real name is Cassandra, Cassie to her friends. We met in London when I was a child; we go back a long way. You know I was a lonely child and, with my mother's unpredictability, I couldn't ever risk asking anyone home, and I was also confused by the powers I felt in me. I had no one to talk to until Cassie moved from a different area and came to my school. We soon realised we had a similar legacy and were inseparable from that moment. No one would have suspected that the two nerdy girls in the corner were anything other than what they seemed." She stopped to take a breath, and I thought that hearing about my mother's relationship with Carol/Cassie made me feel even more excluded than I already did.

"As we got older, we realised it probably wouldn't be good for us to be seen together too often, it could be dangerous. We kept our friendship secret for years, even from you and your father, but she's always been there when I needed her. You should know that she has more power than the two of us put together, and we are in the top echelon."

I had more questions, but she shook her head. "Let me finish first. It was Cassie who cast the spell for Mike, Alice, and me. She could see the danger we were putting ourselves in. She took the time to teach me the magic, too, so if I had to use it, it would be used accurately and safely. It has certainly started to save lives."

"That's all well and good," I said, "but you do know what Carol/Cassie, whatever her name is, charged me? She practically blackmailed me into paying."

Sandy grinned. "She can be a tough cookie but it's not for her own gain, she's been using the money to help others like us and some of it has gone to foot the spiralling legal bills witches have been running up in defending themselves according to the law of the land."

"So where do you come into all of this?"

"We," she included Alice with a wave of her hand, "were already well respected in the legal community, so we've been defending as many individuals as we can. It's not been easy." Her understatement didn't detract from the bravery I appreciated they'd shown in helping. The whole thing smacked far too much of the Dark Ages for my liking, but my respect for Sandy, Alice, and Mike was growing by the minute. I'd lived my whole life not knowing my mother and felt ashamed.

Mike had been quiet up until then, but he chipped in to explain his involvement due to his own family background – it was that which had drawn him and my mother together in the first place.

"My mother was a witch," he grinned, "but she kept it under her hat." I laughed, visualising a pointed black witch's hat. I was relieved by this small lightening in the tone of the conversation. "My father was in the US forces during the Second World War, in the 1940s, and based in Gloucestershire, but he was born and brought up in Salem. Living in Gloucestershire, as you can imagine, they had to be careful, and his background wasn't even mentioned."

I understood the reluctance, I'd studied the Salem witches and been appalled at how arguments between warring families had led to so many accusations thrown, and lives lost.

"The role I took on as your driver," Mike went on, "was to support and protect you from the danger all around. You see, Ellie, many people don't realise what they are. Remember that girl at work, Sophie, I think her name was, you always had a bad feeling about her?" I nodded. "Well you were right, she wasn't to be trusted, she didn't know it herself, but she was a witch of the worst sort."

I took that in for a moment and then had more questions, "How did Carol— err, Cassie, find me? I'd changed my looks completely."

My mother took that one. "I had a sixth sense you'd head for London."

Alice piped up, "We were so desperate to find you. I even went to Lavender Cottage, but you'd gone off radar. And I knew you'd never switch off your phone unless you were in deep trouble." She shrugged. "No one I asked had seen you for an age."

Sandy said, "At the same time, Cassie was methodically working her way around all the London hospitals – that's how we eventually found you; it didn't matter that you looked different, there's more to anyone than what's on the surface. Cassie was certain she'd found you, and I confirmed it when she described the scar from the mole removal, and then I came to see you. I couldn't risk being visible, but I think you sensed I was there."

"I was certainly aware of someone's presence but had no idea it was you." And then something else occurred to me. "I wouldn't have put Cassie and you together as friends, you're so different. She looks far more the archetypal witch than you, she even has a black cat!"

"Well, she certainly lives a quiet life now, but back in the day she was a stunner, as she grew up, she became a Bridget Bardot-type. But she doesn't need to impress anyone any more, she loves her animals more than people, and she's doing great things in helping our kind."

I smiled. "OK, you've justified the cost, and I certainly am happier at the thought of it being used for a good cause."

"Right," said my mother, lightening the mood, "that's enough heavy information, let me show you my repertoire." And she launched into several spells, encouraging me to match her with some of mine. Even though I now knew I hadn't inherited directly from Sandy, for the first time since I'd left Hampstead, I felt I'd come home, and we were finally in tune with each other. She seemed to feel the same way about our new dynamic and gave in to my demand to learn the invisibility spell and, of course, flying. She took me into one of the other rooms, placed me in front of a mirror and helped me master the words of the spell. Within seconds my reflected fingers disappeared, then my arms, and gradually the rest of me. What a brilliant spell, this was in a whole different league.

And then on to the flying – she made it seem so simple, and in no time, we flew around, onto the landing, then darted through the upstairs rooms. It felt as though I was in an amazing dream – one from which I didn't want to wake because I could finally see my mother for the amazing woman and witch she was. I could have gone on all day, but she called a halt.

"OK, Ellie, that's enough for now. I'm exhausted, it really takes it out of me, I'm going for a nap. Shoo, go play with Alice."

For once, there was a level of frivolity in all of this, which was much needed.

CHAPTER 36

It was a bracing day, and the air was as fresh as it could be if you discounted the pungent aroma of manure, one of the joys of living on a farm. Alice turned to me as we trekked over the field. "What are you smiling about?"

"Just enjoying the fresh air and ignoring the pong."

She grinned too. "You get used to it."

"You know I've been running for so long now, I can't go back to Yorkshire, or Hampstead, but maybe it is time to stop and smell the roses – and the manure!"

She laughed loudly. "Darling, I've been hoping you'd say that, I can't bear to lose you again."

I linked arms with her. Unlike me and my mother, Alice and I had always been on the same wavelength. Words weren't always necessary because she knew how much I'd missed her.

As we walked, I was considering the Cotswolds. I'd never really thought of it before, but there was no doubt how picturesque it was, with the big plus that I could lie low and hopefully be left well alone. After all, the nearest neighbours were the cows and sheep and the odd farm labourer, who popped in and out. I had to ask again – being here in the Cotswolds, where Sarah used to live, I couldn't help myself. "When are the girls going to appear, I'm sure you are hiding something from me. Are you sure Sarah isn't still around here?" She was shading her eyes as she looked across the fields. She sighed. "Look Ellie, there's something you need to understand. The work we're doing is ... a little sensitive. It's not great timing to bring them back into the fold." I opened my mouth to ask more questions, but she hurried on.

"I'll leave it for Sandy to tell you more." I sighed, my ease of mind slipping away again. Surely there weren't more disclosures to come.

When we returned to the farmhouse, Alice wanted to show me the other farm buildings and their detailed plans. I hadn't taken much notice of what looked pretty derelict and neglected. The stables had already been renovated, one of the priorities for Sandy, and they were in full use now, a hive of activity. They made me feel nostalgic, there'd always been a pony in the background as I was growing up.

"The livestock buildings and hay barns are also going to be restored. There's an arrangement for some of them to be used by one of the local farmers, and rather than paying rent, they're going to supply us with fresh produce."

I laughed. "That makes sense, I can't imagine Sandy, or Mike for that matter, getting their hands dirty growing things themselves. I know Sandy's always said she loves her garden, but between you and me, all she used to do was wander around snipping the tops off the roses, wearing dainty gardening gloves, with matching secateurs."

Alice laughed and went on, "If all goes according to plan, the household will always be stocked with vegetables, potatoes and meat." She opened the chicken coop and put some eggs in the basket she'd picked up. "We're OK for free range eggs too." Indeed, in addition to the chickens now squawking indignantly at being disturbed, ducks and geese were wandering around the yard. "And these are so much better than anything you'd get in a supermarket, the yolks are so yellow."

"You've become a real country bumpkin," I commented. "And to think how much you all laughed when I moved to Yorkshire." It felt good to be back to our gentle teasing of each other, just like old times – except they weren't, were they?

The last building we came to was a barn conversion, still a work in progress. A caravan was parked alongside, although nothing as luxurious as the motor home I'd had during the Lavender Cottage restoration.

"The pièce de résistance," Alice announced. "We must have known you were on your way back to us! The scaffolding's coming down shortly and then there's just finishing touches left to do, mainly cosmetic. It's got two bedrooms and its own garden and parking. How does that sound?"

I looked at her in astonishment. "You mean I could live here?" She nodded. It would certainly be perfect for me and was far enough away from the house to maintain my privacy, but they must have other plans for it? Alice read my mind. "There was talk of using it as a holiday let, but we think now it has your name on it."

I didn't want to get too excited, but the idea had huge appeal, although I wasn't entirely sure whether Sandy really did want me back home, after all she had the perfect surrogate daughter on site already.

"We'll talk about it later," said Alice.

As we made our way back into the kitchen, I couldn't help but smile as I saw my mother freely using her magic. She'd heard us come in and, taking the glass jug from the coffee machine, poured two full mugs. The jug promptly replenished itself – like magic! At the overflowing sink, full of cutlery and crockery from our last meal, she clicked her fingers, and sparkling clean plates, bowls, knives, and forks flew into ready-opened cupboards and drawers. In minutes, the kitchen was pristine.

Back around the table for more revelations, it was Alice doing the talking this time. She confirmed again that she wasn't a witch, but she was a sympathiser and had thrown herself into helping with the practical side of the business, working closely with Mike and my mother.

"I came on board to use my legal experience to help protect and represent the witches in the best way I could," she told me. "There are so many haters and persecutors out there, as you know, so there's a level of risk involved." On the surface, they were like any other family law firm, helping people with divorce and mediation, and they had a fearsome reputation, but since Geoff had died the business gradually changed direction, and they started to represent witches. Although over the past few years it seemed witch-hunting had become a national sport, there was, in fact, a legal process, and this side of the business had grown from strength to strength. And, as word of their success spread, their services were much in demand, getting convictions quashed and ensuring other charges didn't stick.

Under cover of respectable law practice, they were also working for the resistance supporting women persecuted and prosecuted by draconian laws. There were all sorts of horror stories, it was like being back in the Dark Ages. Even with what I knew already, it was hard to believe what I was being told, and my admiration for their bravery grew by the minute. There was so much more going on in the background and most of this was not reported in the news. Maybe since the start of the Purge it was old news anyway?

Under cover of their law work, they intended to extend the powerful protection spell to as many as possible, now they felt they had perfected it and could spread the word. The spell would last a lifetime, and the risk of something going wrong, as it had with me, was outweighed by the benefits. I had voiced my nagging doubt about the spell – how could I be certain that I was protected? I wasn't absolutely sure that Cassie had administered the spell, she went through so much with me but hadn't touched on the spell again. But then I cast my mind back to the horrendous experiences in the US, so maybe she had? After all, I had survived three attempts on my life. Or maybe just had lucky escapes. I was conflicted, not one hundred per cent convinced that I was fully protected. Sandy reassured me that in the right hands, it was safe. It was an unimaginably huge undertaking, and I'm not sure how it could be practically done but, as I listened, I understood why I should stay and help however I could. You'll be proud, I hope, to note that for once, I wasn't thinking just of myself. I had a purpose now, I could do my bit to help humanity – well, maybe that was a little ambitious, but I'd have to see what I could do.

"Trust me," Sandy said, "we've been through some pretty gruesome testing." She and Alice exchanged a look.

"We had to try and murder each other," Alice put in. My eyes widened in shock.

"That wasn't easy," added Sandy wryly.

"There are lots of ways to kill someone," said Alice. "We needed to make sure we were protected against everything."

"And if it had failed?" I asked.

"Well, as we're here to tell the tale," said Sandy, "obviously it didn't."

Even though I knew I wouldn't be hundred per cent sure unless I tested it for myself, I was still quaking in my boots.

"You know it protects you against death at the hands of another?" Sandy poured me yet another drink as I nodded. I realised I'd been so intent on what they were telling me that I'd been draining glasses without really paying attention. I felt quite squiffy. But maybe given what was to come, that wasn't bad.

"Let's just say we were pretty thorough," Sandy continued. "Stabbing, asphyxiation, burning – that's medieval, but you'd be surprised – and of course, drowning, it's a long list."

"You tried them all?" I kept my tone even.

"And we can do the same with you," Alice said. "It's all about trust."

Considering what had happened last time, I was justified in feeling scared, but I needed to do this, and the following morning we all woke early as planned and made our way through the fields to the river. A small bonfire had already been set up. For one horrific second, I was convinced I would be burnt alive; the thought of being murdered this morning wasn't a welcome one. But they had reassured me and explained in detail how my body would repair itself. I had to trust, and we went ahead.

To my unspeakable relief, as we worked through the list – and of all my surreal experiences that has to take the prize – they were proved right time after time, although it was an experience I'd never want to repeat, and I suspect they were just as exhausted and drained as I was. We'd saved the worst for last. It was time to confront my worst fears. My nightmares, plus my past and recent experiences with water, still haunted me, the same fear that had been with me since childhood.

For my modesty, my mother had brought a towelling robe. I stripped off. If I'd hated all the stuff that had gone before – the stabbing, throttling, and burning – going back into the water again was worse and brought back my immense, almost uncontrollable, fear of drowning. I had a sudden horrific thought, was it possible they meant me harm? Were they really on my side? Maybe this was the time I really did drown. But I was being ridiculous; these were the two women I trusted most in the world. If I couldn't put my faith in them, there was no hope for me or the future. As I dipped my toe into the river, my mother was frenziedly chanting the familiar words, for safety's sake administering the spell again. But I knew it worked – after all, we'd just tried so many ways to extinguish my life, and none had worked. I was invincible.

I turned once to look back at Sandy and Alice for reassurance. The sun was rising behind them. They looked angelic, framed by the light. Did I see a wicked glint in their eyes? No, of course not, just my overheated imagination. I felt an upsurge of love for them both.

Alice moved forward, "Go get them, Ellie, you can do it." She added softly, "Then it's all out to wreak revenge, kick some ass, this needs sorting, and you have the power to do it, to save so many souls." I smiled weakly at her and turned away to submerge my shivering nakedness in the freezing water, as I'd done a million times before in my nightmares.

Sinking into the water, the feeling familiar, I was now up to my neck, and took the last few deep breaths before submerging. The icy cold hit me first, as I sank deeper and deeper, my mind foggy, but then I had a shockingly crystal-clear image of Lavender Cottage. It became animated, like an old Victorian flicker book machine, its strobing pictures flickering, and each image, a different season, a different year, a different century, going way back through time, through its own past until it was no more than a heavenly ray of light, illuminating the river where the cottage had once been, all the lives lived there, no more, extinguished. What does this mean, am I travelling towards this light, my own life at an end, or am I crying wolf? Through Lavender Cottage am I returning to my own creation, of who I am? Slowly losing consciousness, now a starry universe surrounds me, as I plumet into space, my life force beginning to slip, then one last malevolent thought: a dark shadowy figure is calling me ... Seb?

LETTER TO MY READERS

So glad you have joined me as we continue on Ellie's magical journey. I hope you are not disappointed with the second book in the series *Not Forever Dead*.

I am currently working hard with my wonderful editor, Marilyn Messik, on the third book in the series, *Where Time Goes*. Publication by Goldcrest Books is expected in Autumn 2023.

When I started writing *Dream Die Repeat* it was only ever intended to be one book, but something magical happened as I started writing about Ellie. It was like she was speaking to me, telling me her story, and she had so much more to tell. I hope you enjoy Ellie's ongoing adventures.

One of the most rewarding things about being an author has been giving away signed copies of *Dream Die Repeat*, as I travel the country. It's been so much fun. Seeing the surprised look on a diner in a café, or someone coming out of a bookshop. I took some copies when on a recent trip to Rome, and the look of delight on the face of the lady working at the Hard Rock Café was heart-warming. And on my quest to spread the *Dream Die Repeat* word in the UK, my last stop was the Goth Festival in Whitby at the end of April. I had a fantastic time!

Jules Langton
May 2023

As an avid reader myself, I follow The Queen's Reading Room on Instagram, and I'm currently reading *The Fair Botanists* by Sara Sheridan. I sent a letter and a copy of *Dream Die Repeat* to Camilla, Queen Consort on 7th March. You can imagine my delight and surprise to receive a wonderful letter back.

CLARENCE HOUSE

15th March, 2023

Dear Jules,

So many thanks for your very kind letter. I am delighted that you have been enjoying the recommendations on my Reading Room and was touched that you thought to send me a copy of your book, which I much look forward to reading!

With best wishes

Camilla R

ACKNOWLEDGEMENTS

My continued love and admiration for my beautiful family has no limits. They are all on this exciting journey with me, listening to new storylines, contributing where they can and giving me advice on social media. A big thank you to Tom for help with the cover, we were scratching our heads for some time. My grandson is encouraging me to write a children's book so he can read the book too – now that's an idea!

So, I have to mention the awesome Kate Bush, her music continues to inspire me. I recently listened to a Radio 6 tribute to *The Kick Inside* – 45 years old, who would have believed it! As Ellie continues her journey with her new friends, I thought it'd be fun to put some more melancholic music within the story. Radiohead, one of my favourite bands, seemed perfect. I have seen them live and they blew me away. I also added a fun track when Ellie is in Salem – *Ghost Town* by the Specials. Whilst writing, it was sad to hear that the lead singer, Terry Hall, passed away in December 2022.

I was introduced to *Voracious Readers Only* by Marilyn, my editor. She found it helpful when she first published her own books. They are a fantastic community of readers, who are connected directly to authors, and the genres they enjoy reading. It seems that magical realism is popular.

It can be a daunting prospect as a new author, attending a book club and meeting your new readers after they have just finished your debut book! Tina Gayle-Walford, Heidi Robinson, and Deb Green have been so supportive, inviting me to their book clubs. I had such a fantastic time and had such a brilliant response to *Dream Die Repeat*. I look forward to meeting you all again soon with *Not Forever Dead*.

Thank you to my ARC readers who read *Not Forever Dead* before it was published and gave me a review: Kay Cobbold, Tania Deane, Jane Godding, Anne Greatorex, Alisoun Macdermid and Lori Reynolds.

Thank you once again to the following bookshops and retailers for believing in me and stocking my book: Old Curiosity Book Shop, Hathern, Wistow Deli, Leicestershire, Wigston Deli, Leicestershire, The Langton Greenhouse, Market Harborough, Fox Books, St Martins, Leicester, and Claridges, Helmsley.

A big thank you to my team: Sarah Houldcroft at Goldcrest Books, Marilyn Messik – my editor, Gail Bradley – my graphic designer and Jacqui Womersley for ongoing point of sale and advertising. You are all so supportive and I know I can pick up the phone and nothing is too much trouble.

www.juleslangton.com

www.instagram.com/jules.langton

www.facebook.com/jules.langton.9

www.tiktok.com/@juleslangtonauthor

ALSO BY JULES LANGTON

Do you believe in a previous life lived?
Book 1 in the DREAM DIE REPEAT series.

Ellie is living the dream – a high flying career in London and a luxurious apartment overlooking the Thames as part of a hedonistic lifestyle. So why does a tumbledown, haunted-looking cottage in the bleak wilderness of the North Yorkshire Moors bewitch her? Why does she feel compelled to buy it?

Her life is about to change: a new lifestyle, new friends, the secrets they keep, and the nightmares that haunt her. What can it all mean?

Gradually, Ellie is drawn into a magical world like nothing she had experienced before - with mysterious, spellbinding and dangerous results.

Available from Amazon.